222

GOLDEN
FLEECE

GOLDEN
FLEECE

Jack Becklund

St. Martin's Press / New York

With all my love to Patti, who believed.

GOLDEN FLEECE. Copyright © 1990 by Jack Becklund. All rights reserved. Printed in the United States of America. No part of this book may be used or reproduced in any manner whatsoever without written permission except in the case of brief quotations embodied in critical articles or reviews. For information, address St. Martin's Press, 175 Fifth Avenue, New York, N.Y. 10010

Design by Amy Mayone

Library of Congress Cataloging-in-Publication Data

Becklund, Jack.
     Golden fleece / by Jack Becklund
          p.   cm.
     "A Thomas Dunne book."
     ISBN 0-312-04983-8
     I. Title
   PS3552.E2835G6   1990
   813'.54–dc20   90-37258
                                        CIP

First Edition: December 1990

10 9 8 7 6 5 4 3 2 1

GOLDEN FLEECE

Harry Potter had been puttering on his boat half the morning, hauling stuff back and forth to his station wagon. Nobody noticed exactly what he was doing, because Harry wasn't the kind of man people watch. At forty-seven his only distinguishing feature was a scraggly, graying beard, worn since it had been dark brown. With his glasses, his medium five-foot-nine-inch frame gone slightly soft in the middle, and his quiet demeanor, he was easy to lose in a crowd.

Between trips to and from the station wagon that bore the name Sawtooth Lodge and its logo, Harry had been down below fiddling with a blown fuse, poring over charts, and listening to the VHF marine weather.

He locked the car, carried a large sailing bag on board, and disappeared below. There, he listened again to the weather announcer.

". . . patchy, dense fog over the north shore will diminish this evening with winds becoming west-northwest at ten to fifteen knots. Sunny and cool tomorrow with seas two to four feet and winds clocking north at ten to twenty."

Harry climbed out the companionway. An off-shore fog

bank had moved in from the southwest. Then he released the dock lines, cast off the spring line, and started the engine. The sleek white sailboat slid toward the fuel dock, slowed, then bruised the pilings with a glancing blow.

Paul Lindner felt the dock shudder and turned to see Potter throwing a stern line at a piling. The line missed, splashed in the water, and Lindner shook his head. He hurried down the dock to the tee-section as Potter gunned the engine in reverse, trying to bring the boat back alongside.

"Hi, Mr. Potter," Lindner said as cheerfully as he could manage. "Throw me that line and I'll pull you over."

"Thanks, Paul," said Potter, fumbling with the dripping line and finally snaking it across to the dock attendant. "Guess I overshot it today."

Lindner nodded silently as he cleated off the line, thinking how it had been half a season and Potter had yet to make a decent approach. The man was pleasant enough, considering that he was one of the town big shots, but he was a menace on that boat.

The boat deserved better, Lindner thought, looking from her reverse transom forward along the sleek lines. A C&C 33 should be in the hands of a seasoned skipper; someone to race her, voyage her, take care of her.

Instead, she was dirty and neglected, her teak trim graying, her hull and keel already battered from too many careless encounters with pilings, rocks, and floating logs.

Occasionally, she was used to haul the Potter family on an afternoon misadventure a mile or two out of the harbor, then back. Mostly, however, Harry Potter used her for trout and salmon fishing. She was fitted out with permanent down riggers and rod holders for trolling, which seemed to suit Harry and his fishing friends just fine.

What a waste, Lindner thought. Might as well pull the mast and turn it into a full-time power boat.

"Trout still down deep?" Potter asked.

"Yes sir. We pulled nets early this morning and they're down about sixty, seventy feet."

Potter nodded. "I hear they're biting good out at Isle Royale, so I'm taking her over there for awhile. Go ahead and fill up the tank and these three jerry cans, Paul."

Lindner's eyebrows arched. "Yes sir," he said. "You going straight across?"

"No," Potter answered. "Thought I'd kinda follow the shore, then go across on the ferry boat route over to Washington Harbor."

"Got a chart?" Lindner asked.

"Yah, there's a map down below somewheres," Potter answered offhandedly.

"Be sure to stay clear of the Rock of Ages light," Lindner advised. "It'll be on your right, and it's surrounded by reefs."

"Okay, I'll do that," Potter said agreeably.

"Going over there alone?" Lindner asked. He wasn't being nosy, just making conversation as he dispensed the diesel fuel.

"Yah, unless you want to come along," Potter replied.

"Nah, I gotta work all day."

"Well, it should be an easy trip. I figure about eight hours, so I'll make it easy before dark. The wife's coming over on the ferry tomorrow morning."

Lindner topped off a jerry can and started another. He looked at Potter sitting all soft and shapeless in the cockpit, wearing blue jeans and an old stained sweater. Some guys have all the luck, he thought. Here's a guy who looks like a slob, can't learn to tie a proper knot, is too lazy to clean up his boat, and he's got it made. He owns a big resort and I pump gas. It's not fair.

Lindner was still shaking his head as he recoiled the long hose and hooked the nozzle back on the pump. "Twenty-eight gallons," he said. "Comes to $33.25."

"Just put it on my bill, Paul," Potter said, starting the diesel engine.

3

"Will do, Mr. Potter."

Lindner untied the lines and pushed the boat away from the dock.

Harry Potter pushed the throttle forward and spun the wheel to point the bow out. The stern kicked around and caromed off a piling, then grazed a second one before it cleared. He turned back and shrugged at Lindner, who shook his head.

Damned idiot, Lindner thought, watching the boat move away under power. On the stern, painted in blue script, was the name *Fishin' Fool.* You got that right, he thought. With any luck, you'll miss Isle Royale altogether.

He was absolutely right.

C aribou County sheriff Ray MacNulty sat behind his big desk, his weather-creased face offset by silvery brown hair and split by a toothy smile. He was a big man, a sheriff of old-time celluloid proportions, standing six foot two in his favorite wool socks. According to the scale at the Caribou County clinic, he weighed 240 pounds, which worrisome Doc Johnson said was twenty-five pounds too much to be chasing any bad guys on foot. Still, people said he looked impressively formidable at fifty in his tan sheriff's outfit.

Today, however, MacNulty was out of uniform, wearing a short sleeved white shirt and the blue tie his wife, Muriel, had picked out to match his dark blue blazer. Despite the tie, he wore the size seventeen shirt neck open; buttoned earlier, it had made his temples throb.

He was not usually the kind of man people would call jovial. Witty, sometimes, bright, even, but certainly not given to silly smiles or cigars, like the one that protruded, looking petite between his meaty fingers. Then again this was not an ordinary day.

This was an election year. MacNulty enjoyed his work and

the prestige of his office, but hated the politics and public appearances that went with it every four years. He had been elected five times, but it never got any easier, and he had dreaded the coming months.

Then today at noon, in the middle of July, it was over. Over before it really started. The deadline for filing as a candidate came and went and he was unopposed. Winner by default. Done with campaigning for at least four more years.

It had been almost a pleasure to address the luncheon meeting of the Northport Lions Club. Instead of dishing out the usual political crap, he had given them some straight talk about drugs and their kids.

He then went back to his office and his jubilant staff, who had decorated the place with streamers and balloons to celebrate their continued employment.

So why not grin like a kid at Christmas, MacNulty thought to himself. You just got a five hundred pound gorilla off your back. Now you can concentrate on enforcing the laws in twenty-five hundred square miles of northeastern Minnesota. So what if half of it is water? Who cares if there's only four thousand people scattered around and half of 'em live in or near the county seat of Northport? You're doing what you've always wanted to do in the only place you've ever wanted to do it. You're one of the lucky few and you've got good reason to glow a little.

Chief Deputy Walt Downing appeared in the doorway and propped himself against the frame. The merriment in his eyes belied the look on the hard, flat face that never seemed to hold a suntan.

"Just got the news, Chief. The word on the street is that you fixed it, bought off some people so you could get your pension."

MacNulty's smile receded, his eyebrows lowered. "Bullshit. You know that's not true."

"That's what they say," Downing shrugged, deadpan.

5

MacNulty hesitated, growing angry, then watched Downing's face crease with a gleeful smile.

"Dammit, Walt, at least let me enjoy myself today. Is that too much to ask?"

Downing, still grinning, walked to the sheriff's desk, hand outstretched. "Glad it was easy for you this time, Ray. Congratulations."

MacNulty smiled and extended his big hand. "Thanks, Walt. Just promise me you won't go getting yourself shot again this term."

"Once is plenty, thanks," Downing replied, settling himself in an easy chair and propping a foot against the coffee table.

MacNulty spun to pick up the ringing phone on his credenza.

"Ray," the voice said, "this is John up at La Rendezvous. I hear you lucked out again."

"Thanks a lot, John," MacNulty said sarcastically. "What I think you meant by that ass-backwards compliment is that you get to keep your job four more years."

"That, too, Ray," said John Brouillard, laughing. Brouillard was chief of law enforcement at the La Rendezvous Indian Reservation thirty miles northeast of Northport, and an official Caribou County deputy.

The reservation was Minnesota's most northeasterly point. Shaped like the tip of an arrowhead, its cutting edges were bounded by Canada and Lake Superior.

"Got a problem you should know about," Brouillard continued in a serious tone. "I just got a call from Captain Jurgenson on the ferryboat Wenonah. Says he's got a hysterical lady on board who lives near Northport. Name of Agnes Potter."

"Good God, that's the woman who owns Sawtooth Lodge—she and Harry, her husband."

Brouillard gave a low whistle. "Jeez, Ray, that's a pretty big operation. Anyhow, she says her husband is missing. Claims he left Northport yesterday by boat and was supposed to meet her at Washington Harbor."

MacNulty covered the mouthpiece. "Walt, what kind of boat does Harry Potter have?"

"Big new sailboat. Something around thirty-five feet."

MacNulty nodded as Brouillard continued.

"Nobody seems to know anything about Potter or his boat out on the island. Jurgenson said he called the park headquarters over at Rock Harbor, but they're in the dark about it. The weather's clear, so Mrs. Potter got some fishermen to look around the west end for him, but he's apparently just not there.

"Anyhow, there was no place for her to stay out there and seeing she's pretty upset, Jurgenson decided to bring her back to La Rendezvous."

"Okay, John, tell you what," MacNulty instructed. "Go down to the landing and get her off the ferry, then drive her down here in her car. I'll talk to her, then I'll take her down to see Augie at the Coast Guard Station.

"One more thing, John," he went on. "Use some of that famous Brouillard charm to keep her from coming unglued. Tell her we'll have him located in no time. Tell her he's probably just got motor problems or something. I'm sure you can handle it."

"Okay, boss, I'll get her there as quick as I can."

"Don't rush it, John. Just take it nice and easy. You'll scare hell out of her for sure if you drive like you usually do."

MacNulty hung up and swiveled around. He stared at his desk pad a few seconds, looked at Walt Downing, and explained Brouillard's side of the conversation.

"Walt, let's get a jump on this thing. I'll call Augie and tell him what little we know. You go find out where Potter keeps his boat and see what you can learn about the boat and his departure. Meet me out at the station in about two hours."

MacNulty looked at his watch. "It's four now. Make it about six. It's still light till nine, so we might be able to do some good yet tonight before dark."

"I'm on my way," Walt said, pulling himself from the padded leather chair.

7

The way Paul Lindner explained it to Walt Downing, Harry Potter had been screwing around on his boat half the morning before he left. Lindner called Potter an asshole, a noun reserved for most of the people he had ever met in his job as fuel dock attendant at Northport Municipal Marina.

Lindner, the self-styled manager of the marina, spent, on average, an hour each day dispensing fuel; the balance of the time he looked after the place, or more accurately, sat aboard the fuel hose box next to the pumps at the end of the tee-shaped dock, smoking Salems, watching seagulls, and thinking profane but rarely profound thoughts.

At twenty-five, Lindner had it made. He lived at home after a failed marriage, spent the four warmest months on the dock, and drew what was locally known as rocking chair pay until spring.

As he later explained, "I didn't know old Potter was goin' anyplace. He just kept haulin' stuff back and forth to his station wagon, ya know?

"Anyhow, I went back towards the shack to catch the phone and there's this *thunk* and the whole goddamn dock shakes. I look around and there's Potter in his big sailboat, scramblin' around with a line in his hand, tryin' to catch a piling before he drifts away.

"I hate to say it, but the guy's a real asshole, ya know? He may have that big resort and lots a money but that don't mean shit. He's the kind of guy that wears a baseball cap with captain on it and lots of gold shit on the brim, ya know?

"Anyhow, I go out to help him, real polite-like even though he's just rammed the dock and somebody should chew his ass. Twice he throws me the line and it falls in the water. Doesn't even know how to coil it up right, so I explain what to do and he finally gets it across.

"So he says, 'Fill 'er up and also fill these three jerry cans 'cause I'm going to Isle Royale.' I couldn't hardly keep a straight face. This asshole can't hardly get out of the harbor without hittin' the breakwall and he says he's going to Isle Royale, forty miles up the lake, and wants to know if I'd like to go along. No fuckin' way, Jose.

"So I tell him, 'Gee, sorry, Mr. Potter, I gotta work.' I mean the guy don't know he's a menace so what do you say? Then he says he's going alone and meeting his wife up there at Washington Harbor and the first thing I think is that he's never even gonna *find* Isle Royale, let alone Washington Harbor.

"I ask if he's got a chart and he looks sorta funny and says, 'Yeah, I think I got a map down below somewhere.' Can you believe the guy? Calls a chart a map.

"So I tell him about the Rock of Ages light this side of the island and all the reefs around it. I'm just tryin' to be helpful, ya know? But he gives me this look like he's off in space somewhere; doesn't know what I'm talking about. Says he's gonna follow the shoreline so he won't get lost. Can you believe it? Shit, man, you can't get to Isle Royale by following the shoreline, but what can I say?

"Anyhow, I give him twenty-eight gallons of diesel. The bill was $33.25. Here's a copy if you want it. And he says, 'Put it on my tab, Paul.'

"Mr. big shot. That's what I hate about guys like that. Got big boats with fancy stuff on 'em that they don't even know how to operate. 'Put it on the tab,' he says, so I do. Then I untie his lines for him and he guns it and kicks the stern around. Hits the dock again like a ton of bricks tryin' to leave. Then he turns around and gives me this wimpy little shrug, like Jeez kid, I'm real sorry, but who gives a shit, you know?

"So away he goes and I can remember thinking, your money can't help you out there alone on the lake, asshole, so bon voyage. Hope you miss the island altogether.

"I know it's not right to think like that, but dammit, sometimes you can't help it, you know? Guy like that might be rich, but he's a fool."

Agnes Potter's eyes were rimmed in red, her round face puffy from wiping tears and blowing her nose.

Ray MacNulty came around his desk and put a comforting arm around her shoulder. She began to sniffle.

"There, there, Agnes. Let's sit you down and hear what happened, then we'll go out to the Coast Guard station together. I'm sure we'll have Harry located and safe in no time."

MacNulty turned to Brouillard. "John, thanks for bringing in Missus Potter. Stick around and go down to the Coast Guard with us. You may be able to help."

Brouillard nodded.

MacNulty looked at Agnes Potter wiping her eyes. She was a stout, matronly woman who showed little hint that she had once been a thin, vivacious charmer, probably the prize catch of the county. The red hair of youth had been replaced by a dyed orange-brown mop. Freckles had become blotches. A five-foot-two-inch frame meant to carry 120 pounds now hauled a cargo of 170.

And yet, he thought, this dowdy little woman and her husband have transformed Sawtooth Lodge from a pleasant, ma and pa place in the little more than ten years since they took over from her parents, into one of the great showplaces of Caribou County and the entire north shore. The couple now sat at or near the top of the Northport social register and were regularly asked to take the lead in civic and charitable causes.

"Agnes," MacNulty said gently, "let me just ask a few questions before we go see Chief Nellis at the Coast Guard station. First, has Harry been feeling okay lately? I mean he hasn't been sick or anything."

She shook her head and blew her nose.

"Has he said anything about the boat acting up?"

"No, I don't think so," she replied, composing herself.

"He was supposed to meet you at Washington Harbor and left a day earlier?"

She nodded. "We planned a few days to fish and cruise around. It was our first real trip since he got the boat."

"Did he seem to know how to operate the boat all right?"

"Oh, yes. Well, sometimes he'd get things mixed up because he was still learning how everything worked. But he was always careful, cautious."

"But you thought he could get to Isle Royale okay? I mean you weren't especially worried?"

"He thought he could. I always worry," she said, sniffling again into her handkerchief.

"I guess that's only normal," MacNulty said. "Why don't we go and get things underway with the Coast Guard. Maybe we can locate him yet this evening."

"John," MacNulty called to Brouillard in the outer office. "Take my pickup and meet us at the Coast Guard station. I'll drive Missus Potter down there."

He helped her to her feet, then slipped into his blue blazer. Harry Potter had left yesterday. Hadn't there been fog then? He wasn't sure, but it seemed like he remembered fog. Was Harry stupid enough to go wandering off in that kind of weather? MacNulty shuddered at the thought. He was no boatman, but it seemed a stupid and frightening thing to do.

B MC August Nellis ran the Northport Station with an easy hand. He was just plain Augie to the many friends he'd made in his three years' duty at Northport. At forty, the balding but burly sailor had eighteen years of service. His rating, Boatswain's Mate, Chief, qualified him for the prestigious job of commanding the Northport station. He had purchased a home in Northport for his family of five and planned to retire there after two more years as station commander.

When MacNulty called him shortly after 4 P.M., Chief Nellis had moved quickly. The station's official mission was search and rescue, which meant boat crews at the ready around the clock. He dispatched the forty-four footer toward Isle Royale without hesitation and a Coast Guard pickup truck to start searching the shoreline.

A call to his group commander in Duluth caused a search plane to be dispatched and readied all Lake Superior units and their Canadian counterparts for search duty. It also generated a quick response from state authorities who supplied the boat's registration numbers, MN-4660-AS.

Augie Nellis could do all this because he had a sharp and well-trained memory of boats and their skippers. He knew the *Fishin' Fool* was a white, Canadian-built C&C 33, vintage 1986 or 1987, with a royal blue waterline stripe and matching dodger and sail cover. Since he knew Harry Potter personally, he was also able to give an excellent, unaided description of the boat's skipper. As far as Nellis was concerned, his scheduled meeting with Ray MacNulty, Walt Downing, and Agnes Potter was pretty much superfluous. The search was already underway and group Duluth was broadcasting a special VHF notice to mariners concerning the disappearance of *Fishin' Fool*.

When Walt Downing arrived, the station's forty-four footer, No. 45300, had reached the halfway point twenty nautical miles west of the Rock of Ages light. The shore search party had combed fourteen miles of shoreline and would continue until dark.

"Chief, how's it going?" Walt asked.

"Oh, it's going," Nellis answered. "The troops are out beating the bushes."

"I figured you'd light a fire under 'em pretty quick," Walt said. "No use wasting summer daylight. Especially when it's sunny and clear."

"So what can you tell me?" Nellis asked.

"According to Paul Lindner over at the fuel dock, Potter

took on twenty-eight gallons, left the dock about ten or ten-thirty and said he'd be following the shoreline as far as La Rendezvous."

"The shoreline, eh?" Nellis mused.

"Yup. And young Lindner wasn't surprised that the boat is missing. Said Harry Potter is a menace; doesn't know what the hell he's doing."

Nellis nodded. "So I've noticed."

"So what do you think?" Walt asked.

"I don't know yet. The fog rolled in and out a couple times yesterday, but it wasn't all that thick. Not enough to make him run up on a rock or a reef unless he was sleeping or something. Staying along shore, he wouldn't be likely to get run over by a ship. I'm sure the answer will be simple enough, once we find him."

"Lindner figured he probably missed the island altogether," Walt replied.

Nellis snorted. "That island is forty miles long and ten miles wide. How the hell could he miss it?"

"I don't know. Just passing along the kid's comments. What have you got out looking?"

"So far, my forty-four footer, a shore party, and an airplane. By now, group Duluth's probably got something coming out of Thunder Bay and the eighty-two footer from the Upper Peninsula, but that's not confirmed."

Nellis stopped as he heard Sheriff MacNulty's voice in the lobby. He went to the doorway.

"Sheriff, we're in here."

MacNulty strode in. "Chief, I don't know if you know Missus Potter. Agnes, this is Chief Nellis."

Nellis offered his hand to the short woman. "Of course we're acquainted. Mrs. Potter, it's good to see you again, though, of course, not under these circumstances."

"Oh dear," she answered. "Does that mean there's more bad news?"

"No, absolutely not," Nellis assured her. "We're already looking, and maybe we'll spot him before dark. That's three hours yet, and the conditions are excellent for a search."

"I'm just so afraid something's happened to him," she said, holding a Kleenex to her face.

"Usually, there's a perfectly logical explanation," Nellis said, "like an engine that won't start, or a line trailing overboard that gets caught in the prop. It happens all the time. Your husband's probably anchored somewhere waiting for help to arrive."

Chief Nellis explained how the search was being conducted, the units currently involved, and his hopes for a speedy solution. He inquired, as had MacNulty, about Harry Potter's physical and emotional condition, then suggested that Mrs. Potter would probably be more comfortable waiting at home. He assured her of an immediate call with any news that might be forthcoming.

"Agnes," MacNulty said, "I'd be glad to drive you out to your place or have John Brouillard go with you."

"No, I feel better, knowing what's being done," she said. "I can drive myself home. You fellows have better things to do than chauffeur me around."

"Well, it's really no bother," MacNulty said, "but if you're sure. . . ."

"I'm sure, Ray," she answered in a firm voice. "Chief, I'm feeling better knowing you've got all those people out looking for my husband. Maybe the best thing for me to do now is go home and pray that you find him safe, soon."

"Yes ma'am, your prayers would be a help," Nellis said. "You know we'll do our best."

"I'm sure you will," she said firmly, and left the room on Sheriff MacNulty's arm. Nellis watched MacNulty escort her to the pearl-gray Cadillac Sedan deVille and wait as she pulled away. MacNulty returned quickly to the office.

"I think your assurances helped. Looks like she's feeling a lot better, Augie."

14

"I wish to hell they did the same for me, Ray."

MacNulty's raised eyebrows caused Nellis to continue. "Walt here has come up with at least one opinion that Harry Potter may be a whiz at running a resort and serving his community, but he's a real Jonah on the water. I happen to agree with that opinion."

"A Jonah?" MacNulty repeated.

"Yeah, bad news. An accident waiting to happen. He doesn't know his boat, he pays no attention to charts, we've had to go fetch him twice already and it's only been two or three months since he got her. Truthfully, Ray, I wouldn't be surprised if he put her on a reef and went blub, blub, blub."

MacNulty stared out the window at the rocky shoreline and the benign waters of the huge lake. He shook his head. "You know, fellas, this just doesn't jibe. The Harry Potter I know is not the guy you're talking about.

"I've known Harry since he came here with a geological survey team back in the sixties. Since then, and we're talking twenty-five years, I don't think he's ever had even a speeding ticket. He's the kind of guy you want as treasurer of your church or club, because he'll have every damn penny accounted for.

"I never heard any rumors about him, never heard of him makin' any dumb mistakes. Old Fred Marquardt thinks he's the greatest son-in-law ever created. Lot of folks figure him and Mike Devon over at the bank got more brains than the rest of the town put together.

"So now you're telling me he's a menace, a dimwit on that boat. An accident waiting to happen; isn't that what you said, Augie?"

Nellis nodded. " 'Fraid I'll have to stand behind that comment, Ray. I don't give a damn what your man has done or hasn't done, he don't know shit about sailboats. It's like if you landed on a strange planet and somebody handed you the keys to a space ship and said, 'Here, take 'er for a spin.' That's how he acts around that boat."

15

"Okay, Augie, I believe you," MacNulty said. "But I know zilch about boats. Give me a for instance."

"Right. We're talking about a sailboat here. Most people use 'em to sail places. Potter uses it like a motor boat, knows nothing about the sails. He tried putting up the jib the other day, that's the sail in front of the mast. Put it on upside down and never knew the difference. Damnedest thing I ever saw.

"So far, we've been out to get him twice. One time, he ran out of fuel. Said there wasn't wind enough to sail back. Second time, he got the halyard wrapped around the spreader and stuck the mainsail halfway up the mast. Half the sail was overboard, along with several lines. He started up the engine and wound a line up in the prop. Really dumb.

"If he's so careful and cautious, Ray, why doesn't he have someone teach him about what to do on a boat? If he manages to screw up in perfect weather, imagine what would happen in a squall or in rough seas. A C&C 33 is a big, safe boat. Hell, you could sail her around the world. But a boat that size can be a real handful in heavy weather, way beyond Harry Potter's ability."

MacNulty shrugged and shook his head. "You're the expert, Augie, but it sure as hell is surprising. Glad I couldn't go fishing with him last month when he asked."

"I got the same kind of story from the Lindner kid over at the fuel dock," Walt said. "Figures one day soon, Harry's just going to demolish the dock. Says the only thing Harry got right on his boat is the name, *Fishin' Fool*."

"Dumbest name I ever heard of for a sailboat," Nellis said, chuckling. "But I got to agree it sure fits to a tee."

"So what's happening with this search you got going?" asked MacNulty. "How does it work?"

"Group commander down in Duluth, a lieutenant, he coordinates it," Nellis said. "We'll hit the obvious, most likely areas before dark, then if we don't locate him, we'll add more units and set up a grid pattern in the morning."

"Weather expected to stay nice?"

16

"Through tomorrow at least. Actually, except for the spotty fog yesterday, it's been about perfect. No rain, no squalls. Flat seas. Couldn't be better."

"One more thing," MacNulty said. "If you don't find him, how long you figure to keep looking?"

Chief Nellis looked out the window and hesitated momentarily. "I'd say three days max. This isn't the open ocean. He's got to be somewhere in a confined area. We can look a second time over that area, but after that, we're just sawing sawdust."

"Supposing he did run up on a rock and sink," Walt asked. "Would it be likely you'd see debris in the water?"

"Hard to say, Walt. Boat like that doesn't have a lot of equipment that would get out through the companionway and stay afloat. Maybe a seat cushion, paddle, a few little odds and ends. Stuff could wash up on the rocks and we'd never know where it came from. Those things aren't easy to see."

"Well, keep in touch, Augie. Let us know what's happening," MacNulty said.

"You'll be the first to know, Ray, but I got bad vibes on this one. If we don't find him by dark...." Nellis hesitated, then shrugged. "Know what I mean?"

MacNulty nodded. "Hope you're wrong," he said, and turned toward the door.

MacNulty pulled off the highway onto a rough, single lane road cut into the forest of birch and spruce. He bounced along slowly for nearly a quarter mile, then emerged into a small, natural clearing. Three pickup trucks, an old sedan, and a Jeep Wagoneer were parked at odd angles. There was no one in sight.

MacNulty pulled off into the weeds and got out. He walked stiffly toward the roar of heavy equipment coming from someplace beyond the screen of spruce trees ahead.

He picked his way over rocks on the path that led through

the spruce, then emerged onto a recently bulldozed clearing. The wood skeleton of a large structure sprawled across the raw clearing. A red crane on caterpillar tracks was swinging a huge laminated beam over the structure.

He watched for a moment, then spotted a trim, sandy-haired woman in sweatshirt and blue jeans watching the crane maneuver. Her back was toward him, and with the noise, she didn't hear his approach.

"What'cha building?" MacNulty shouted. "A hotel?"

The woman spun around backwards, startled. "Jeez, Ray," she said, holding her hand over her heart. "You scared me."

"Sorry," he shouted. "Just thought I'd stop and see how you're doing, Prentice."

She nodded. "They're setting the big beams today. Does it really look like a hotel?"

MacNulty shook his head. "Naw. It looks great. Bigger than I figured though."

She shrugged. "It just kept growing. We didn't want to leave anything out."

The crane was lowering the beam into place and they stopped talking to watch. Below the beam, an older man in a plaid shirt with a baseball cap and carpenter's apron was gesturing, guiding the crane operator.

Then another man, taller and looking lanky in a loose red T-shirt, began to gesture violently. When it became apparent the crane operator wasn't responding to his signals, he strode angrily to the crane and motioned, with a hand across his neck, to shut it down.

The roar subsided suddenly, beam still hanging suspended, and an argument ensued.

"You're supposed to be at least three feet north."

"I was watching Axel. Doesn't he know where it's supposed to go?"

"If you were watching, you sure as hell weren't responding."

"Why don't you go talk to Axel and figure out who's giving orders, then let me know."

The older man walked over to the crane, adjusted his baseball cap, and talked quietly to the lanky man and the crane operator. Then the lanky man threw up his arms in frustration, turned away, and walked toward Prentice and her visitor. MacNulty saw that one hand was heavily bandaged.

She shook her head. "Nels can't understand why they're taking so long," she said to MacNulty. "He thinks you can build a house in two weeks."

"How's it going, stranger?" Nels said as he approached MacNulty, hand outstretched.

The sheriff gripped the lanky man's good hand and squeezed briefly. The two were of equal height, six foot two and change, though MacNulty had fifty pounds on the younger man with the peculiar sun streaks in his hair.

"Thought you were going to do some trout fishing," MacNulty said, "but now I see by the hand you're in the house-building business."

"The hand? Got it caught between some two-by-fours," Nels answered.

Prentice rolled her eyes.

"I'm serious," Nels said. "If I thought I could leave these clowns alone. . . ."

"These clowns, as you call them, are the best builders in Northport," Prentice replied. "They'd do a lot better if you weren't nagging them all the time."

Nels rolled his eyes expressively. "Come on," he said. "Northport's got only a thousand people and not a builder in the lot."

"No, I'm serious," she said without humor. "You can't talk to people the way you're doing and still expect them to care about doing a good job."

MacNulty offered his opinion. "Axel over there is a pretty fair hand. You ought to see some of the places he's built."

Nels shrugged, "Well, maybe I'm too impatient, I don't know."

"That's an understatement," Prentice said.

"Hey, guys," MacNulty interrupted, "I didn't stop by to start an argument. I thought maybe I could talk Nels into lunch if I offered to buy. I need to pick his brain."

"Well, I don't know," Nels said, looking back to the beam still dangling from the crane cable.

"Take him with you, Ray," Prentice said. "That's an order." She turned to Nels. "I'll stay here and watch things. Besides, Axel always brightens up when you leave."

Nels smiled down at her and playfully hugged her close. "Something going on between you and Axel that I should know about?"

The big crane roared into action and Prentice pushed Nels away, smiling. She pointed in the direction of the parking lot. "Go to lunch," she yelled over the noise. "Now."

The roar diminished as the two men passed through the screen of spruce and reached the parking lot.

"Want me to drive?" Nels asked, pointing to the Wagoneer.

"No, better take mine," MacNulty said, "just in case."

They climbed into the sheriff's pickup and drove slowly over the rocky road.

"Those old Norwegian carpenters can be a handful," MacNulty said. "But from what I know, they're best left alone. Start riding 'em and they'll just get more stubborn."

"You're telling me I should go fishing?" Nels asked.

"Sure, why not," MacNulty said. "We can take the canoe up to Frying Pan Lake on Friday and see if those big Brookies are biting. Hell, you can come by evenings to see what they're doing on the house. Life's too short to get all worked up over it."

"I just wanted it to be perfect for Tizz," Nels said, using his pet name for his wife.

"Then let her be the straw boss," MacNulty said. "Hell, she'll have old Axel eating out of her hand in no time."

"I'll think about it," Nels said, then hesitated. "What's this about picking my brain?"

"What about Friday?" MacNulty asked.

"Sure, what the heck," Nels replied.

"Great. Now for the brain picking," MacNulty responded.

The sheriff started from the beginning, with Harry Potter's departure from Northport on Thursday and Agnes Potter's return from Isle Royale on Friday.

"Today's Monday," MacNulty said, "which means the Coast Guard's been looking almost three days without finding a trace. The weather's been quiet all this time, but nobody's reported seeing him, hearing from him, nothing. He just went off Thursday into the fog and vanished.

"Now, based on that evidence, what do you think could have happened?"

Nels was silent for a moment. He knew boats, especially sailboats. For the past eight years, he and Prentice had operated Paradise Charters, a successful sailing operation based in the United States Virgin Islands. The business owned nine boats, ranging from thirty-six to fifty feet, and also managed more than a dozen others for their owners.

"Ray," he said finally. "Almost anything imaginable could have happened. I mean that, literally. Put an inexperienced man on a complicated piece of equipment and the smallest molehill can become a mountain. I've seen it time and again."

"You mean it could have sunk in perfectly quiet weather without a trace?"

Nels nodded. "Yup. Let's say the water intake line breaks or comes loose. Then the engine overheats and stops. He looks below and there's water pouring into the boat. Probably coming in too fast to keep up with. If he can't figure out where the water's coming from, the boat sinks. Same thing if he throws the shaft or breaks the line connecting any thru-hull fitting."

"Wouldn't the boat stay afloat?" MacNulty asked.

"Not for long," Nels said. "Boat that size has got five thousand pounds of lead in the keel for stability. That same weight is going to pull you down fast if the boat starts filling with water."

"Wouldn't he send out a radio call for help?" asked Mac-Nulty.

"Maybe he couldn't. Maybe the water came in fast enough to cover the batteries, short out the radio. No electricity, no radio. I've seen it happen."

"If he sank, wouldn't there be some debris? Chief Nellis said he could go down without a trace. I find that hard to buy."

"Nellis is right. In the Caribbean, boats vanish without any evidence quite often. It's not because there's no debris; it's because the stuff that's floating consists of small items that are hard to spot from a search plane or a cutter."

MacNulty shook his head. It just didn't seem possible that Harry Potter and his beautiful new boat had simply vanished.

There was a parking space across from the bus stop, where the bus from Duluth had just disgorged its load of a dozen passengers. MacNulty pulled in.

"Amazing," he said. "With the place full of tourists, you can hardly ever find a spot downtown."

Nels and MacNulty got out and walked across to Sid Richardson's Bus Stop Cafe, a local institution. The place was nearly full, as always for lunch, and they had to thread their way to the far corner of the dining room section.

It was a slow process. After six weeks in town, it was Nels's first real chance to meet the business community.

Everybody knew MacNulty, and the sheriff in turn introduced his friend to table after table. "Fellows, this is Nels Dahlstrom. He's building a place on the lake out west of town. George, Ernie, say hello to Nels."

In rapid succession, Nels met the postmaster, the banker, the vet, the restaurant proprietor, and several others. Nels was embarrassed by the attention to his red T-shirt and bandaged hand, but was grateful for the chance to meet the people he would need to know as a summer resident.

Mike Devon, whose bank was handling the construction financing for the Dahlstrom house, was especially interested in the lanky newcomer.

"Nels, I was out of the bank the day you were in," Devon said. "Couple of things that I'd like to ask you about, whenever you've got time."

Nels nodded, "Sure, how about tomorrow morning? I've got some questions myself."

The questions concerned loose ends in his father's estate, which Nels had been trying to sort out. As an only child, Nels had inherited everything after his father's tragic death last spring. It was a sizeable estate, made up of many small bits and pieces that had still not been completely accounted for. There were stocks, bonds, CDs, property, several bank accounts, an airplane, two cars, and multiple insurance policies. As the pieces were liquidated and the cash accumulated, Nels had simply been depositing everything in a savings account at the Northport State Bank. It was probably past time to take a look at what he had and what should be done with it. So far, he had left it untouched, financing the construction of his house with surplus cash from his business and a construction loan that Mike Devon would probably tell him was a waste of interest.

Having met Devon, who seemed a nice man in his mid-thirties, made things easier, since Nels often had a hard time dealing with strangers. Meeting Devon also made him eager to sit down at the bank and review the assets that had suddenly made him comfortable, if not exactly wealthy.

Nels and MacNulty took a table in the far corner and ordered the liver and onion special. Nels hadn't had liver for years, since Prentice wouldn't touch the stuff.

"Quite a treat," he said, explaining his wife's antipathy.

MacNulty grinned. "I got the same problem, so I come in on Mondays when it's on special. Sid's got a way with liver."

The waitress brought both of them iced tea, which Mac-Nulty sweetened liberally with three packages of sugar.

"You ready for the second half of my question?" he asked.

Nels looked up, puzzled. "Second half?"

"Yeah," MacNulty said. "What happened to the boat if it didn't sink?"

"You think that's an option?" Nels asked.

"I don't know if it is or not. I'm just asking, 'What if?' "

"Well," Nels began, "it's not just floating around loose out there. Somebody would have seen it long before now.

"I saw a chart of the lake two, three weeks ago, and if I remember right, there's a couple hundred islands up on the Canadian side. A boat might be pretty hard to find back in those islands, especially if there are lots of little coves."

Nels looked down at his silverware, rearranging the knife and spoon as he thought. Finally, he looked up at MacNulty.

"Maybe they didn't find it because it's not there any more. He could have sailed it out of Lake Superior through the Soo Locks. Or he could have taken it someplace there's a travelift or some other equipment for lifting boats and had it lifted onto a semitrailer—it would have to be a lowboy—and just hauled away. There are people who specialize in hauling boats that would think nothing of it. A thirty-three footer would be easy for them to handle, no problem at all."

MacNulty was staring into his iced tea glass. He looked up. "That whole idea never occurred to me. Hell, the boat could be out on the Atlantic or maybe down on the Gulf Coast by now. By the time we figured out who hauled it and where they went, the boat could be repainted or changed somehow so we'd never find it."

"I was talking hypothetically. You think it might really have happened?" Nels asked, surprised. "Would he have reason to do it?"

"No, I don't think so," MacNulty replied. "What I'm thinking is that somebody else might have done it."

24

"Like pirates?" Nels suggested. "I know things like that happen in the Caribbean sometimes, but up here on Lake Superior? You ever hear of anything like that before?"

"No," MacNulty said, shaking his head. "I was just stretching my brain, airing it out a little with some fresh thoughts. Truth is, I don't have a clue what happened.

"Actually, this is the kind of thing that drives me nuts. A man disappears without a trace. There's no sign that any law's been broken, so my hands are tied. I can put out a bulletin, which I've already done, but that's about it. The Coast Guard can search, which they've done, but that's the end of it. Nothing more to do.

"So I go to Agnes Potter and say, 'Sorry, Agnes, we've looked, but he's gone. Maybe he drowned, maybe he took off, maybe pirates got him. Who knows? But since I don't know of any laws being broken, I can't be bothered with it. Good luck, Agnes.' "

Nels shook his head. "Frustrating."

"Drives me nuts," MacNulty repeated.

"So what can Agnes Potter do? What are her options?" Nels asked.

The waitress served the plates of liver smothered in onions. MacNulty began to cut his meat, then stopped.

"Offer a reward. Print up posters and put 'em around. Hire a private detective to check all the possibilities. No end to what she can do if she wants."

"But won't the insurance companies send investigators?" Nels asked. "They stand to pay out on life insurance and boat policies."

MacNulty shrugged. "Maybe, maybe not. They're not going to spend penny one 'til the thing gets in front of a judge. The burden of proof is on her that the man and his boat have been lost."

He resumed eating, then glanced up at Nels, who was staring out the window.

Tuesday morning, with the rising sun still a mustard smudge in the eastern sky, a C&C 33 entered the locks at Sault Sainte Marie.

A clean shaven gray-haired man stood at the wheel maneuvering the boat, while a younger, dark-haired woman handled lines on the bow. The white hull bore an Ohio registration sticker and number, OH-4357-1M.

The skipper gave their names as Bud and Norma Lacey, Cleveland, Ohio. The recording officer noted the boat had royal blue cove stripe, matching bimini folded back, matching sail cover, and bore the name *Whisper* in blue across the transom. Below the name was the port, Cleveland, Ohio, in small block letters.

"Is she documented?" asked the locks officer.

"Yes, number 23801, out of Cleveland," replied the skipper.

"How long have you been on the lake?" asked the officer.

"About ten days," Lacey replied.

The officer flipped through pages on his clipboard, then stepped away and talked into his hand-held radio telephone. After a minute, he stepped back to the sailboat.

"We don't show you entering her at the Soo," he said.

"Ah, no, that's right," Lacey responded. "We had her trucked to Bayfield and put in there, at the yacht basin. Wanted to see Lake Superior but didn't have time to sail her all the way from Cleveland and back. Only got two weeks vacation, ya know."

"You're taking the boat to Cleveland?" the officer asked.

"Yup, that's right," Lacey said. "Heading home."

The officer nodded, stepped back for another look at the boat and talked again to the radio.

The line handlers had secured the small fleet of pleasure and work boats and the locking down process began.

By the time the boats had dropped more than twenty feet to the level of Lake Huron, the officer had verified Ohio registration and U.S. documentation of the C&C 33 *Whisper*.

He checked the Coast Guard description of the missing boat once more and assured himself that this was not it. Then he watched as the Laceys released the lines and pulled out into the adjoining waters of Lakes Huron and Michigan.

T he deeply tanned, sandy-haired man sat in the cockpit of his sailboat as the sun burned the Tuesday morning haze away. He was braiding a wire to rope halyard, a difficult and time-consuming job.

His boat, a white-hulled C&C 33, was tied bow and stern against a low rock ledge on the eastern side of a small island in Nipigon Bay.

He listened to the deep rumble of a diesel approaching at low speed, then watched as a red-trimmed, forty-four foot Canadian patrol boat slid into view between islands to the north. It was the first boat of any kind he had seen in days.

The bright colored double-ender altered course and idled toward him, its hull reflected in the calm waters of the cove. The boat commander, a petty officer, stepped from the wheelhouse as the heavy patrol boat glided to a stop alongside.

"Good day, Captain," the officer said. "May we ask you a few questions?"

"Sure, fire away," the tanned sailor answered.

"I note you have no registration numbers. Is this a Canadian yacht?"

"Nope, American."

"I see," said the unsmiling but polite officer. "And what might the home port be? I am assuming you're documented?"

"That's right. U.S. documents, port of Mobile."

"That's Mobile in Alabama?"

"Right again."

"We would like to see your papers and inspect your vessel, Captain."

"Really? What's the problem?"

"No problem, Captain. You are in Canadian waters and we are authorized, as is your own Coast Guard, to make routine inspections of safety equipment and documents."

The sandy-haired sailor shrugged and stood up. He was wearing khaki shorts, a long-sleeve sweatshirt, and tan boat shoes.

The petty officer and a boatswain's mate stepped over the double lifelines.

"If you would get your documents, the bosun will have a look below," said the Canadian officer.

The sailor went below to the nav station and returned with a certificate of documentation. It was studied silently.

"And you are Commander Ross Trawick?" the officer asked.

"That's Trawick as in tray, and it's Commander, U.S. Navy, retired," said the sailor. "Here's a military ID for verification.

"Maybe I should explain," he continued. "I retired about a year ago after twenty-three years in the Navy. Bought this boat down in southern Ontario at the factory and sailed her up here to a summer place I have on Madeline Island, that's in the Apostles. I spend five months a year there and the rest down in Baldwin County on the east side of Mobile. Since I have residency in Alabama, the boat hails from Mobile, even though she's never been there."

"This address says Bayfield, Wisconsin. . . ."

"That's where I get my mail while I'm on Madeline Island. The boat sits at a mooring in the cove near my house."

"So the boat is more or less permanently situated on Lake Superior?"

"About as permanent as a wandering old sailor can get," Trawick said, grinning.

"I see no sail cover, Commander. Do you have one?"

"It's black. Rolled up down below if you'd like to see it."

"No, that won't be necessary. I see you've done some recent repair work on the decking outboard of the cockpit."

"Very observant. I do some racing and thought it might be handy to mount extra winches for spinnaker work as well as single handing. Turned out they were in the way. They were Lewmar 48s, same as the primaries. You can measure the thru-deck holes for yourself, if you'd like."

The bosun came up the companionway with his checklist completed.

"Well boats, she look shipshape to you?" Trawick asked.

"Yes sir, pretty well loaded, I'd say. Everything handy and well-marked. Didn't see any bolt cutters, though. They might come in handy in an emergency."

"Overhead compartment, port side up in the bow. There's the cutter, a long-handled nicropress, and an emergency tiller. You miss 'em?"

The bosun's face colored. "Yes sir, I guess I did." He turned to his boat commander. "Everything in order safety-wise. His list is longer than mine."

"Well sir, sorry to bother you," the petty officer said. "Thanks for your cooperation." He turned and stepped over the lifelines onto the cutter. "Oh, one thing more. I forgot to ask you the name of your yacht."

"*Golden Fleece,*" Trawick said, hooking his thumb toward the stern. "Says so right on the transom."

The Canadian officer gave an odd little salute and disappeared into the wheelhouse. The lines were cast off, the fenders removed, and the big diesel rumbled as the cutter backed away.

N ext morning at 11 A.M., Sheriff MacNulty was back at the Dahlstrom construction site. The weather had turned to that mixture of fog and light rain that the Lake Superior coast can experience in any season. It's the stuff that sends tourists home a day or two early.

Nels was alone, clad in a red foul weather jacket, shorts, and baseball cap, checking the dimensions of the stud walls with a long tape measure.

"Neither rain nor snow nor dark of night," teased MacNulty, picking his way through the open interior walls.

"Prentice said about the same thing," Nels replied, grinning, "and she added something about being crazy."

"I was just coming to that part," MacNulty said. "You remind me of the old Norwegian fishermen around here when I was young. They never liked it much unless their skiffs were coated in ice from the cold and waves."

"No way, Josè," Nels replied. "I draw the line on ice. I may be crazy, but I'm not a complete fool."

"That's why I stopped by to see if you got a minute in your busy schedule to talk."

"Talk about what?" Nels asked.

"About that sailboat that may or may not have sunk," MacNulty replied.

"Got something new on it?" Nels asked, his interest obvious to MacNulty.

"Just got some ideas," the sheriff said. "Come sit in the car where I can stay dry and have a cigarette."

"Sure, I can spare maybe a minute, minute and a half," Nels replied lightly.

The two men walked through the spruce trees to the sheriff's cruiser, where Nels pulled off his waterproof coat and shook it before climbing into the passenger seat. "So what's happening?" he asked.

"Augie Nellis from the Coast Guard called me first thing this morning. Said they were discontinuing the search about an hour from now, at noon. They've turned up zilch. They ran into two boats the same as Harry's. . . ."

"C and C 33s?"

"Yeah, that's the kind. Anyway, both seemed to have papers in order and logical stories. Both skippers, surprisingly, were about Harry's size, but different enough to eliminate suspicion. One's a retired Navy man poking around the islands in Nipigon Bay. The other's a guy from Ohio who exited the lake through the Soo locks yesterday. He's on his way home with his wife aboard.

"Anyway, the Coast Guard plans to check out both boats further, but at this point, hasn't had the time. They're out of the picture now and the family had to be told.

"So I went out to Sawtooth Lodge to see Agnes, that's Harry's wife, and her dad, who's helping to run things right now. Actually, he's running the whole show, because Agnes is a wreck, which isn't all that surprising.

"Anyhow, I talked to Agnes, but mostly to her dad, Fred, who's still a pretty sharp old guy. He's about seventy now, I'd guess, but he doesn't miss much. You meet him yet? Name's Fred Marquardt."

"No, I don't think so. Doesn't sound familiar."

"No matter. Anyhow, I explained the situation to them about the search and all, told them I was a skeptic, which I am, and suggested that instead of giving up, they should push even harder.

"They agreed, but not for the reason you or I might expect. She holds out hope for her husband, but I think he figures Harry and his boat have sunk. So he got real interested when I explained that if worst came to worst, a good investigator, tracking down all the leads and checking all the possibilities, could influence a judge to declare Harry dead a lot sooner than seven years.

"And they both got real excited when I told 'em I had someone who could go at it right away and spend full time tracking down every possibility. Someone who is not only an expert about boats and sailing, but comes from a local family and can be trusted completely."

"Whoa, wait a second, Ray. You're not suggesting. . . ."

"I certainly am. In fact I've already told 'em that Nels Dahlstrom is the only man who can do the job."

Nels colored, as he always did when his temper rose quickly. "Goddamn it, Ray, you got no right to start telling me what I will or will not do. You understand that? You can go right back and tell 'em you made a mistake. It's the craziest thing I ever heard of."

"Okay, maybe I jumped the gun, but calm down, will you?" MacNulty urged.

"Of all the stupid goddamn things I ever heard," Nels muttered, looking at the spruce trees out the car windshield. "You take the cake, Ray, you really do."

"Okay now, simmer down, MacNulty said gently. "No need to fly completely off the handle. If you're too busy watching Axel build your house, or if you don't want the responsibility of helping out your neighbors in their time of trouble. . . ." He left the sentence unfinished, throwing up his hands and shrugging his big shoulders.

"Come on, Ray. Dammit, you're not playing fair. You know I don't know anything about this kind of thing. What do I know about being an investigator?"

"You know about boats. You know about people who run boats. You know about the sea and the weather and the way they lift boats out of the water and about a hundred other things a typical PI wouldn't even guess at.

"You said last spring that you wanted to get out of your father's shadow, that you wanted to be known as Nels Dahlstrom, not just Bob Dahlstrom's son. Let me remind you that your dad threw a hell of a big shadow around here and this is the kind of thing you're going to have to tackle if you ever expect to get out from under it."

Nels still smoldered, as much now from embarrassment as from anger. "I don't know. I just don't think I can handle something like this. I wouldn't know where to start."

"We'll talk it through, then go see Agnes and Fred together. You know I'll give you whatever help I can, grease the skids to help you get things done. Tell you what, you think about it, talk to Prentice, and I'll come over later, say about five, and buy you a drink."

"Even if I say no?"

"Yes or no. Without any more pressure from me. I think you're the man for the job, but if you think it's too much for you, that'll be the end of it. Fair?"

"Fair," said Nels, taking MacNulty's offered hand.

P rentice sat in the dining room at the Lakeview Lodge, staring out at the rain-washed rocks and the cold, gray lake that surged around them.

The rustic room, its rough-sawn walls covered with trophies from Ollie Alderson's lifetime of hunting and fishing, was filled, as it always was when the weather turned ugly.

Nels joined his wife at the window table and sat down heavily with a groan, his shoulders slumped. She knew without glancing up that something was wrong.

"Just looking out there makes me feel cold," she said. "Did you get wet, chilled?"

"No," he said. "I feel fine."

Now it was his turn to stare out the window. She turned to him, took in his sun-streaked hair, matted from the rain.

"What is it, then?" she asked. "Something wrong at the house?"

He shook his head and kept staring out the window. She waited, becoming exasperated with his overdramatized actions.

Some day I'm going to just blurt it out, she thought. Tell him to stop acting like a kid. Why does he overdo it? Doesn't he think I can read him? Instead, she looked sympathetically at him and said, as gently as she could, "Tell me what's wrong."

"MacNulty came by again," Nels answered. "Wanted to talk some more about that missing boat. They've called off the search, but Ray convinced Mrs. Potter and her dad to hire an investigator to keep looking. He's trying to talk me into being the investigator."

"Oh?" she replied. "Isn't that sort of a dangerous thing?"

"Dangerous? No, I don't think so. More like studying the possibilities and checking them out. Like, did he sink or did he just want people to think he did?"

"If it's dangerous, you should say no. We had enough of that last spring. I'd be worried sick if you were into something dangerous, Nels."

"No, it's not, Tizz. But it bothers me that MacNulty is pushing me to do this, and I know zilch about being an investigator."

Now it was Prentice's turn to stare out the window, contemplating the idea. After what seemed like several minutes, during which time Nels ordered soup and a sandwich, she turned back and said simply, "Do it."

"Do it?" he questioned.

"That's right; take the job. At least get into it and see what happens. I can handle most of the house things. You'd be free to investigate to your heart's content."

"Have you forgotten that Graham will be here within a week with *Island Girl*?"

Graham was their right hand man at Paradise Charters and a skilled charter captain. He was taking a busman's holiday during the off-season by delivering their favorite boat, the J40 *Island Girl*, up the Atlantic and through the St. Lawrence Seaway to Northport. He had called them two days earlier upon entering Lake Huron north of Detroit.

"No, I haven't forgotten. You promised to keep him busy when he arrived, and I think he'd make a fine investigator's assistant, don't you?"

"Tizz, come on. Neither one of us knows the slightest thing about being an investigator."

"I know, honey," she said, then laughed. "Sort of like the blind leading the blind."

"It's not funny. We're talking about a very serious thing here. Harry Potter was well-respected. A town leader. This is definitely not fun and games."

Prentice subsided. "No, I know it's serious business. But I think you can find out whatever there is to find out. And I think Graham can be a big help to you. And then there's the real reason. . . ."

"Which is?"

"That Axel needs to get out from under your impatient glare so he can get on with the house. You're not exactly Frank Lloyd Wright, you know."

"No, I don't suppose I am," he replied glumly.

"Don't start sulking. I'm not saying you haven't tried, and tried hard. It's just that you're more likely to be a good boat investigator than a good house builder."

"I don't know. I just don't like MacNulty's pressure tactics."

"No, but you've got to admit it's probably the only way he'd get you to consider it."

"Yeah, I guess you're probably right."

"So do it," Prentice repeated.

"Okay, I'll give it a shot, but I'm still not convinced it's the right thing to do. My name could be mud around here if I screw up."

"Somehow, I don't think you'll screw up, but think about the alternative. If you keep nagging Axel, he'll quit and your name will be mud anyhow, so what've you got to lose?"

It was not the same Sawtooth Lodge that Nels remembered from his boyhood, when his father and friends occasionally used it as a hunting headquarters. There must be a hundred cars in the lot, he thought as he looped through it in search of a parking space.

The pathway to the main entrance led through a glade of

pines and past the outdoor portion of the huge heated indoor-outdoor pool. Despite the unseasonably raw weather, several children laughed and splashed in the steamy warm water before ducking back under the glass divider wall into the tropical indoor setting, complete with poolside palms and a thatched hut bar.

Nels went through double doors into the two-story lobby where a fire crackled comfortably in a circular stone hearth. The decor, he noted, was Indian, with solemn totems and wall-hung blankets vying for attention. He went to the front desk and asked a young woman in a buckskin squaw dress for Mrs. Potter.

"Down the hall on your right side," she said, gesturing to an open doorway.

He followed her instructions into a corridor. To the right was a secretarial bullpen with three desks. One of the desks was occupied by a middle-aged woman.

"I'm here to see Mrs. Potter," Nels said.

"Your name, sir?" the woman asked.

"Nels Dahlstrom. She's expecting me."

"Oh yes, Mr. Marquardt will see you, if you'll come this way."

She led him to an unmarked door that opened into a spacious office overlooking the lake.

"Mr. Marquardt? Mr. Dahlstrom is here to see you."

Fred Marquardt stood and walked around the desk. "Nels, I never would have recognized you. Somehow I expected someone younger. College kid. You're what, thirty-five?"

"And then some, sir," Nels answered, shaking the short, square built man's hand.

"None of that 'sir' business around me, Nels," Marquardt said with a head shake. He gestured at the large and beautifully finished office. "This isn't my style. Harry and Agnes, they like it plush. I had me a cubbyhole in a big closet back when I was running the show."

He shook his head again. "But that was years ago, back when me and Ivy had the place. Sit down, Nels, sit down, and call me Fred. That's my name."

Nels sat in an easy chair, uneasy at having arrived before MacNulty.

"Knew your Dad well, back when you were so high," Marquardt continued, holding out his hand at waist height. "Used to stay right here with his big shot friends. Brought you along sometimes. Don't know if you'd remember."

Nels was nodding and about to speak when Marquardt went on.

"Hell of a swell fellow, your Dad. Terrible shame about him and his young wife, my condolences. Guess we've got the same problem here with Harry turnin' up missing. Agnes is taking it hard, doesn't know what to think. Wanted to sit in on this meeting but she can't talk about it. Falls apart completely.

"Well, what say we get started. The sheriff thinks you're the man for the job and now that we've talked awhile, I agree. So fire away."

Nels was numbed by Fred Marquardt's rapid-fire, one-way conversation. "Well, ah, Fred, I was kind of hoping we could wait for MacNulty before we got started."

"Ah, I completely forgot to mention the sheriff called. Something about an unexpected problem. Said to go right ahead without him. So fire away, Nels."

"Oh, okay, let's see. . . ." Nels started.

"Why don't I just start with Harry. Tell you about him, how he was, how he thought about things, okay?"

Nels merely nodded.

"Well, first off, Harry came here in '63. No, maybe it was '64. Let's see. Me and Ivy went to Palm Springs in '63. Must have been the spring of '64 he got here. Stayed with us here at the lodge while he and this team was out lookin' for minerals or metals or whatever you call 'em. He wasn't rowdy like some of 'em. Clean-cut young fellow. Had a draft deferment on account of school—doing some graduate work. This bunch of people—geologists, seismologists, you name it, we had 'em all right here at the lodge. In those days, some of 'em had that longer hair, but not Harry. Clean-cut, like I said.

"Anyhow, Harry was from Minneapolis. City boy, but he liked it out in the woods, chippin' at them rocks. His folks are nice people, they come up every year for a couple weeks. Anyhow, where was I? Oh yeah, his dad's a retired engineer. Worked at Honeywell. Nice people.

"So Harry was here and next thing we knew, the summer was gone and he and Agnes wanted to get married. Guess they must of fell in love or something when we weren't lookin'. Course we were hard workers, didn't have all this extra help in those days. Now, God almighty, the overhead'll choke a horse. I don't even know 'em all by name. We might not of had as big a place, but when I tell you we did okay, you can believe me.

"So we went down to the Cities and met his folks and figured they was okay so we said, 'Sure, go ahead and get married,' so they did in the old lobby—that's the game and rec room now—I never go in there 'cuz they got those damn video games that'll make you deaf from what I heard—and he just stayed on and helped me out around the place. Said he'd rather learn the resort business than keep on with school.

"So the next thing you know our little Cindi comes along—me and Ivy practically raised the little darlin'—and one day, oh I guess it was maybe ten years ago, Agnes sez, 'Daddy, when you gonna retire to give me and Harry a chance?' I never thought about it that way. We were all doing okay and I was giving them a full 50 percent of everything anyway, so I didn't see the hurry. But she nagged and begged and cried. Said Harry was gonna go off somewheres if he didn't get a chance.

"So I figures, what the hell, give 'em a chance. I worked out a deal they could handle to buy the place—long-term pay-off, you know, so me and Ivy wouldn't want for comfort—and we turned it over.

"At first, nobody knew the difference. We were all still here at the lodge and people kept comin' back like always, so no problems. And then one day a semi haulin' a bulldozer pulls up and the bulldozer crawls off and starts tearing up part of the parking lot, two of our old cabins, even my vegetable garden. You can imagine how I felt about that when I seen what was goin' on. So all hell breaks loose and Harry tells me he's expanding the place and tells me he's got new financing and here's a check for what I owe ya. Wham, bam. Me and Ivy are suddenly out the door and Agnes is tellin' me, 'Daddy, it's best for everyone.'

"Here I take 'em under my wing and show 'em the business and now I'm out on the highway on my keester with a big check and no place to go. And Harry is suddenly the big shot around town who's got the biggest resort in Caribou County and a new Cadillac car.

"For three, four years, I can tell you things was mighty cool between us. We took care of Cindi when they went off places, but that's about it.

"Then, about three years back, Agnes comes over one day and says, 'Daddy, how come you never come around the lodge? Don't you like us any more? Come over and help out if you want.' Well, I came over and saw the way things were in the dining room and told 'em how to fix it and they asked me why don't I fix it for 'em?

"So the next thing I know I'm back workin' my fanny off runnin' the restaurant and I got Ivy out front bein' the hostess and things are all like a big family again. Damnedest thing you ever saw, Nels. Then they start takin' more time off 'cuz things are goin' smooth and they got me back runnin' things while they're gone. Except now I'm workin' for wages instead of half the take. Guess I'm crazy, but what the hell. It's somethin' to do."

Nels nodded and glanced at his watch. Surprisingly, Marquardt seemed to understand.

"So anyhow, that's been going on awhile. Harry and Agnes play with their toys like the boat and go to meetings and parties and me and Ivy sort of look after things.

"Guess I ramble on a little. But if I missed anything, just ask."

Nels smiled and nodded. "Tell me about the boat. I don't mean a description, but how come Harry bought it?"

"I haven't got the damnedest idea why he bought it. Turns out he never used them sails much anyhow. Made a good fishing boat though, after he got it all rigged out. Me and him went out a couple weeks back and caught three cohos. It's a nice, roomy outfit."

"Yes, but did Harry ever do any sailing that you know of?" Nels asked.

"Well, you wouldn't know it, 'cuz he wasn't at all handy with it, but he always said he wanted one of those big sailboats, like you see on the bad breath ads on TV. Said he would love to sail; wanted to go sailing out on the big lake. But I never heard of him doing any sailing 'til he got that boat."

Nels nodded. "Any possible reason you can think of that he would want to leave here?"

"Whoa, there, young fella. Harry and Agnes, they been happy together, if that's what you mean. Hell, he's got the world by the tail right here. Why go someplace else?"

"No problems you know of?"

Marquardt shook his head. "Naw, he's got it made. Him and Agnes will be well off in a few more years. That's not to say the resort business is easy. Some of these tourists nowadays are looney, downright peculiar. You got to put up with 'em. But Harry, he is good at it. Never blows his stack, nice and friendly to everybody. Me? I sometimes tell 'em where to go. Getting too old to put up with all the baloney you see these days. But not Harry. He isn't like that at all."

"Okay," Nels said. "Sheriff MacNulty suggested you offer

a reward for information so I can make up posters and put them around. What kind of reward would you be willing to put up?"

"I s'pose Agnes would pay about anything to get Harry back in one piece, but I don't know. What's fair? Five thousand? Ten thousand? I s'pose one thousand would look too chintzy."

"Five thousand might get people's attention," Nels said. "I don't think you need to go any higher."

"As long as we're talkin' money, Nels, how much we talkin' about for you?"

"To tell you the truth, Mr., ah, Fred, I'm not doing this for the money. If you'd be willing to pay my expenses, I'd be happy."

Marquardt eyed him carefully. "Huh-uh. No deal. If you're goin' lookin' for Harry, I want you to go at it hard. You need some incentive to keep at it 'til the end. Tell you what, you find Harry, dead or alive, or find proof what happened, you get ten thousand dollars."

"Wait a minute," Nels interrupted, "that's way too much."

"No, it's not," Marquardt said firmly. "First off, I don't think it's going to be easy. Second, Agnes wants him back. Money's no big deal. Finally, if he's not coming back, I want to be able to prove to a judge what happened. Harry's got three insurance policies worth a total of $325,000 for Agnes. I don't want her sitting around for seven years watching inflation chew up that money before she gets it."

"Okay," Nels agreed, "we'll do it your way." He held out his hand to Marquardt. "You got a deal, Fred. Expenses plus the bonus if I prove what happened. I'll keep you informed what's going on."

"Okay, Nels, you do that. If you're anything like your old man, you should be able to handle it."

Nels pushed himself up out of the chair, stared hard at the older man, and nodded slowly.

"I'll do that," he said, and turned away.

U nlike some of the old logging roads that led to remote fishing hot spots and were well traveled by sportsmen, this one led nowhere in particular. Where it turned north off the Quill Mountain forestry road, grass grew knee deep in the twin ruts. Small spruce were taking possession of the space in between. It was, at a glance, abandoned and probably impassable.

Mark Ferrell often drove the Quill Mountain Road doing wildlife counts for the U.S. Forest Service. Today, he was checking wood duck nesting boxes on several small lakes around Quill Mountain. As his green pickup rattled over the rock and gravel surface, he heard the familiar croaking calls of ravens and spotted them circling ahead and to the north.

He slowed the truck, curious about the cause of the commotion, which had attracted more than a dozen of the big scavengers. Something dead, he knew. Probably a wolf kill, he guessed, which meant the wolves, foxes, and smaller carnivores had already eaten their fill, leaving slim pickings for the hungry birds.

He stopped. The proximity of the ravens and the convenience of the old, abandoned road on which to walk made a quick look irresistible. He set out through the knee-deep grass and noted immediately that there were tire tracks.

Someone had tried to drive the old road. He smiled and shook his head. Some tourist and his four-by-four had gone exploring, he thought. Some of them will spend their entire vacations exploring abandoned logging roads, hoping to find God knows what.

The old road led downhill and squeezed through a thick screen of alders. Ahead, he could see a big white spruce blocking the road. Lightning strike, he thought. Maybe just rotting from old age.

The ravens circled and croaked just beyond the deadfall.

42

Two of them perched on the downed spruce. Whatever it was lay just ahead.

Ferrell reached the fallen tree, scattering the ravens. He saw the big spruce had been cut to fall across the road. Something scurried away through the brush. He peered through the thick screen of branches and needles, looking for an easy way to crawl past. Then he realized he was looking at the hood of a dark blue pickup truck and froze. He spent his days studying the habits and habitat of wild creatures. They lived and died, ate, and were eaten. All this was familiar, a system to be studied.

Man's intrusion always interrupted things. It was unnatural and somehow angered him. How was he supposed to count the wood ducks when there were fishermen with a loud radio near the nesting box?

He stood unmoving, listening to the silence of the forest, broken only by the croaks of the circling ravens and the hum of flies around the pickup. Then he moved to one side to circle the deadfall. Faded white letters stenciled on the door of the pickup indicated it was the property of Hoffman and Sims Logging.

He came up alongside the pickup box and looked in. It was empty except for a length of chain and a few tools. The tool box behind the cab was closed.

He moved forward to the cab decisively, without thinking. Putting his hand on the door handle, he leaned toward the open window. The smell and sight hit him simultaneously as he stared into the eyeless sockets of what had once been part of a man's face. He stumbled back and fell to his knees among gnarled alder roots, where he gagged.

Inside the cab, lying on the seat, was the partially eaten and decomposing body of a man.

As Ferrell climbed frantically through the fallen spruce and hurried toward his pickup, he glanced back only once.

The ravens were already settling back to their feast.

At Ray MacNulty's suggestion, Nels went first to see Chief Augie Nellis at the Coast Guard station. Though Nellis was gracious and easygoing, he bristled quickly at any implied criticism of his abilities. Not understanding this, Nels plunged in with what Nellis perceived as sarcasm.

"How could we lose a big, safe boat between here and Isle Royale?" Nellis repeated. "Hell, man, we didn't *lose* the boat; Mr. Potter did that. He did it so well that we couldn't *find* it again, which is not surprising when the boat happens to be sitting on the bottom in five hundred feet of water."

"You think she sank then, Chief?"

"Yah, I think so, but what the hell do I know, right?" Nellis shot back.

"Wait a minute," Nels said. "I came in here to ask a few questions and suddenly your nose is out of joint. What gives?"

"Somebody comes in here and acts decent, I go the extra mile. But you come in here with a chip on your shoulder, I'm gonna knock it off for you."

"That's a load. I just asked you how you could lose a boat between here and Isle Royale. No offense intended."

"I heard you the first time," Nellis snapped, and the two men stared hard at each other.

"All right, Chief, if you want an apology, you got it," Nels said quietly. "You got me pegged half right. I don't know much about Lake Superior and I'm trying to learn. Maybe I ask stupid questions because of it."

He hesitated, noted the chief's unwavering glare, and went on. "Just don't give me any shit about boats and the people who run them, or I'll hand it right back to you in your hat. I hold an ocean operator's license—unrestricted tonnage. I own and operate a fleet of sailboats in the Caribbean where I get to deal with assholes like you every day. And I take care of those boats,

44

which is more than I can say about your chief engineer, who's got the injectors fucked up on the port side engine of your forty-four. I also train and evaluate skippers for those boats, and based on that experience I know you got a bosun's mate first running one of your boat crews who shouldn't be allowed out of the harbor."

Augie Nellis continued to stare at the lanky man in front of him, his face red, as if ready to explode. Then he exhaled loudly and seemed to sink a bit in his chair.

"Shit, for an asshole, you don't miss much," he said, "I suppose you'll tell me next you can fix those damn injectors."

"Sure, any afternoon," Nels replied, grinning. "So long as you hold hands with your engineer while I'm doing it and fix his bleeding hemorrhoids later."

Nellis shook his head and returned the grin. "That would be more trouble than the smoking engine."

"Now that we understand each other, what can you tell me?" Nels asked.

"Well, for openers," Nellis replied, glancing in the direction of Lake Superior, "this little pond out here is about the size of New England. Three hundred fifty miles by a hundred sixty. It's cold and deep. Even now, in midsummer, you'd be lucky to last ten to fifteen minutes.

"This one lake has as much water in it as all the other four combined; the waves are steep and short. Don't underestimate it. The storms come up fast and there's not many harbors to hide in."

"You figure a storm got Harry Potter?"

"Naw, just stupidity. He didn't know the boat and he was in a lot of fog. Combine those two things and you got trouble."

"No debris?"

"Didn't spot any. That doesn't mean it wasn't there, as you well know."

Nels nodded. "Maybe I'll get lucky."

Nellis smiled. "You strike me as a lucky asshole."

Nels grinned back. "You should know." He got to his feet. "Augie, if I can call you that, I appreciate your help, and this time I mean it."

"Anytime, Nels. And yes, you can call me Augie. I prefer it slightly to asshole."

The two men grinned and shook hands, knowing they had each found a friend with whom he would gladly go to sea.

Ray MacNulty stood leaning against the tailgate of the blue pickup long after they'd taken the photos and the measurements and removed what was left of Carl Hoffman's corpse. After the ravens, blow flies, ants, and God knows what else had finished, there wasn't much of poor old Carl to cart off.

MacNulty was feeling sick, the kind of deep, tired sick that made him want to go off somewhere and lie down. This was a murder, pure and simple. Nothing could disguise the fact that Hoffman's skull had been bashed in. Maybe crushed was a better word for his report.

He wondered what the hell was going on around here. Four murders in five months. He'd solved the other three, but that didn't seem to help. After years of seeing petty theft and vandalism cases, he was seeing people killing each other.

He shook his head. This didn't make sense. Carl Hoffman was a hard man, not exactly your chamber of commerce type. He worked hard, lived hard, took the edge when he could get it, but never bit off too big a piece. Now somebody had smashed his skull. If the loggers of Caribou County took to settling their differences with blunt, heavy instruments instead of fists, the place would be uninhabitable.

He looked north along the old roadway, unused except for the tracks made by Hoffman's pickup. The truck had been driven in past this point, turned around and returned. He'd checked the tracks and gone over the ground carefully. Whatever had happened had not happened here. He figured his next move was to follow the road to where the tracks ended.

It was quiet, so MacNulty could hear a pickup door slam back on the Quill Mountain Road where his cruiser was parked. A second door slammed. Two people, he thought, so he decided to wait at Carl Hoffman's pickup to see who they were and what they wanted.

He knew word of the murder would soon be oozing in whispered tones around Northport. Spreading gossip was a favorite pastime, and, by now, the sidewalk detectives had probably dispatched themselves to come out to the scene of the crime to see what was doing. Pain in the ass, he thought, watching as two men came over the rise.

Couple of loggers, MacNulty thought immediately. The work clothes and rolling gait gave them away. Both big men, probably six feet or better and built solidly.

As they approached, he recognized the one on the left as Virgil Sims, Hoffman's partner. He studied the one on the right, then realized it wasn't a man at all; it was Big Charlie.

MacNulty maintained a purposeful nonchalance, leaning against the pickup box as the two came up. "Hi, Virgil, Charlie," he said, nodding at each in turn.

Sims nodded to the sheriff, then looked at Hoffman's pickup, studying it as if it had fallen from outer space.

Charlie looked at Virgil, then at the ground. She stood with her fingers stuffed into her blue jean pockets, the way people do when they don't know what else to do with them.

MacNulty hadn't seen her for months, so he didn't know if the puffiness in her face was from a lot of drinking or from crying. He couldn't imagine it being the latter, since Big Charlie Mittner stood six feet tall and weighed about 160 pounds. She had raven black hair, an angular face weathered by years of outdoor living, and was rumored to have fought, drunk, and loved her way through most of the logging outfits in northeastern Minnesota.

MacNulty knew the rumor to be true, since he'd had her in the lockup twice for assault, public drunkenness, and disorderly conduct. She could swing an axe or a right hand with just about anybody, and her temper, especially when drinking, was legendary.

Still, the most amazing thing about Charlie, the part nobody ever forgot, was the color of her eyes. Set in an unremarkable face were the most vivid green eyes anybody had ever seen. People called them cat eyes, and when she fixed you with them, you stayed fixed.

Nobody spoke. Sims continued his study of the alien craft while Charlie, standing back two steps, now looked at the grill.

Finally, Sims pulled out a cigarette, lit it with a scarred Zippo windproof and asked, "What happened?"

MacNulty rubbed his chin and stared at Sims. "Thought you might tell me, you being his partner," he replied.

Sims shook his head. "All we know is what we heard, that he was found here in the truck."

"So when did you see him last?" asked MacNulty.

Sims shook his head again. " 'Bout ten, twelve days ago," he replied.

"And what exactly did you figure he was doing all this time?" MacNulty shot back.

Sims shrugged. "Don't know," he said. "Been acting strange. He went off sometimes."

MacNulty stared at the logger. "You mean to tell me he went off all this time and you never wondered what the hell had happened? Never told anybody he was missing?"

"Oh, I was starting to wonder," Sims replied.

MacNulty switched his attention to Big Charlie. "So what are you doing here, Charlie?" he asked.

Her green eyes flashed briefly at him, then resumed their study of his boots. "I work for the Hoffman and Sims outfit," she said.

"And Virgil here's your new boyfriend?" MacNulty asked.

Her eyes flashed again to meet his. He saw the angry tears coming.

"Charlie bunked with Carl," Sims said.

MacNulty continued to meet her eyes with his own steady glare. "And how long since *you've* seen him, Charlie?"

She shrugged and looked away. "Like Virgil said. 'Bout ten days," she said in a husky but definitely female voice.

"And it doesn't bother you when your boyfriend goes off for ten days without you knowing where?"

She rubbed her left eye with a knuckle. It came away wet.

"Charlie, I asked you a question. I expect an answer," MacNulty snapped.

"Hey, Sheriff, ease up on her," Sims interrupted.

"Shut up, Virgil. I'm not asking for your opinion," Mac-Nulty's voice was hard, his eyes still staring at Charlie.

"He always came back," she replied, her voice unsteady with rising emotion.

"So he went off like this before?" MacNulty said quickly.

She shrugged.

"So where'd he go? Got some cute little number stashed away close by?" MacNulty asked sarcastically, testing her response.

"A lot you know about it," Charlie said derisively.

"So tell me about it, Charlie. Tell me how he could go off for ten days without you gettin' mad at him."

"I don't know where he went," she repeated, steadying herself. "But he always came back."

"Not this time, he didn't," MacNulty said. "This time, he got his head smashed in. And whoever did it was strong enough to put him in the pickup, drive it here, and hide him behind that big white spruce, which was cut down to make it look like a deadfall.

"He's been laying here dead for over a week makin' a tasty diet for the ravens, but neither one of you bothered to report him missing. How convenient. So now, Virgil, you got the logging business all to yourself. And you probably got Charlie out of the deal, too."

MacNulty stopped, waiting for the response.

"Wait just a damn minute, Sheriff," Sims replied indignantly.

"You son of a bitch," Charlie growled, her green cat eyes narrowing dangerously.

"That's right, Charlie. Take a run at me, like I'm some drunken logger. I'll put you on your ass so fast you won't know what the hell happened. Then I'll throw you in the MacNulty Hotel until you come up with a reason why you couldn't possibly have killed your boyfriend.

"You, too, Virgil. If you got half a brain, you better use it to remember what you were doing and who you were doing it with about ten days ago. Because I'm gonna check things real careful and then I'm gonna come back and we're gonna go over every fucking detail to see if you can convince me that I shouldn't arrest you both for the murder of Carl Hoffman.

"Now get the hell out of here," MacNulty shouted, waving them away with the back of his hand. "But don't leave Caribou County without letting me know."

The two loggers turned sullenly and walked south through the tall grass. Charlie hesitated momentarily to throw him one of her if looks could kill glances, before turning her back and continuing.

MacNulty watched them go. Prime suspects, the both of them, he thought. Yet he was guessing that neither was the killer.

Whoever did this would have been quick to report Hoffman missing, he thought, or would have laid back even after the body had been found. They had done neither, he thought, wondering if his hunch and his logic was right.

Still, he thought, they know something; maybe even know who did it. Somehow, he'd have to pry the information out of them before he could put the pieces together. And that, he knew, would be very difficult.

He turned away and began walking north along the old, alder-lined logging road. His first job was to find out where the tire tracks led.

Nels Dahlstrom came into Northport as the pink-trimmed gray dusk was fading. He had been driving five days, all the way around Lake Superior, and he was tired. Moreover, having drawn a near blank in the search for Harry Potter, and *Fishin' Fool*, he was discouraged.

This morning at 6 A.M., he had started at Michipicoten, Ontario. Since then, he had spent fifteen hours traveling four hundred miles with stops at Richardson Harbor, Otter Head, Peninsula Harbor, Port Munro, Port Caldwell, McKellar Harbor, Jackfish Bay, Schrieber, Rossport, Nipigon, Thunder Bay, and La Rendezvous.

In five days, he had distributed or posted 150 reward notices, talked to dozens of fishermen and sailors, checked every travel-lift operation and fuel dock, and looked at every marina and anchorage for C&C 33s.

From Canadian authorities, he had learned today that the C&C 33 skippered by retired Commander Trawick had been seen at anchor off one of the islands southeast of Black Bay Peninsula, some fifty miles west of where it had been boarded earlier and only seventy-five miles from Northport.

In Munising, Michigan, two days ago, he had learned that a boat which its owner described as a C&C had been lifted out and trucked away a week earlier. However, the boat, which belonged to a Tom Jenkins, according to the travel-lift operator, could have been anything from thirty to thirty-five feet. Instead of charging by the foot for the lift out, they had simply collected one hundred dollars in cash, well above the going price. They had no recollection of the boat name or registration, though they scrambled madly through their records when shown the five thousand dollar reward poster.

In Superior, Wisconsin, he spotted a C&C 33 but later verified personally that it was owned by a Canadian couple cruising the lakes.

At the Soo Locks, Nels checked the records of the Ohio boat that had locked down shortly after Harry Potter's disappearance. There was nothing in the documents to indicate that it might have been the *Fishin' Fool.* He had tried calling the phone number in Cleveland but there had been no answer.

So now he was back in Northport with nothing else but a pile of receipts to show for his effort. He had serious doubts about his abilities as an investigator.

He pulled up in front of the darkened room at the Lakeview Lodge. There was a note on the bed.

"Nels," it began, "we're down at the small boat harbor enjoying your favorite toy. We'll hold the steaks 'til ten. Hurry down. Love, Tizz."

Nels smiled. Graham Jackson had arrived safely with *Island Girl,* as he had expected. He'd missed Graham by only a few hours at the Soo two days earlier, so he thought they'd be arriving today.

He hauled his sea bag into the room, showered quickly, and threw on clean boat shorts and a light sweater. It amazed him, as it always did, that he could revive so quickly with good news and the prospect of a happy evening.

He drove the six blocks to the small boat facility with haste and anticipation. Parking, he looked at the end of the dock and saw his beautiful *Island Girl* bathed in the soft glow of her own spreader lights. Three people were sitting in the cockpit, talking and laughing.

As Nels walked along the dock, he was met by a teasing British accent.

"M'God, 'tis Sherlock himself come to investigate."

"Bet your ass, Limey."

"And would Mr. Holmes be fancyin' a sample o' the ship's grog?"

"Only if it's genuine British gin, with a touch of vermouth and the bitters."

"And who said all you bloody Yanks are daft?" Graham laughed, extending a hand.

"You pushed her hard to get here so fast, old buddy," Nels said, grinning. "Good show." He looked at his wife and another woman sitting in the cockpit. "Looks like I'm just in time for the welcome home festivities."

"I told them that you'd make it, hon," Prentice said, pulling herself up to the coaming for a hug and a kiss.

"God, what a trip," Nels sighed. "I feel like I could write a book on little known ports and harbors of Lake Superior."

"Here's a proper British drink, skipper," Graham said, holding out a glass half filled with clear liquid.

"No ice?" complained Nels.

"Her Majesty's finest should not be bollixed up with American ice," Graham replied sternly.

"Nels," Prentice interrupted, "I'd like you to meet Graham's date, Margie Kirkpatrick."

"Glad to meet you, Margie," Nels said to the shadowy figure sitting back near the big steering wheel. He could make out a dark, curly mop of hair, but not much else. "Did you arrive here on the boat, or are you a more recent addition?"

"Quite recent, I'm afraid," the young woman answered pleasantly. "I met Graham at the fuel pump while I was gassing up my uncle's boat for tomorrow's fishing trip. I'm visiting from the Cities."

"Well, then, welcome aboard," Nels said, "but beware the slippery Brit."

They all laughed as Nels carried on. "So, Tizz, how's the house going? Ready to move in?"

"You'll be amazed," Prentice replied. "The roof's on and it's all enclosed except for windows and doors. Old Axel is doing wonders; you won't recognize it."

"Meaning I should stay away so Axel and his troops won't pout?"

"No, of course not, hon, but he *has* been very cheerful the last week."

"Sounds like another good story," Graham interjected. "Captain Bligh and the builders."

"Come on, you guys," Nels complained. "I was just trying to be helpful."

Prentice and Graham erupted.

"Oh God, I can see him now," Graham chuckled. "Just like the time on Antigua when he tried to race with those hung over rummies, poor blokes. Bligh was screaming orders like, 'Sheet the main, tighten the vang, prepare to tack, hard alee,' and those poor, sick buggers just staring at each other, wonderin' should we put 'im over the side or just ignore 'im?"

"Don't remind me," Nels said in mock horror. "That was the time they hauled the chute right up into the masthead sheave and we never did get it down."

"And yours truly had the honor of going aloft in those eight-foot seas to cut it loose," Graham added.

"You were the only one who wasn't sick," Nels replied. "That was truly a nightmare. Makes me shudder to think of it."

"Here's to nightmares forgotten," Graham announced, glass raised. "We had a lovely trip up here; sixty-two hundred nautical miles in thirty-eight sailing days."

"Not bad at all. Where'd you hide the crew?" Nels asked.

"Ah, the boys are put up at a room across the way," Graham said. "By now they've had a pint or two, no doubt. They're ticketed to leave day after tomorrow."

"And all went well?"

"Cup a tea," Graham replied. "But this lake of yours is quite something. Reminds me of the western approaches at home."

"Game for a little cruise in a couple of days?" Nels asked. "I want to go up and have a look at a C&C 33 sitting in the lee of some islands about seventy-five miles northeast."

"Prentice has been telling us about the missing boat you're hunting. Count on me to have a go."

Nels told them briefly of his five-day excursion around the lake's perimeter and of his curiosity about the *Golden Fleece,* currently moored in Canadian waters.

"Five days to drive around? That's no surprise," remarked Graham. "Doesn't look like much on a chart, but it was three hundred miles of cold, empty sea from the locks to Northport. Not precisely a pond, eh?"

They were interrupted by a shout from the far end of the dock.

"Hey, out there."

The group turned together to watch a man emerge from the shadows and stride toward them on the springy planking. Backlit by the shorelight, they could see only his silhouette. He appeared to be wearing jeans, sneakers, and a short sleeve, Hawaiian style shirt.

"You're in violation of the county boating ordinance," the man said sharply.

There was a momentary silence.

"What's that?" whispered Prentice.

"Get lost, you turkey," Nels called, a grin creasing his face.

"Nels, for God's sake," hissed Prentice.

"What's that you said?" the man asked crossly.

"I said, how about letting us buy you off with a drink?" Nels said as the man came into the glow of the boat's spreader lights.

"Oh my God," Prentice exhaled, "Walt. I should have known. You guys are terrible."

"You didn't know my voice?" Walt asked, grinning mischievously.

"So can you have a libation or are you on the clock?" Nels asked.

"No, I can't, and no, I'm not," Walt said. "Ray's been trying to get you at the motel. Naturally, when he couldn't reach you, he called trusty old Walt to track you down."

"What's up?"

"Something about a prowler or some kind of break-in out at Sawtooth Lodge. Ray's out there and thought you might be interested."

"Sure. You going out there?"

"I'm not on duty, but what the hell, why not?"

"Hey, I'm sorry. Almost forgot to introduce you to our friends. That's Margie back there and this is Graham Jackson. He brought the boat up from the Caribbean. Graham, say hello to Walt Downing, chief deputy sheriff around these parts."

The two men stretched to clasp hands.

"Hi. How ya doing?"

"Pleasure to meet you."

"Walt, if it's okay with you, I'd like to bring Graham along," Nels said. "We won't be long, Prentice, and we'll be starved when we get back. Right, Graham?"

"Oh, yes."

"Let's do it, then," Walt urged. "I'll have that drink when we get back."

R ay MacNulty was waiting with Fred Marquardt in the plush owner's office at Sawtooth Lodge. His limited reservoir of patience had been exhausted by Marquardt's lugubrious recounting of the break-in and by the long wait for Nels Dahlstrom.

Marquardt was enthusiastically prattling on about the lack of good help. MacNulty had tuned out and was about to excuse himself when the three younger men trooped in.

He eyed them momentarily in tight-lipped disapproval, taking in Walt's loud flower print shirt and faded jeans, then scanning Nels and the other man in their shorts and T-shirts. None of them were wearing socks, which somehow rankled him more than the casual attire.

" 'Bout given up on you boys," he said. "Somebody steal your socks?"

The three looked down simultaneously, then at each other, and shrugged in confusion.

"Who needs 'em, right?" Nels said, uncertainly.

Walt knew at a glance that MacNulty was in no mood to be trifled with. "Sorry we're late, Ray. I had to track 'em down on the boat."

"The boat?" Marquardt asked hopefully.

"My boat," Nels said. "This is Graham Jackson, my right hand man in the islands. He took a busman's holiday to bring *Island Girl* up here for me. Graham, this is Fred Marquardt, Harry Potter's father-in-law, and Sheriff Ray MacNulty."

MacNulty had been eyeing the deeply-tanned young man, who stood as tall as Nels at six foot two but was considerably bigger through the chest, shoulders, and neck. His dark hair was shaggy, but not especially long, and his blue eyes were set wide in a deceptively rounded face.

"So you're the British fellow Nels has been telling us about," MacNulty said, offering his big, beefy hand. It was met by a hard hand of equal size and the sheriff knew that he had not felt such latent power since he first shook hands with the big Finn, Arvo Juntinen, some twenty-five years earlier.

"Yes sir. I hope he's been generous in his praise," said Graham, smiling as he shook hands.

"Oh yes, and I'm sure it's well deserved," MacNulty replied.

"I hear there was some kind of break-in out here?" Nels inquired.

"You can say that again," Marquardt answered eagerly. "The way I've got it figured. . . ."

"Excuse me, Fred," MacNulty interrupted. "Why don't I

57

tell the fellows what happened. That way, I can be sure I've got it right."

Marquardt looked disappointed, but nodded. MacNulty had no intention of hearing the rambling discourse a second time.

"A few years back," MacNulty began, "Harry took one of the older cabins out of the rental program for use as his own personal workshop and storage facility. Seems he's always kept on doing some geology consulting and needed space for his equipment and projects. Then, too, he wanted a place to store all his odds and ends, like fishing equipment. There's some sailboat stuff in there, and Fred here stuck all the stuff in the cabin that Harry left in the wagon the day he vanished.

"I looked around but couldn't see what was missing. Fred couldn't either. There's no doubt that somebody broke in, though. The door had a hasp with a padlock on it. It's been removed, the whole works.

"Whoever was in there made the mistake of leaving a light on when he left. That's how Fred discovered the break-in. He figures it was done earlier this evening since he would have seen the light last night, if it was on. He doesn't think anybody would break in like that at random and he doesn't figure it to be the work of anybody who's staying here.

"That's about it. Maybe three new sets of eyes can see something neither of us did. At least I'd like to give it a shot. Any questions?"

"No, I'm ready to have at it," Nels said. "But Fred, if you could spare a few minutes tomorrow to dig out more photos of Harry, and anything else you've got showing the boat, I'd be grateful."

"Sure, be glad to," Fred answered. "See you got back from your trip around the lake."

"I'll tell you about it when I pick up the photos," Nels replied, standing.

MacNulty led the way around the hotel's west side, past several log cabins that were occupied by guests. He stopped at the one closest to the parking lot.

"Built all these log cabins myself," Fred said, pointing to the dark-stained wood. "When they expanded the parking area, this one sort of lost its appeal." He opened the door and reached into the darkened interior for the light switch.

The harsh brightness of an overhead light revealed a room that Nels estimated at twelve-by-twenty, plus an alcove containing the corner kitchenette. The doorway at the far side led to what Fred described as a "nice-sized bedroom and a full bath with tub and shower."

The original furniture in the main room had been removed, leaving only a table and chairs, plus a desk near the fireplace. The place was cluttered with boxes, piles of rocks, and assorted gear.

"Okay, take a look around," MacNulty suggested. "Save your questions and ideas 'til the end. We'll have a quiz."

"Swell," muttered Walt, leaning down to open a cardboard box with the flaps closed.

The three men looked for fifteen minutes, talking quietly, showing each other the finds they considered interesting. The sheriff and Fred Marquardt stood just outside on the small porch.

MacNulty's face was illuminated briefly as he drew deeply on his cigarette. "Pretty night, eh, Fred?"

"Yessiree. Warm, no bugs. Can't beat it. Me and Ivy sat out last night watching the northern lights. You see 'em?" Marquardt asked.

"Nope" MacNulty answered. "Muriel and I used to go out on nice summer nights and listen to the loons, watch the lights, things like that. Don't seem to have time for it, anymore."

"Know what you mean. In a few weeks, the nights get cold, summer's over, and you've missed it."

MacNulty looked at the dimly-lit parking lot, nearly full now with late model cars. "Looks like you get a nice clientele, Fred, judging by what they drive."

"Yup. Took a long time to build it up. Harder to get repeats these days, too many choices. We sure don't need no prowler scarin' 'em off."

Walt stepped out the open doorway. "I guess we've seen about all of it," he said.

"Okay, Walt," the sheriff replied, then turned back to Marquardt. "Let's step inside and find out what ol' eagle eye here has figured out." MacNulty loved to showcase his chief deputy's keen observation.

"First of all," Walt said, "I want you to know this is a joint effort. There's some stuff here I wouldn't have figured out without the help of Nels and Graham.

"Anyway, we start with the three, four boxes of rock. These aren't the weathered rocks that the tourists find. They're broken pieces with unweathered edges. This first box is just interesting odds and ends: mica, quartz crystals, fool's gold, that sort of thing. The other boxes contain samples with minerals, traces of precious metals, like copper and silver.

"Then over here, where the tin floor is installed and the pots and forms are sitting, is a little minismelter, where you can melt lead, separate the metals like brass or bronze into their basic components, and take impurities out of base metal, like silver or copper. These little bars of silver and copper might have been purchased, but it's more likely he made them himself out of raw materials that he found."

"I'll be damned," MacNulty said.

"This silver here is about five hundred dollars worth, if you figure a hundred a pound. Whoever came in here probably didn't know what it was or they'd have grabbed it.

"Then we've got odds 'n ends that have to do with fishing and sailing. The thing that's interesting here, according to Nels, is that he left behind quite a lot of fishing gear, rods, reels, tackle and such, but not a bit of sailing gear. That would mean he took all seven sails aboard when he left for Isle Royale."

"How do you know there were seven?" Marquardt interrupted.

"I can explain," Nels answered. "From the photos you gave me, I knew the mainsail and sail cover were built by North Sails. I called their Chicago loft, and found that he had purchased seven sails from them this spring; a main, a high tech 150 genoa, a 110 jib, two storm sails, a ginnaker, and a full-radial spinnaker.

"I talked to the North rep who sold him the sails. He said Harry didn't ask for advice. Knew exactly what he wanted and sent an itemized list."

"What are you driving at?" Marquardt asked.

"Only that seven sails seems a bit excessive for somebody that mostly used the boat for fishing. Then, too, the fact he wanted North sails, which are generally known to be high quality with a price to match. It just seems a bit strange."

"You didn't know Harry," Marquardt answered. "He always had to have the very best."

"Maybe so. Maybe that's all it is," mused Nels.

"Back to our inventory," Walt said. "We've saved the best for last. What we have here are two strange-shaped pieces of lead that weigh about a hundred pounds apiece. They look sort of ratty because they're partially enclosed in fiberglass."

He looked mischievously at MacNulty and Marquardt. "Either of you figure out what they were?"

When they both shook their heads, he continued. "Neither did I, so don't feel bad. But our two sailing experts think they've got it figured out. Nels, I'll let you explain this little surprise."

Nels squatted next to the odd-shaped lead objects. "Sometimes, when new sailboats are designed, they don't float quite right; not 'on their lines' as the designers say. Or maybe they're a bit more tender, more tippy, than the designer intended. In either case, the easy remedy is to add internal ballast in the bilge, under the floor boards.

"They'll cast the lead in a shape to allow it to fit against the bottom of the hull, then glass it over. Bingo, it becomes part of the bilge and nobody ever notices.

"But it can be removed if somebody has a reason to do it, such as lightening the boat for racing. Why he did it, I haven't a clue, but there's no doubt these two pieces came out of *Fishin' Fool*'s bilge. Maybe he replaced them with something else, something that he wanted concealed. Right now we just don't know."

MacNulty cleared his throat. "Looks like you boys have raised some interesting questions about Harry's disappearance, but haven't learned much about whoever broke in here."

"There's one more little tidbit," Walt said. "Harry didn't smoke, right?" Marquardt shook his head. "If you take a look in that shell ashtray on the table, there's one cigarette butt that doesn't match. Those two with brown filters are yours, Ray, but there's one that's white. It should be easy to figure out what brand it is, unless you already know someone who was here that smokes white-filtered cigarettes."

The sheriff and Marquardt looked at each other, then back at Walt. Both shook their heads.

"Okay, the way we figure it," Walt continued, "is that someone broke in here looking for something in particular, something large enough so he'd have seen it without tearing everything apart. It's not a petty thief; he would have taken the fish finder and some of the equipment. And he wasn't after the silver, or he'd have taken that bar of it. Other than that, we're stumped."

"Ya know," Marquardt said, "I never realized Harry had found enough silver to refine it down into a bar that big. People would call him sometimes to go out and have a look around, or they'd bring him a rock to look at. He always said you could find pretty near anything around here if you really went lookin'.

"In the old days, they had mines up north of here that took out copper, iron, some silver even. I used to know a fellow who had a little mine on a creek near here; it produced nearly pure copper from a vein that he worked with a pick and shovel. Trouble is, most people don't know what they're lookin' at, including me."

"Well Fred," MacNulty said, "we'll be going along now. If we come up with something, you'll be the first to know. Meanwhile, I think you can probably put a new lock on that door. I don't think your prowler is likely to come back."

The men said their goodbyes to Marquardt and walked toward the parking lot.

"Walt," MacNulty said, "when you get in tomorrow morning, we'll take the Bronco up towards Quill Mountain and go back up that old road beyond where we found Carl Hoffman. Something's been going on up there and I want to see what you make of it."

"How early should that be, Ray?"

MacNulty paused, thought about the question, then grinned. "Hell, you guys have a good time tonight. Make it ten-thirty or eleven."

"Thanks Ray," Walt said.

The Bronco followed MacNulty's cruiser onto the highway and headed for Northport. It was followed by a dark pickup truck that had been sitting with its lone occupant in the parking lot.

When the Bronco turned off the highway into the small boat marina, the pickup slowed noticeably, then went on around the block, stopping where its driver could watch them go out on the dock.

63

The Bronco jounced along over rocks hidden by the deep grass of the logging road. It passed the point where the deadfall had been cut away and continued north through the multihued greens of the forest.

"So what time did you finally get supper last night?" MacNulty asked.

"I think it was about 1:00 A.M., and it consisted of an extra two olives in my third martini," Walt answered, grinning.

"Jeez," MacNulty grimaced. "Those things'll kill you, but you don't even look like you're hurting. How the hell do you do it?"

"Actually, I took two extra strength Bufferin when I hit the sack at 2 A.M. and woke up at ten this morning feeling great."

"You young guys," MacNulty said, shaking his head.

"It's the first time I've had a martini in five or six years, Ray, and I know better than to have any more anytime soon."

"So I imagine you hashed things out pretty good last night."

"Oh yeah, mostly whiskey talk, but a pretty definite consensus that there's more to Harry Potter's disappearance than meets the eye."

"Motive; I need a motive."

"We don't have one, not yet at least, but things just don't add up. Did you know that Nels talked to Harry's father and found out that Mr. Incompetent was actually a first-rate sailor in high school and college? Apparently, he raced small boats on the lakes around the Cities and crewed on a couple of ocean races during his school holidays. Nels says sailing is like riding a bicycle. You never forget it. He figures there's something real fishy about Harry's sailing performances since he got that big boat."

64

"Very strange," MacNulty mused. "Just like what you're gonna see up ahead."

"Oh really? How much further does this road go?"

" 'Bout a mile, I guess, to where we're going," MacNulty answered. "It goes on north from there, but I haven't been on that part of it."

The two men continued on in silence along the old road that led through a second-growth conifer forest. It was rugged going, which held their speed to between five and ten miles per hour.

"Stop right here," MacNulty said suddenly. Walt pulled the Bronco to a halt. "What is it?" he asked.

To the right, a steep meadow, covered in places with bushes, rose several hundred feet to meet the pines and poplars above.

"I know we're on county business," MacNulty said, "but I promised Muriel I'd bring her some fresh raspberries if I saw some along the way. Looks like we got about half an acre of 'em in that meadow and there's enough ripe ones to get a quart or two in a hurry. Do you mind?"

"Mind, hell, I got a couple of big coffee cans in back, just in case, Ray. Best way I know to pick up brownie points."

The two men climbed out into the warming midday sunshine and had soon stripped off their uniform shirts and were picking in their T-shirts.

"Must be gettin' up around eighty," Ray said across a wide expanse of raspberry bushes. "Too hot for my taste. Glad it always stays cooler down by the lake."

He poked a handful of berries into his mouth and munched contentedly. Then he saw Walt watching.

"One handful for Muriel, one for me," he laughed.

Walt shook his head and kept picking. "I'm a blueberry man myself," he said. "Couple weeks from now they'll be out and I can go on a rampage. Blueberry pie, muffins, pancakes. I can hardly wait."

Within minutes, they had finished filling a can apiece and climbed back into the Bronco, still in T-shirts. "A little R&R never hurts," Walt said.

"Yeah, I don't know if this job of catching crooks is getting tougher or if I'm just getting older and dumber," MacNulty said absently.

"Maybe the bad guys are just getting smarter and meaner," Walt mused.

MacNulty looked at his chief deputy's flat, angular face. He had almost lost him last spring during the big blizzard when Walt had been gunned down from ambush by the same man who had killed Nels's father and his pretty young wife. Shot in the back, Walt had almost died.

That had been three and one-half months ago. Funny how he rarely thought of it anymore, after Walt had recovered so quickly and came back to the job without complaint.

"So how you been feeling?" MacNulty asked. "Any problems?"

Walt's mind was traveling the same path, as it often did. "I saw Doc Johnson about three weeks ago, regular checkup. He keeps calling me Lucky, says there's no long-term damage. I can still feel it though, like right now when I'm bouncing over rocks and logs."

"Shit, if I had any brains, I wouldn't have suggested you come along."

"No problem, Ray, seriously, if it was hurting me, I'd let you know. I'm no hero."

"Uh-huh. That's bullshit and you know it."

"No it's not. I can feel it, but it's not exactly a pain; more like a memory my body's reminding me of. It's hard to describe."

"Okay, but you tell me if it's a problem," MacNulty ordered. "I mean it, Walt."

Walt glanced at the sheriff, grinning. "Okay, Uncle Ray, whatever you say."

66

"Ah, forget it," MacNulty said, waving a hand at his side-kick.

They were silent again as they reached their destination, a small clearing whose features had been totally rearranged by the work of a bulldozer.

"Holy shit," Walt said, leaning forward over the wheel as he stopped the big four-by-four.

"Let's leave 'er right here and walk," MacNulty said. "You haven't seen the half of it."

Beyond the small meadow, which looked to have been lowered by a depth of four or five feet, a narrow stream flowed. To their right, along both sides of the stream, boulders and chunks of gray rock lay piled in confusion. Just downstream from the devastated bedrock, a new culvert had been installed. Below that, a delta of dirt and gravel had been deposited, several feet deep and twenty yards wide. They stood where the dirt had been piled atop the culvert to allow vehicles to cross the creek.

"Now, you tell me what the hell's been going on here," MacNulty said.

Walt shook his head. "Did you ask Sims about it?"

"Yup," said MacNulty. "He told me their outfit has the contract to log this area. Said his partner, Carl, our latest murder victim, took a D6 with a bucket over here to put in a new culvert and fix up the crossing for truck traffic when they're ready to start cutting. Said he hasn't been over to look yet, but that Carl had the Cat over here two, three weeks, then brought it back and said the road was all set.

"Somebody had a big bonfire over there, like the loggers sometimes use to burn stumps. But it looks like they've been burning planks and boards beside the stumps.

"Somebody put one hell of a lot of dynamite into those cliffs up above to blow them to pieces. I'm no demolition expert, but I know it took twenty to thirty sticks to do what we're looking at.

"And look downstream at all that dirt. It didn't start down there; it got washed down by the water."

Walt was still shaking his head when MacNulty stopped. "Maybe there was a lot more water in the creek when he tried to stop it up so he could lay the culvert. Maybe he used all that dirt from the meadow to do the job. That would account for the delta effect downstream, everything but the rock that's been blasted loose.

"The only possible explanation for the rock is that he thought he might have to stabilize the crossing with an apron of boulders."

MacNulty glanced at his chief deputy. "Wouldn't you say he overdid it a bit?"

"Absolutely," Walt agreed. "I'm just trying to recreate what might have happened, trying to make it all seem logical. But of course you're right; no logic can explain all this. The logic all falls apart when you realize that anybody with half a brain would have simply waited a couple of weeks until the water level receded."

"Does the word mining come to mind when you look at all this?" MacNulty asked.

"You thinking about last night and the rock boxes?" Walt asked.

"Well, I wouldn't bet much on it," Walt said. "Carl Hoffman sure as hell was no miner, and we've made no connection between him and anybody who was."

"I know it," MacNulty agreed. "I just didn't want to be the only one to have seen all this before something happens to it. And truthfully, until we got to talking about mining last night, it was the farthest thing from my mind."

"Probably a farfetched connection," Walt agreed. "But you never can tell."

"Well, you've seen it," MacNulty said. "Let's sleep on it and see what develops. I'm planning to talk in more detail to

Virgil Sims and Charlie Mittner, and when I do, I want you along to ask some tough questions, okay?"

"I'll be there," Walt said, "and you're right. You've got to see this place to believe it."

T he big sloop rolled steadily northeast, shouldering the sloppy, three-foot seas aside. Nobody was on deck, an autohelm self-steering arm was attached to the wheel and kept *Island Girl* on a course of seventy-five degrees magnetic.

The apparent wind was twenty-two knots at an angle of forty degrees. Her number two genoa was sheeted to an outboard block, enhancing the wing effect of the two sails and driving her at a steady 8.8 knots. Down below, Nels Dahlstrom and Graham Jackson studied the chart.

"Three hours out," Nels said. "Make it another six or seven to our destination, if the wind holds. She feels mighty good to have underneath you."

"She's going liké horses," Graham agreed. "Really flies when she's cracked off a bit."

"What say we grab a beer and watch the sunset," Nels suggested. "Then we can rig her for night running. He looked at his watch. "I make it 8:40. At this pace, we'll be there just at dawn."

"Hope we can find his lordship on the C&C," Graham said.

"Oh, I think we'll track him down," Nels said, smiling in anticipation. "There's about a dozen islands to check. With all the photos Fred dug up, I'm sure we'll know soon enough whether the commander and his boat are legit."

The two men climbed out the companionway and perched on the weather deck to watch the sun begin its vanishing act behind the bluffs and hills that loomed a thousand feet over the lake. Mushroom-topped thunderheads lay to the south and southwest, but seemed static and benign.

"Deja vu," Graham said. "Isn't that what the frogs call it when you've got that been there before feeling?"

"That's right," Nels said. "So where is it you've been that looks and feels like this?"

"The Irish Sea. East of Ireland, running northeast of a summer's eve. Cool and crisp, sea a bit muddled. Almost dead on, visually."

"I never got up that far," Nels said. "What amazes me is the clarity. Those bluffs are what, ten miles away? Yet they stand out in sharp relief. Compared to this, the islands seem like they're in a constant haze."

"Uh-huh," Graham said, watching the quarter wave boil and foam away behind them. He glanced off to the unbroken sea to the south. "Are those thunderheads coming up on us?"

"Mmmm. Can't really tell," Nels said, swiveling around for a better look. "Forecast calls for fifteen to twenty becoming twenty to thirty from the southeast, with occasional thunderstorms. I thought we'd run a jackline to the bow, get our harnesses and foul weather gear out so it's handy, just in case."

"Want to shorten sail a bit?" Graham asked. "We won't lose much with the 110 blade. Be easier to handle in case of a squall."

"Yeah, we're not exactly in a race," Nels agreed. "Let's run the jackline up and shorten to the blade before it gets pitch black. I've seen a couple of squalls up here this summer that were pretty bad. No sense getting caught with our pants down."

"Brrr," Graham shivered as he swallowed the last of his beer. "Time for the heavy sweater and the oilskin pants."

"I'll take the jackline forward. Hand up the blade while you're below," Nels said. He snapped one end of the plastic-coated wire to a stern padeye and began uncoiling it as he went forward to the bow, where he snapped the steel carabiner at its end into another padeye. Then he helped pull the smaller jib through the forehatch onto the deck.

As he prepared to leave the foredeck, a small wave slapped the black hull and splashed on deck, soaking his back. "Holy shit," he yelled, scrambling back to the cockpit, where he quickly peeled off the dripping shirt.

Graham peered up through the companionway. "Brisk and bracing?" he asked, grinning.

"Coldest damn shower I've ever had," Nels said. "And this is the middle of summer."

"A swim in this lake would not be good for your health," Graham said, as Nels climbed down into the still-warm main cabin.

Both men emerged on deck wearing sea boots, foul weather pants, and oiled sweaters. They went forward and began the time-consuming job of changing to the smaller head-sail to reduce power. It was almost dark when they finished hoisting and sheeting the blade, dropping the larger number two, flaking and bagging it, and stowing it below.

"What say you take a watch 'til midnite, I'll stand 'til three, and you can do the three to dawn," said Nels. "We'll reverse the watches going home."

"Fair enough," Graham said as he snapped the tether of his safety harness onto the jackline and settled back in the cockpit to watch the soft glow of light from the digital compass and a bank of instrument readouts that told him the boat's position, speed, wind velocity and angle, and the water depth.

Nels went below and climbed into a pilot berth to feel the easy motion of the boat's progress through the waves. The excitement and fresh air had tired him, and in five minutes, he was asleep.

A few minutes before midnight, Graham roused him for the change of watch. "Your watch, Nels. Here's a nice hot tea towel to wipe away the cobwebs. Fresh coffee's on the burner."

Nels had slept hard and it took him a moment to get his bearings. "How's it going?" he asked in a monotone.

"We're midchannel between Isle Royale and the coast. Still boiling along at eight point five," Graham replied. "Lovely light show astern on the horizon. Come up when you're ready."

Nels clamored out of his snug cocoon, wiped his face, poured coffee, and climbed far enough up the companionway ladder to watch flickering lights of a violent electrical storm that lit up the western horizon line. "Hell of a storm," he said.

"Long way off yet," Graham replied casually. "Could pass behind us. Maybe die off altogether."

"Uh-huh," Nels said doubtfully, then climbed into the cockpit to commence his watch as Graham went below.

The storm closed slowly from astern like some ponderous beast whose growls and footfalls grew more audible as it stalked them. Lightning bolts became visible in the western sky, casting their eerie white light across the darkened deck.

Nels watched in apprehension, willing the danger to pass them to the north or south. It was a big storm, whose trailing edge ran off to the southwest horizon; it came on with plodding certainty.

A glance at his watch, easy to read in the flashing light, told Nels that an hour and a half had passed. He waited, alert now, for the first hint of the storm's power.

It came suddenly as first the jib, then the main, began to luff. Nels adjusted the autopilot to a more northeasterly course to fill the sails, then hollered below to Graham. "Storm's coming; time to go to work."

Unlike Nels, the Englishman popped awake instantly, listened momentarily to the crack and rumble of thunder, and began to throw on his oilskins, as he called the waterproof outerwear.

The wind had gone fickle now, a certain sign that the storm was nearly upon them. The first big wind, just ahead of the main squall line, would be coming soon.

Graham popped through the main hatch and was met by a hail of instructions.

"Hook up your tether and let's get forward," Nels said. "I want the jib down and the main reefed. We've got to hustle."

Without words, Graham scrambled to the foredeck. "Release the halyard," he called back, and immediately began gathering in the rapidly-falling sail.

Nels was beside him now, helping to haul the sail down onto the deck. "Let's get the bungee cord around it fast and get on that main."

The wind had headed them again, but was not light and fickle. It caused the long boom to snap dangerously back and forth above the cockpit. With the sail tied along the foredeck rail, they turned attention to the main. Without a word, Nels found the halyard and began to ease it, while Graham pulled the sail down the mast track. Foot by foot it dropped, until Graham was able to get the reefing cringle into the horn and yell "made."

Nels tightened the halyard and scrambled to wind the reefing line onto a secondary winch, while Graham released the vang. They worked silently, but with furious haste, knowing the new wind would reach them in moments.

"Got it," Nels yelled, and Graham tensioned the vang. They had reduced the mainsail area by 20 percent.

"I can hear it coming," shouted Graham, dropping cat-quick into the cockpit.

Nels released the autopilot arm and grabbed the wheel as the first fingers of wind clutched at the mainsail and shook the rigging. "Hang on," he shouted, "and get ready to ease the main."

The first sustained gusts hit the sail like fists, sending the boat careening northward. In the lightning flashes, he could see they were heeled thirty to forty degrees.

"Wind's gonna come from the southwest," Nels yelled over the whine of the rigging and the roar of the gale. "If we get a break, let's jibe her and run off to the east."

As if on command, the wind eased slightly and Nels spun the wheel, turning *Island Girl* to the east. For a moment, the main hung suspended as Graham sheeted, then snapped around above them with a rush and a loud pop as the sail filled.

"Big wind coming," Graham shouted, looking astern as the wind-driven sheet of water approached.

"Too late now for the second reef," Nels yelled. "Hang on."

The wind that hit them was impossible to measure, except against memories of other times, other storms. It drove the big boat forward, then sent her skidding on her side through the black water.

A lightning flash gave Nels a visual snapshot of the scene; they were heeled almost ninety degrees, with the tip of their sixty-foot mast less than ten feet above the roiling water. It was impossible to run off before the roaring wind. The rudder was out of the water, allowing the wheel to spin helplessly.

They were pinned for what seemed like a long time, hanging on for their lives. Nels was draped over the steering post while Graham hugged both arms around the main sheet track. Huddled fearfully in the lee of the wind, they watched the awesome roaring, shrieking scene.

"Son of a bitch," Nels yelled. "Just hang on."

"Bloody awful," Graham shouted.

Nels knew the wind was ripping past them at sixty to seventy knots. It would take that much to pin the forty footer on her side. He knew that at forty to fifty knots, they could get *Island Girl* back on her feet and run off to the east, surfing before the storm. Until then, they were helpless; an eight-and-one-half-ton package of flotsam at the mercy of the elements. God only knew what might happen next.

When the wind eased, it was imperceptible at first. The

rigging still shrieked and thrummed, the boom still dragged in the water, cutting a frothy furrow beside them. But the difference was enough. The four-ton keel resumed its role as a counterweight and the mast tip lifted.

As the boat slowly righted herself and the rudder bit into the water, Nels instinctively turned the wheel to drive her off the wind. The wind caught the sail and *Island Girl* bulled her way through a wave and gathered speed toward the east.

"Pretty hairy," Graham exclaimed, shaking his head.

"Still touch and go," Nels answered, straining to keep the boat upright in an easterly course.

They roared down a wave and buried the bow in the wave ahead. Immediately, the boat began to broach.

"I'm losing it," Nels yelled, as he fought futilely to keep the boat upright. Then he was hanging on again as *Island Girl* tried to round up and was driven over on her side.

"Jesus, we gotta reef," Nels screamed, frightened now as the boat wallowed helplessly. He could feel his muscles shaking from the exertion of merely trying to stay on board.

Through the blinding rain, he could see that Graham had somehow climbed forward to the mast as they went over. He was astride it, clawing at the sail.

"Let go the fucking wheel and help me," Graham shouted angrily, pulling the sail down the track to the second reef point.

Nels released his death grip on the binnacle post and struggled forward, wedging himself into the hatch. He was able to tension the main halyard just as a brief lull brought the boat up to a forty-five degree angle. The sail was snapping and popping, threatening to shred into confetti.

"Hurry up with the reef line," Graham bellowed. "I don't fancy a fuckin' swim." Nels responded with speed and quickly had the second reef snugged to the boom.

"Get back in the goddamn cockpit," he yelled at Graham. "She's coming up."

Nels barely reached the wheel in time to drive the boat

downwind. This time, he could feel the control, and soon had *Island Girl* surging east.

In minutes, the lumpy sea had been blown flat by the wind. Now it was already forming sizeable waves that lifted the stern and sent the boat surfing ahead.

"What's the apparent wind speed?" Nels asked. "I can't read it."

"Bouncing around. Thirty-five, thirty-four, now thirty-seven," Graham said.

"We're doing twelve to fourteen, so the true wind is forty-five to fifty," Nels said, shaking his head. "No wonder she broached with one reef."

"That was bloody fucking close to disaster," Graham said.

"You got that right," Nels replied tightly, his wet face suddenly lit by a white flash that was joined to a ripping, grinding roar of thunder.

"Shit. Now she's trying to fry us," Graham shouted in the sudden darkness that followed.

"Too damn close," Nels muttered, hoping the grounding system would do its job in the event of a direct hit.

Tethered in the cockpit, silent with their private fears, the two men sailed on through the storm and the building seas. A half hour passed.

"Wind's almost due west now," shouted Nels, his words torn away by the still-roaring storm. "Still holding thirty-five to forty true. Let's check position; see if we need to jibe."

Graham pushed open the hatch, unsnapped his tether, and descended into the quiet chaos of the cabin. He was gone only a minute, then climbed back out into the wind-blown rain.

"Closing fast on the north side of Isle Royale," he shouted. "Not much sea room, shoals a couple miles ahead. Let's get the hell outta here."

"Okay, we'll pick a good wave and jibe as we surf," Nels directed.

With the sea already running four to six feet, it was not difficult to find a surfing wave.

"Okay, the wind's eased a bit. Here we go," shouted Nels.

Graham took in the main sheet quickly, controlling the sail, then Nels steered slightly to the northeast as they slid down the wave at thirteen knots with the sail flipping across with a bang. Graham let the sheet run out and they continued surfing without letup.

"How was that one?" Graham shouted, grinning for the first time in an hour.

"Slightly better than perfect," Nels laughed. "You take her awhile. Hold her about seventy-five degrees while I check position and course. I'll be up in a half hour."

"Aye, aye, your lordship," Graham said, still grinning. "Don't look too close at the mess down there; it'll make you sick."

Below, Nels waded through a twisted jumble of clothes, bedding, and kitchen ware. Ignoring it, he braced himself at the nav station and studied the chart. He checked his watch: only two-forty. He measured the distance again and shook his head.

We're not out of the woods yet, he thought. In fact, the hard part's still ahead. If the wind holds, we'll come up on the narrow approaches to the islands in ten or twelve-foot seas. We don't have a chart that shows the depths in there and it'll still be dark.

He pondered the problem, studying the chart. Not worth the risk, he knew. But a turn north would take us up through the Montreal Channel into North Bay. Then, after dawn, we could slide in close and get out of the wind.

Nels zipped his foul weather jacket, feeling suddenly exhausted, then climbed out to discover the rain had passed ahead. Only the roar of the sea and the moan and whistle of the wind greeted him now. It was menace enough.

"Looks like we should head up to about fifteen degrees, Graham. Put her on a beam reach and we can make the channel leading into North Bay. It's about five, six miles. Should be a ten-second flash to starboard."

"You really want to beam reach in this sea?" Graham

asked, looking up as a ten-foot comber with foaming top roared past to port. "Won't be a dry ride."

"Don't have much choice," Nels said, "unless you'd rather run past the islands and beat back at daylight."

"No way," Graham responded. "Let's try your first idea. If you'll sheet the main, I'll come to fifteen degrees."

"Let's go for it," Nels nodded, as the boat turned northward on the crest of a wave.

Within seconds, a breaking wave slapped the black hull and a wall of ice water cascaded across them into the cockpit. "God a'mighty", Graham shouted. "let's go to the North Pole, where the fuckin' water's warmer."

"Only a few miles, if we can hang in there," Nels said, shivering from the first drenching. "Let's tough it out."

"Let's not both suffer," Graham said, shaking from the cold shower. "I'll take a turn; you relieve me in fifteen minutes."

Nels nodded and went below, bracing himself on the settee. Contorted and cold, he fell asleep instantly. He was pulled awake a half hour later by Graham, who was shaking him hard.

"What? Huh? What's happening?" Nels mumbled.

"You're sleeping like a dead man," Graham responded. "Got to get up there. I need to warm up."

Nels blinked and focused. Graham's red-rimmed eyes and wet, shaking face told a story of the savage conditions above.

"How long did I sleep?" Nels asked in a tired monotone.

"About thirty minutes. I've got her on autopilot, but it won't hold; too much wind. Ten second-flash is about two miles ahead."

Nels pulled himself up and waded through the tangled mass of watersoaked belongings to the ladder. Before climbing out, he turned to Graham with a wan smile. "Are we having fun yet?" he asked.

A big wave surged against the hull and sprayed him with

freezing water as he emerged. He shivered and hunched deeper into his foul weather clothes. "Welcome to Lake Superior," he muttered.

The sky was just beginning to gray with that subtle light they call false dawn when *Island Girl* drew abreast of the 25-foot light that marked the Montreal Channel.

Nels left the mark well to starboard, recalling the charted shoals and reefs that lay just outside it. Another half mile and they'd be through the channel and protected by the headlands of the Sibley Peninsula, famous for its outline of the Sleeping Giant.

He had never felt so cold; his fingers were numb and his boots were half full of icy water. Unable to penetrate his hooded coat, the water had found its way down his neck and up his sleeves. And still the wind-whipped waves fought him for every yard, stinging him with spray, filling the cockpit with waves sheared off by the powerful hull.

In the dull light, Nels could make out the spray of breakers to the right and left. Straight ahead, through the black water, lay the course to safety and peace, blessed, restful peace and quiet. In the rigging, the wind still shrieked and moaned its warnings.

They hit the great dark unyielding slab of granite doing ten knots in the trough of a wave. In flat water, the keel would never have touched its hidden face.

It happened fast. The keel hit with a jolt and a shudder, tipping the bow forward and throwing Nels against the wheel. The grinding sound of lead meeting rock was interrupted by the explosive bang of the backstay parting.

Then, as if in slow motion, the boat was lifted gently from the rock and the mast fell forward over the starboard bow.

Graham reached the hatch in seconds to find Nels hunched over the wheel, staring with open-mouthed disbelief at the wreckage.

"What happened?" Graham asked, not comprehending.

"We stopped. The mast kept going," Nels answered in a calm monotone.

Graham spun around and saw that the mast had snapped six feet above the deck. He stared several seconds, then turned back. "You okay?" he asked.

"Sure," Nels said in a hollow voice. "Just freezing to death."

"God bless us all," Graham muttered, and ducked below. In seconds, he reappeared with long-handled bolt cutters and a hacksaw.

"Come up here and give me a hand," Graham said. "It'll help you warm up. We've got to clear this mess and try to save the three big things: mast, boom, and mainsail."

Nels crawled stiffly from behind the bent wheel and took the bolt cutters. He found he was so cold that he could negotiate the heaving deck only on his hands and knees.

Working silently on the wave-washed deck, the two men cut away the standing rigging, salvaging what they could. It was all they could manage to loosen the mainsail and pull it on deck. The boom was next, and they got it, too, before literally collapsing.

"Fuck it," Nels gasped. "Pull the halyards through and let's cut 'er loose. No way we can save the mast."

They cut the last of the wires and watched the mast, a ten thousand dollar investment, settle slowly into the clear gray water.

With the wreckage contained or thrown overboard, Nels crawled back into the cockpit. "I'll crank up the diesel," he said. "You look below for water coming in. Let's get the hell out of here."

The turbo diesel caught immediately and ran smoothly as Nels brought the forward speed up to six knots.

Graham crawled back out of the hatch. "There's water below but I think it's from before. Can't see any serious leakage around the keel."

"Thank God for small favors," Nels said solemnly. "Put in a call to the Coast Guard. Tell 'em to call Prentice and tell her we're fine. Tell her we'll be back tomorrow."

"The aerial went down with the mast, Nels," Graham said. "I took the spare off when I cleaned the boat out. No way to call anybody right now."

Nels nodded in silent understanding.

Running up the channel, they left the fearsome cold waves behind and entered flat water.

"Anything dry down below?" Nels asked. "I could use a nice warm sweater or jacket, mine are soaked."

Graham returned minutes later with an armload of dry clothing. "This is the lot. We'll have to pick and choose."

He watched as the boat closed with the shoreline of a small bay. "Looks like good protection," he said. "Want me to put out the hook?"

"That's the general idea," Nels said stonily. "Go up front and I'll tell you when."

He slowed the boat, then reversed the engine to stop. "Well? What are you waiting for?"

Graham let the anchor slip into the water, followed by twenty feet of rattling chain. "Want to back her off to test the bite?" he shouted.

Nels shook his head. "Hell with it. Let's just quit screwing around and pay out some extra line. She'll set herself," he said. The two men slowly pulled off their wet clothing and scattered it around the deck to dry.

"Listen, mate," Graham said quietly. "I know you're upset with losing the mast; lucky it wasn't worse. But don't lay your troubles at my feet, okay?"

Nels stared dully at his friend, then shook his head. "I've about had it," he said. "The last thing I need right now is for you to lecture me, okay?"

"I'm not lecturing," Graham replied evenly. "Just telling you, plain and simple, to get off my back."

"Sure, wash your hands of the whole deal," Nels responded, his face reddening. "It's not your boat, so it's not your problem. Is that what you're saying?"

"Hey, I didn't run us on a rock," Graham said, more loudly now. "You did and the bloody rock is marked clear as day on the chart. So it's your own damn fault."

"Sure. My boat, my problem, my fault. I'm tired, Graham, so just fuck off, okay?"

"Oh, you can be bloody well sure I'll do that, soon as we get back, mate. Meantime, you can kiss my bleedin' arse."

"You've just dug your own grave, asshole. When we get back, you're gone," Nels snapped. "Now I'm tired of wasting my time with you. I'm going below and get some sleep. I don't much care what the fuck you do."

With that, he swung himself through the hatch and dropped below, leaving Graham staring angrily at the rocky shoreline nearby.

R ay MacNulty and Walt Downing trooped into the office dejectedly. Their brown shirts were ringed with sweat stains and the sheriff was mopping his face.

"Too damn hot to work around here," he muttered. "Must be ninety. We need some air conditioning in this place."

"It said eighty-four at the bank," offered Mary Jo Collins, who was working the switchboard in the wind generated by MacNulty's personal floor fan.

"I'll take that fan back, Mary Jo, unless you want me and Walt to die of heat stroke right here and now," MacNulty said. He continued on into his office and began opening all the windows. Walt stopped for the fan.

"Anything happening?" he asked Collins.

"One call on a stray dog. Another on a bad check," she answered. "Both are taken care of."

She hesitated, "You guys look sort of wilted," she said.

"Been up in the woods working the Hoffman case. Must be ninety-five up there. Bugs like to have carried us off."

It was a rare day when the temperature reached eighty degrees in Northport, though inland a few miles, away from the lake's cool breezes, it often reached ninety. The cool summer weather was a source of pride for local residents, as well as income from the hordes of tourists seeking escape from the three-digit heat of the central plains. Air conditioning, therefore, was usually considered a frivolous extra in the purchase of a new car or the construction of a home. Because their personal thermostats were aligned to long winters and cool summers, locals complained whenever the thermometer exceeded the low seventies.

The switchboard lighted and Mary Jo Collins answered as Walt hauled the fan into MacNulty's private office.

"It's your wife, Ray," Collins called. "She's on line two."

MacNulty cradled the receiver between ear and shoulder as he rolled up his sleeves to the elbow. "Hi," he said. "What's happening?"

He listened, then answered. "No, I didn't forget. We stopped on the way in to get it, but it's not done. Earl says it's too hot to work on it."

He listened again. "I know, I know. Maybe we'll have to get a couple sheep to eat it."

He chuckled at his own joke, then became serious. "Muriel, I will somehow get it cut before your book club meeting, trust me. Okay, love you too. See ya about six."

He hung up the phone and stood in the flow of air generated by the fan that Walt had plugged in.

"How's your mower working? I might need to borrow it," MacNulty said. "Muriel's hosting the book club tomorrow morning and she's in an uproar about the grass."

"Mine's fine. Why don't I bring it over when we leave? Hell, I'll even help you mow it, provided that you serve gin and tonics during and after."

"You got a deal."

"You want to talk some more about today?" Walt asked.

"I'd rather forget the whole works," MacNulty replied. "But I guess we better rehash it some."

He unbuttoned his shirt and pulled the wrinkled tail out of his pants, letting it hang. Then he sat down.

"Okay, we were in agreement that the other loggers we talked to were either slick liars or they didn't know anything, right?"

"Right. Then we discounted the slick liar part," Walt said.

"So that leaves us with Sims and Charlie, the dynamic duo," MacNulty added. "Which is right back where we started."

"Right," Walt said, staring at the desk top.

"So where's the motive?" MacNulty asked, leaning forward. "What's the scenario?"

"That's our problem," Walt said. "There isn't any. Sims alibies Charlie; says she and Hoffman were bed buddies, happily in love. Charlie alibies Sims; says he and Hoffman were friends, making good money, never argued. And the crew backs 'em both up, right down the line."

"Happy horseshit," MacNulty growled. "See no evil, hear no evil, speak no evil."

"Nobody connects Sims and Charlie, nobody knows what Hoffman is doing all that bulldozing and blasting for, nobody knows nothin'," Walt mused. "What we have here is a totally happy and compatible logging outfit, which is about as common as finding a two-headed albino cow."

"It's got something to do with the bridge site," MacNulty said. "So who does that implicate?"

"My guess is Charlie. They're lovers, right? He's gonna talk to someone about what's going on. She's the logical choice. She's got a brain and she's aggressive. I think she'd insist on it."

"So she knows more than she's telling," MacNulty said, pondering. "So how do we crack her?"

Walt chuckled.

MacNulty stared at him, then smiled. "You young guys, dirty, dirty minds. Hell, she's bigger than you, Walt. Probably eat you alive."

Walt nodded, still smiling. "Probably, but let's save that as a last resort. There must be a way, but right now I'm drawing blanks."

"Me too," MacNulty nodded. "I think this heat has fried my brain. What say we go mow my lawn and get about half in the bag."

"Let's do it. Maybe we'll get a brainstorm."

"Yah, gin hits me the same way," MacNulty said, grinning.

T he word that a dismasted sailboat was coming toward the harbor was enough to draw spectators to the small boat dock. On a warm summer evening, with two hours notice, there was sure to be a crowd.

Augie Nellis at the Coast Guard station had received a phone call from a resident east of town. He called Ray Mac-Nulty, who was hard at work cutting grass. MacNulty called Prentice Dahlstrom, who said she had been sick with worry ever since the big thunderstorm two nights ago. Prentice passed the word to Avis and Ollie Anderson in the lobby of the Lakeview Lodge, and so it went.

By 9:00 P.M., these and fifty other people had gathered in the marina parking lot to await the arrival of *Island Girl*. The crowd was growing steadily, as passersby saw that something was happening and stopped to find out what it was.

"I figure they're about a mile east," said Nellis. "I would have sent a boat out, but they seem to be moving right along. We'll see 'em in a few minutes."

"I get so scared when he's out there in a storm," Prentice said. "But he never thinks to call and tell me he's okay."

"Must have hit quite a storm to take the mast," said Mac-

85

Nulty, who had showered and limited his intake of gin in deference to the occasion.

"We'll have to give him a little razzing about it, I suppose," Ollie Anderson added. He and his wife Avid owned the lodge and were old friends of both MacNulty and Nels's late father, Bob.

"Oh God, Ollie, please don't," Prentice said, looking at the small clots of people standing nearby in the lot. "He'll be embarrassed enough having to dock her in front of all these people."

Augie Nellis pointed to the eastern breakwall. "There it is. You can just see the stump of the mast above the breakwall. They'll be coming through in just a few seconds."

The black hull burst into view from behind the breakwall. "There they come," somebody shouted.

"Oh my God," Prentice muttered. "They lost almost all of it. Must have been a terrible storm."

The boat cut straight across the mirror-flat harbor, reflecting the sun's last rays. It slowed as it came, reducing its wake to a ripple. Graham stood on the foredeck, coiling a length of line. Nels stood behind the wheel, steering.

The damage was immediately visible: three stanchions missing or bent over on the starboard bow, lifelines missing, the hull chipped and gouged where it had been raked by the mast alongside.

Nels swung the starboard side along the dock and reversed the engine to bring *Island Girl* to a stop. Graham tossed lines to waiting arms on the dock.

"Both of you okay?" Nellis asked.

"Yah, sure, we're just fine," Nels answered. "My pride got a little scuffed up, along with the boat, but we're okay."

Nels looked at Prentice, who stood silently with tears in her eyes; he shrugged. "I'm sorry, hon, the antenna went over with the mast. No way I could let you know."

He shut down the engine, stepped to the rail, and lifted her over with a hug. "We're okay, that's all that matters," he said quietly in her ear.

"So what the hell happened, Nels?" It was Ollie who spoke up.

"Well, we got hit by a pretty good storm two nights ago. Everything was okay and we were running her into Black Bay for some shelter. I just screwed up and ran her onto a rock. There was a lot of wind on our quarter, so when the boat stopped suddenly, the mast decided to keep on going. What can I say?" he shrugged, grinning and holding out his arms, palms upraised.

"Sure are taking it well," said MacNulty, thinking that Nels seemed unduly nonchalant about the whole episode.

"I am now; I wasn't at the time, as Graham will tell you. But I've had two days to get used to the idea. What's done is done, no sense worrying about it."

The conversation moved to the bow as someone asked Graham a question about the bent stanchions.

Nels bent down toward Prentice and spoke quietly. "Tizz, talk to Graham. I got mad, said some things. I tried to apologize, but he's still upset, talking about flying home. See what you can do."

She shook her head and glanced up at her husband, who was looking plainly chagrined. "The famous Dahlstrom temper," she said. "I'll see what can be done."

Having satisfied themselves that the disaster was of a minor nature, people began drifting away.

"Tell you what," MacNulty said in as jovial a voice as he could muster. "Me and Walt were just about to pour us a couple big gin and tonics up at the house. Augie, why don't you and Ollie and Prentice and the shipwrecked sailors come on up and have one?"

Ollie demurred. "Me and the Missus got to get back to the lodge before the help cleans out the till, but you youngsters go ahead and have one for me."

"I'm game," Augie said. "Nels, you look like you could stand one."

"Why not," Nels said with a shrug. "Prentice, how about giving Graham a ride? I'll go with Ray so I can ask him a couple things."

The sheriff and his cadre wandered back toward the foot of the deck as Prentice went below. There was no sign of disarray; in fact, the main cabin was spotless. Two sea bags on a settee were ready to be off-loaded.

Graham followed her down into the cabin. She turned, "I can't believe you've been through a storm. Everything's so, so perfect."

He nodded. "Fresh water and a day of sunshine to dry everything. Not the same as having salt water about."

"And there's no keel damage?" she asked.

He shook his head. "The bolts held. She's tight as a drum, though I rather expect the foot of the keel is dashed up a bit."

"You ready to go?" she asked.

"You go ahead," he replied. "We've been running since seven this morning and I'm a bit tired."

She had expected the refusal. "Nels told me he had one of his infamous tirades after the mast went. They can do a lot of damage to a relationship, as I well know."

"There was no reason for it," Graham said.

"I know. He says things he doesn't mean, things that hurt. He probably feels worse about it right now than you do."

Graham shrugged. "I think I've been too long on this boat. I need a change of scene, thought I'd fly home to England for awhile."

"Graham, don't leave us. We need your steady hand on things in the Caribbean, this year more than ever. And right now, Nels needs you. This business of playing detective might lead nowhere, but it could also cause him to go blundering into something he can't handle alone.

"You may not believe this, Graham, but he thinks of you as his best friend. He respects you and your opinions more than he'd ever let on. I know he's not the easiest person to get along with, but he means well. Don't let one angry flare-up destroy all that."

"Well, I don't know," Graham said. "We always get on famously, but it all just sort of exploded."

"Give him another chance," Prentice asked. "Put the past, both the good and bad, out of your mind and start fresh. What could be fairer than that?"

Graham stared for several seconds at his sea bag on the settee. "What you say makes perfectly good sense, Prentice. I know I shouldn't begrudge him a second chance, after all this time. It's just that I feel hurt and maybe angry at what happened."

He hesitated, then nodded. "I'll have another go."

"Great," she said, putting a hand on his forearm. "Let's start with a drink of your British gin up at the sheriff's house."

"Hear, hear," he agreed, a grin edging into the corner of his mouth.

Somewhere in her dream, the phone was ringing. Prentice heard it sound twice before she snapped awake and clambered over Nels's inert form to reach it. "Hello," she said sleepily.

Out of a background of noisy talk and laughter, a voice asked for Nels.

"Ah, can I get a number where he can reach you?" she asked.

"Have him call Paul Hunter, 218/695-1202, in Duluth. It's about his boat."

"Okay, sure," she said, writing down the number. "Tomorrow morning?"

"Yeah, after nine," the voice replied, then the circuit went dead.

Prentice crawled back over Nels, who muttered and turned

over. Some drunk, she thought, and fell back asleep, leaving her scrawled note on the pad by the phone.

In the morning, she had forgotten it entirely. She dressed and went into the dining room for breakfast without waking Nels, who was still sleeping soundly.

Sitting alone at her favorite window table, Prentice was looking out at the sunshine sparkling off the benign wavelets of the lake, when Ollie Alderson appeared. "Sorry we couldn't come up to Ray's for a drink, but you know how it is in the summertime. You look like you survived it all right."

"I had one glass of chablis," she said. "The gin drinker is still asleep."

"So the party was a success?"

"I think for everyone but Muriel."

"Uh-oh. Tell Uncle Ollie all about it."

Prentice laughed. "Well, after we heard all the sea stories Nels and Graham could think of, Walt decided he'd better load the mower back in his truck. So he pulls up on the lawn and the guys all lift the mower into the back end and push it forward. Unfortunately, the truck starts moving forward, too, and runs downhill into Muriel's rose bushes. "No problem," says Walt, and he jumps in the truck to back away. But the ground is soft from all the rain and his wheels start spinning. Well, before anybody can stop him, he's dug up half the front yard and Muriel is screaming. Seems her club is coming this morning. Last I saw, Walt and Ray were out there with shovels and a flashlight, trying to repair the damage. Otherwise, the party was just fine."

"Now I *am* sorry I missed it," Ollie said. "Oh, I bet Ray's really in the doghouse right now. I suppose I should call him and rub it in a little."

"Oh God no, Ollie, I'm sure things are bad enough."

"Well maybe I'll just call and sort of draw it out of him slowly, like a porcupine quill," Ollie said gleefully, walking toward the lobby.

90

P rentice returned to the motel after a morning at the new house, where plumbers and electricians were running pipes and conduit. Progress seemed distressingly slow during this mechanical phase of construction, as Axel had promised it would be.

Nels was sitting in pajamas, drinking coffee, and reading the morning paper, when she arrived.

"Well, if it isn't the old salt risen from the dead," she said.

"Was I really that bad?" Nels asked, refolding the sports section.

She shrugged. "At least you were happy and humorous," she said. "Probably no worse than any of the others."

"Where did Graham go?" he asked. "Back to the boat?"

"Uh-huh."

"Thanks for talking to him, Tizz. He was pretty upset after my little outburst."

"That's what I'm for, right? To make apologies after your 'little outbursts?' "

"C'mon, hon. Let's not start with the heavy guilt trip. I can't handle that right now."

"God forbid I should bring up something you're not ready to handle," she said sarcastically.

"Hey, I just don't need to have a heavy lecture on my failings just now, okay?"

"Sure, Nels. We'll talk about it later."

"Talk about what, for God's sake?"

"Never mind. Let's just drop it."

"Okay, I fly off the handle when I shouldn't. I'm a spoiled, impatient child. Anything else?"

"No, that about covers it."

"If I'm so rotten, how come you married me?"

She looked at him, then looked away, shaking her head.

"You just don't understand, do you? You think a quick admission of your faults absolves you. Poof. No more problem.

"But I'm not your confessor, I'm your wife," she continued. "I love you for being charming, gracious, steadfast, thoughtful. There's a lot of reasons. But every so often, the other Nels surfaces. The one who is petty, spiteful, superficial, bullying. . . ."

"Bullying?" Nels asked incredulously.

"Yes, bullying. You push people who can't fight back. The carpenters at the house, Graham. You pay people to do things for you, then you second-guess them for not doing it your way. That's what I call bullying, and it's not a very nice trait."

"Right; I'm not a very nice guy. So what else is new."

"Not a thing. You're just the same old you."

They sat in silence, depressed by the turn of conversation.

"So where does that leave us?" he asked.

"I don't know," she said. "All I know is that I'm going to have lunch and go back to the house."

She stood, arms folded, to leave. Then she glanced at the phone and saw the note.

"Someone called during the night. I was half asleep, but it sounded like some sort of party. Here's the number if you're interested." She retrieved the note and handed it to Nels.

"I'm going to have some lunch," she said, and went out the door, leaving Nels sitting in silent anger.

"Thhis is Nels Dahlstrom returning your call."

"Are you the guy offering the reward about the boat?"

"Yes, I'm the one. Do you have some information?"

"Well, I'm not sure, but maybe. Let me back up and explain. My name is Paul Hunter; I just finished the Trans-Superior race last night and saw your notice in the Seaway Bar. That's where we sometimes stop to do a little celebrating."

92

"Right. I'm following you," Nels said.

"Anyhow, a couple days ago, in the afternoon, we were beating out around the Keewinaw Peninsula. Northwest wind about twenty-five knots, big sea running.

"I'm on the helm at the time, beating north to clear the end of Manitou Island. I keep going just about due north for about ten miles beyond the island. Then we tack west for Duluth.

"Anyhow, the sea's running about eight to ten feet, pretty nasty, when I see this boat running south, heading for the protection of the peninsula. I knew she wasn't a racer. Going the wrong way."

"Was the boat a C&C 33?" Nels asked.

"Oh yes, I know my boats. It was one of the new models they've been building for two or three years. Looked to be only one man at the wheel, wearing a red foul weather outfit. He passed pretty close, crossed our bow, and passed just to the east. Knowing our course, I'd say his course was about 150 degrees. I looked at a chart this morning; his course would have taken him from the east side of Isle Royale to where I saw him. He was running with a reefed main, no head sails."

"That's good information," Nels said, "I appreciate it. If it leads anywhere, I'll call you."

"That's okay, I just wanted to help. Reward or no reward," Hunter replied. "Oh, one thing more."

"Yes?"

"We were close enough so I'm pretty sure of the name of the boat. She was called the *Golden Fleece.*"

"You sure?"

"Yeah, I'm sure. Hell, she passed about fifty yards away, no more than that. I got a good look at her."

"Colors," Nels said. "Did you notice anything about the boat's colors?"

"Hmmm. Just the white hull. Can't recall anything about trim."

"Well, once again, Mr. Hunter, I want to thank you for calling. It might just be important," Nels said.

Paul Hunter's phone call got Nels moving. He phoned the insurance carrier in Bermuda to check the procedure on replacing the mast, then talked to his agent on St. Thomas, assuring him the original mast was standard in all respects, as would be the replacement.

The people at J Boats in New England were helpful. Yes, they had extra spars on hand and they could ship in two days. He explained what had been saved and would not need replacing, and they promised to omit those items and charge accordingly. They estimated that his new mast would arrive, ready to install, in less than two weeks.

Good news, he thought, dressing quickly. Prentice had not returned after lunch, but her car was gone, so she must have come back to the house. He'd leave her alone and go see Graham, who had probably slept all morning. He walked to the marina and strode down the dock in renewed good spirits.

Graham had been busy. He was sitting on the cabin top, detaching fittings from the mast stump, which he had pulled out of the boat.

"I figured you'd be sleeping in," Nels laughed, "but you've been a busy beaver. What time you get up?"

"About eight, I reckon," Graham replied. "The broken mast was attracting a crowd, so I figured I'd best remove it."

"The new one will be here in a couple weeks," Nels said. "I talked to J Boats and they're shipping one from stock. Pretty lucky."

"Thank God it's not custom," Graham said. "We'd be waiting six weeks or more."

"You know the boat we went looking for when all this happened?" Nels asked. "Well, it's not there anymore. Got a call from a fellow who saw our commander and his *Golden Fleece* off Keewinaw Peninsula the day before yesterday."

Graham stared off across the harbor, thinking. "Same day

we went into Black Bay Channel and laid up. You don't suppose he saw us, do you?"

"I don't know, maybe. Let's take a look at the chart and I'll show you his course and where he was spotted."

"You sure it was the same boat?"

"No question. The boat we were looking for and the boat that was seen are one and the same. It's called the *Golden Fleece.*"

Graham nodded. "Let's have a look on the chart." He slid easily through the hatch and returned with a large rolled chart of the lake. He unrolled it and laid a turning block on each end to hold it flat.

"He was seen about here, running a course of 150," Nels explained. "Wind was northwest, strong with big following seas; carrying a reefed main."

He stopped and looked up at Graham. "So, what do you think?"

"Hmmm. He could be anywhere on the leeward side of the peninsula or down in this bay. Or for that matter, anywhere along the south shore over to Munising."

"That's a big area," Nels said. "Over a hundred miles of shoreline, lots of little coves. Only one good thing; if my memory is accurate, there's only a half dozen marinas where he can fuel up along there."

"You want to go looking?" Graham asked.

"No, I don't," Nels said, "but I don't know any other way to check this guy out, once and for all. If he looks okay, and if the guy in Cleveland is really somebody else, we've got to make the assumption that Harry Potter and his boat probably went to the bottom."

"But you don't think so, right?"

"A few days ago, I'd have said 'right,' but now I'm not so sure. That storm the other night was pretty hairy. If he hit one like that, he could have lost it. Especially if he was alone."

"So when do we leave?" Graham asked.

"You game?" Nels asked.

"Sure, why not. Can't do much sitting around here," Graham said.

"We'll leave in an hour. Drive around to the south shore, find a spot to stay, and start looking at first light tomorrow."

"Prentice won't mind?" Graham asked.

"Mind?" Nels repeated, grinning. "Hell, she'll be delighted."

The telephone rang at ten o'clock. Prentice had just returned to the room after sitting on the rocks for an hour watching the pinks and purples of a spectacular sunset.

"I need to talk to Nels Dahlstrom right away," the woman's voice said.

"He's not here," Prentice replied. "May I take a message?"

"No, no. I got to talk to him right away. He's the one lookin' for that missing boat, right?"

"Yes," Prentice said, "but he's not here right now. He's out of town."

"Do you know where I can reach him?" the woman asked. "It's real important that I talk to him tonight."

"Well," Prentice hesitated, "I know where he's staying, if you want to try him there."

"Oh, that's great. Tell me where and I'll call."

"Okay. He's staying at the Holiday Inn in Houghton, Michigan, at least tonight. If you want. . . ." She stopped when she heard the click disconnect the caller.

Strange, she thought. I should have asked who it was. Maybe I should call Nels and tell him about the call. She hesitated, then decided not to bother him right now. Whoever it was that had called would probably be dialing his number by now, anyway.

I'll wait an hour, she thought, then give him a ring and find out what all this is about.

The two men were sprawled on their beds, watching Ted Koppel on "Nightline," when the phone rang.

"I got it," Nels said, groaning as he stretched across the bed. "Hi Tizz, what's happening?"

"Did you get a phone call in the last hour?" she asked.

"No, no calls. We got back from supper at least an hour ago. Been watching the news on TV."

"A woman called; said it was very important she talk with you tonight. I told her where you were staying. She didn't call?"

"No, no calls. Did you recognize the voice?"

"No; never heard her voice before. It was sort of gravelly, deep. But I couldn't tell how young or old," Prentice said.

"Strange," Nels said.

"I'll say. I called you because I was curious. She sounded so insistent that I figured she would have called right away."

"Tell you what, Tizz, if she does call, I'll get back and fill you in. Otherwise, we're off in the morning to look and I'll phone tomorrow night to tell you where we are and how we're doing."

"Okay; I didn't mean to worry you. And I'm sorry about the argument this morning," Prentice said. "Just remember I still love you."

"I know, hon, and I'm sorry, too. Talk to you tomorrow, if not before. Night."

He hung up the phone. "You hear that?" he asked Graham.

"Something about the boat?"

"Woman called her an hour ago, said she had to talk to me right away about the missing boat. Prentice gave her our motel and town, but no call. Very strange, eh?"

"Quite so."

"Guess we just wait and hope for the best."

"Maybe we'll get lucky tomorrow."

"We could use some."

The Keweenaw Peninsula knifes fifty miles into the belly of Lake Superior. Along its eastern shore, there are no cities and few natural harbors. Nevertheless, the two men covered it thoroughly, mile by mile, talking without success to shoreline residents, fishermen, marina attendants. Nor did the *Golden Fleece* miraculously appear in any of the anchorages.

By early afternoon, they had reached L'Anse at the peninsula's base and were preparing to work east toward Marquette and Munising. It was a tedious and frustrating search; Nels was reminding himself to hold his natural impatience in check as they walked from the marina office toward the jeep.

"God, don't you just love some of these guys?" he remarked sarcastically. "When they give you that huh? with the open mouth, you know they'd never remember the damn boat if it was sitting right in front of them."

Nels opened the door and slid behind the wheel. "Well, looks like it's Eastward Ho from here. What's the number of the road that follows the shore?"

"Tell you in a minute," Graham said. He smiled broadly.

"This may sound rather dramatic and a bit silly, but I think we're being followed."

Nels chuckled. "You're shitting me, of course." He glanced across at Graham. "No, you're not. This whole day has been so bizarre, you *must* be telling the truth. Okay, who and where?"

"Just keep looking toward me. Now, behind my head and about halfway up the hill, there's a dark blue pickup. Dirty. See it?"

"Uh-huh."

"Well, I've seen that same pickup now for the third time today. At least I think it's the same. A woman with long dark hair."

Nels was still grinning. "She's probably just hot for your body, Graham."

"No, I'm quite serious, Nels."

"Well, there's one way to find out, old buddy. What say I pull up next to her and ask?"

"Would that be the proper form?" Graham asked.

"How the hell do I know?" Nels laughed. "Let's just do it."

He started the Wagoneer and drove easily up the hill, swerving into the downhill lane as he approached the pickup and stopping five feet away, cutting off a downhill departure.

If she wants to leave, she'll have to back up the hill, Nels thought, stepping out confidently.

As he did, the pickup roared to life, but did not move.

"Excuse me, ma'am," Nels said in a loud voice.

The woman rolled down her window. "What is it?" she asked, her face emotionless.

Nels fixed her in his memory. Thirtyish, long, straight black hair, suntanned or weathered face, dark glasses, dark sweatshirt, no makeup.

"My friend and I are heading toward Marquette and we don't exactly know the way. Wondered if you could help us."

"No, 'fraid not."

"Meaning you don't know the way or you don't want to help?"

"Whichever."

"My friend and I also are wondering why you're following us?"

"Listen pal. Why don'cha just go on your way and quit bugging me."

"What's your name, lady?"

"Piss off. Want me to spell it for you?"

"No, I got it, and I just want to give you a piece of advice."

Nels put his hand on the rolled down window and leaned forward to speak.

The door burst open, catching him hard on the forehead and sending him staggering back over the hood of the jeep. Then she slammed it hard, popped the clutch in reverse, and spun the tires backing uphill.

Nels bounced off the hood just as she shifted gears and came at him, swinging out to miss him but catching the corner of the jeep with a jolt and shattering its yellow turning light.

The pickup went by fast, turned the corner, and was soon obscured by the dust it left hanging between the leaf-green walls of the back country road.

Nels leaned against the hood with one hand, using the other to tenderly explore the emerging egg on his forehead.

"Let me have a look at that," Graham said, peeling Nels's hand from the bump. "Aw well, it'll mend. A few weeks in hospital and you'll be good as new."

"Right, big guy," Nels grinned. "Stunned me for a minute though. You get the license?"

"I didn't think to do that, sorry," Graham replied.

"Damn. I want another shot at her."

"If it's a help, her sunglasses slipped and I got a look at her eyes."

"Yeah? I don't know if that'll help much."

"Oh, I think it might," Graham said. He hesitated, staring past Nels in search of the right description. "They were bright emerald green; really quite startling."

"I'll be damned. They were unusual enough for people to remember?"

"Unforgettable," Graham mused, staring down the gravel road at the setting dusk.

"At least we know one new fact," Nels said. "We're involved with something more than a simple accident. And I want to find out what the hell it is."

"Which means we keep going," Graham said.

"Now more than ever, we keep going," Nels said, a grim expression on his face.

They followed the shoreline all afternoon and into the evening. Their journey had taken them through Marquette and eastward. The sun was setting in the northwest.

"Will the master be wanting to stop for supper this evening or should I fetch out the crumbs from this noon's gourmet hamburger in a bag?" Graham asked.

Nels grinned. "What time is it getting to be?"

"Nine o'clock."

"Anything interesting ahead?"

"We're coming to a place called Shelter Bay. Doesn't look to be much activity there."

"Let's check it out, then head for Munising and get a room," Nels said.

They crossed a bridge over the Sable River and slowed to look out at the empty bay. A power boat of the type favored by local salmon fishermen was pulled up against a short concrete pier, but there were no sailboats in sight. Beyond, a dirt road led to a waterfront fishing shack with an old car pulled up alongside.

"Let's give it a try," Nels suggested.

They bounced through the puddle-filled depressions and pulled up behind the tan and rust-colored Dodge.

"Anybody home?" Nels called.

On the beach side of the shack, an old man appeared. His sparse white hair was tousled from sleep and his shiny dark pants were hung loosely over his thin frame and held up by narrow suspenders. A green T-shirt and furry slippers completed his wardrobe.

"Excuse me, sir," Nels said, walking casually toward the man. "We're looking for a friend with a sailboat. We were supposed to meet him a couple days ago along here, but we got hung up. It's a white thirty-three footer called the *Golden Fleece.* Maybe you've seen it?"

The old man finished lighting a cigarette and coughed several times before he spoke.

"What'd you say the name was?"

"*Golden Fleece.*"

"Uh-huh," the old man said, and coughed up something to spit into the sandy dirt.

"That's right. Have you seen her?" Nels repeated.

"I dunno. Sometimes I see things that ain't there, so maybe I seen it . . ." he paused to hack and spit again, "and maybe I ain't, like I tole the girl."

"Girl?" Nels asked, glancing sideways at Graham. "Was there a girl asking about the boat?"

The man eyed Nels, who continued. "We're supposed to all meet at the boat. The girl's got long black hair and unusual-looking green eyes; she's a friend of ours. Is that the one?"

"Like I said to her, maybe I seen it and maybe not. White boat was anchored over by the pier a couple days back."

"A sailboat?"

The old man nodded.

"Was it called the *Golden Fleece*?"

He shrugged. "Never saw the name. Anyhow, you're too late. Boat was gone yesterday."

"Do you have any idea where she went?" Nels asked.

"Boats come, boats go. I don't pay no attention anymore."

Nels looked beyond the old man at a skiff turned over in the weeds. "I see you got a boat there. Do any fishing?"

The man looked away, then glanced up with yellowed eyes. "Did a fair amount in my day, but not no more." He drew in the smoke and coughed it out. His eyes watered from the spasms. "Just don't care about it no more."

Nels looked at the ground. "Well, you've been a big help, sir, and we appreciate it a lot. If we happen to get back this way, we'll stop and say hello," Nels said with a small wave. "Thanks again."

The two men turned and walked silently through the fading light to the jeep. When they turned back again to climb in, the old man was gone.

"What do you think?" Nels asked.

"I think our green-eyed friend knows enough about what we're doing so that instead of following us, she can take the lead. She's after the boat, not us, and I think the old man really did see it here a couple days ago. And that, Sherlock, is my last word on the subject until I've been properly primed with food and drink."

"All in all, an interesting day," Nels said. "We'll start tomorrow's session right here, eh Watson?"

"Ask me during dinner," Graham replied.

The two men stood hunched in their windbreakers at the end of the short concrete pier scanning the shoreline for other residences that might be visible. Surely someone else had seen the white sailboat three days earlier.

Nels's eyes watered as he watched the windblown waves pound the concrete pilings, spraying the pier with cold water. "God, what a lovely day," he said, turning away and leaning into the gale.

"Bloody awful," Graham agreed, stuffing his hands into his pockets. "Likely we'll see as much from the car."

No further urging was needed to send them skittering downwind to the jeep, where Nels started the engine, cranked up the heater, and sat blowing warm air into his cupped hands.

"What do you reckon the temperature is?" Graham asked.

"Forty-five, with a wind chill of fifteen or twenty."

"Nasty place. No wonder there's nobody about."

"Before we look around any more, I want to stop at the old man's place and give him the whiskey we picked up," Nels said. "Poor old codger looks like he could use it."

He drove the short distance to the unpainted frame shack and pulled up behind it, out of the wind.

The man appeared, dressed as before with the addition of a buttonless maroon cardigan that he clutched together at the chest.

Nels got out and offered the bagged bottle. "Thought you could use a little something to help fend off the chill," he said.

The old man's eyes sparkled briefly as he clasped the bottle against himself. "Mite cold today. Got a fire in the stove if you boys want to come in."

"No, we gotta keep looking for our friend and his boat, but thanks anyway," Nels said.

"Sorry I can't help you out, but after they loaded it on the trailer, I never saw which way they went."

"They what?" Nels asked in amazement. "You say they loaded the sailboat on a trailer?"

The old man's eyes narrowed. "That's what they done, all right. Figured you'd know, being friends and all."

"We're friends all right," Nels explained. "But he didn't say anything about hauling the boat away. Just asked us to come help him move it."

Nels stopped, shaking his head. "What kind of rig did he put it on? Big pickup and some kind of lowboy trailer?"

"Don't know what you call it. Guess that's what it was."

"And they hauled it right over there at the pier?" Nels asked. "How did they lift it out?"

"One of them big log trucks with a crane on it," the old man said.

"Do you know whose outfit lifted it?" Nels inquired. "Or maybe where the hauler came from?"

"Nope, don't know none a that. Not the nosy kind."

Nels looked down and scuffed his feet in the dust. "Damn," he said half to himself, "wish there was some way to get in touch with him." He looked up. "Sure you don't have a name? Make it worth your while."

"Sorry, fella," the old man said. "I'm gettin' cold and thirsty, reckon I'll go inside and warm up some. Good luck to ya." He turned away and rounded the corner, hunching against the wind.

"Thanks again," Nels called, turning back toward the jeep.

"Damn," he muttered, pounding the side of his fist against the steering wheel.

"What's happening?" Graham asked.

"He pulled the boat out right over there at the pier and had it hauled away."

"Good God," Graham exclaimed. "Where to?"

"Didn't say; claimed not to know. Says he's not the nosy type."

"Any clues?" Graham asked.

"A few," Nels said, describing the kind of pickup truck, trailer, and logging truck that he imagined had been involved.

"So all we have to do now is find the logging truck that was used to lift the boat," Graham exclaimed happily.

Nels eyed the big Englishman skeptically. "Right," he said. "But at least we're on some kind of trail here that leads back to Northport. Good chance the *Golden Fleece* and the *Fishin' Fool* are one and the same. The commander may be Harry Potter or he may be somebody else, but I really do think the boat's the same."

"You really think so?" Graham asked. "How can you be sure?"

"Can't, but there are two clues. First, the commander, whoever he is, isn't doing what he told the Canadians he was planning to do. Second, this is an unusual way to remove a boat from the lake, very isolated and unorthodox."

"Ah, just so," Graham said, nodding. "So where do we go from here?"

"I think we go back home and lay it all out for MacNulty," Nels answered. "We could use some official help and Mac-Nulty's the guy who can provide it."

MacNulty leaned back in his armchair and listened to Nels spin the tale of the mysterious green-eyed woman and the removal of the *Golden Fleece* from the waters of Lake Superior. Despite the serious nature of the story, Nels saw that the sheriff was unable to suppress a broad smile that creased his face. His eyes almost danced with glee.

"So that's about it, Ray," Nels said, puzzled by the sheriff's canary-eating grin. "We probably could use some help in finding the logging truck that lifted the boat on the trailer."

MacNulty threw himself forward to the edge of his chair, slapped both hands down on the desk, and leaned forward toward the two sailors. Nels thought he looked like a kid about to attack a pile of Christmas packages.

"Hah," he shouted, "hot damn. We got us a whole new ballgame."

Nels had never actually seen anybody rub their hands together in gleeful anticipation the way MacNulty was doing.

"Connie, get me Walt on the radio, pronto," he shouted to the dispatcher.

"Men, we got two cases that just rolled together into one," he said excitedly. "We got a murder and a disappearance and God knows what else all wove together.

"Damn," he shouted, slapping a big, meaty hand on his desk. "This is gettin' interesting."

"Sheriff," the dispatcher called loudly, "I've got Walt on the radio."

MacNulty keyed his desk set. "Walter, this is Uncle Ray. You still back up over the hill somewhere?"

"Uh, yeah, I'm about ten miles north, headin' for the barn," Walt's voice replied.

"Make yourself a little U-turn and shag your ass up to the Hoffman and Sims logging operation. I want you to pick up Big

Charlie for questioning. Hell, on second thought, make it an arrest. For conspiracy, that's a good one. Lay on the full bit, cuffs, the reading of rights, you know the routine. I want to see a scared prisoner comin' in here."

"You want to give me any hints, or just keep me in the dark?" Walt asked.

"Too complicated. Just play it dead serious, because it is."

"Breakthrough time, eh?"

"You got it, Toyota. I'll be waiting with open arms."

Nels sat silently for several moments following the conversation before his impatience broke through. "Can you tell us what any of this is all about, Ray?"

MacNulty's grin tried to spread ear-to-ear. "I can only tell you one little thing to hold your interest. Your little miss green eyes is none other than Charlene Mittner, aka Big Charlie, aka the girlfriend of Carl Hoffman, who was found murdered last week. How about them apples?"

"Good God," Nels exclaimed, "Are you sure?"

"Bet my job on it. Yessiree, we got us a live one. You fellas run along and I'll call you later for a positive ID"

W alt Downing and his prisoner were almost identical in height and build. They entered the sheriff's outer office silently and with grim faces.

"Connie, I've got a prisoner here to be booked and logged in. You might ask the sheriff if he wants to talk to her now or later."

Walt began writing an arrest report while Connie Roper disappeared into MacNulty's private office. Nobody spoke to the woman, who stood handcuffed but defiantly erect, jaw set and eyes blazing like green sparks.

"Mr. Downing," Connie said to the chief deputy, "the sheriff would like a private word with you in his office."

Walt put his pen down and walked to the sheriff's closed door, which he opened and closed behind him.

"Any trouble?" MacNulty asked.

Walt shook his head. "Only if looks could kill."

"Got her by surprise, eh?"

"Yeah, I think so. She wasn't working, just got back from a couple days of vacation time, according to her boss."

"Virgil Sims told you that?"

"Yeah, the dead guy's partner."

"Okay, here's what we got," MacNulty said, and followed with an explanation of Nels's story and his own deductions.

"Wow, that's a helluva twist," Walt agreed. "I can see why you were hopped up."

"Let's have at it here in my office; do it informally. I'll ease up, you keep the hammer down. We'll see how it goes."

Walt nodded and went out to the outer office. Charlie met his cold, hard eyes with a glare.

"Okay Mittner, sheriff wants a word with you before we throw you in a cell. I told him it's a waste of time, but he insists; come with me."

He took her arm and led her into the private office, where MacNulty was studying papers. He looked up.

"Ah, Charlene, good to see you again. Please, have a seat right there."

Walt held her arm tightly and pushed her into the chair.

"Easy there, Mr. Downing. We're not dealing with a hardened criminal here. And for God's sake, let's get those handcuffs off. I'm sure Miss Mittner would feel a lot better if she could relax and have a cigarette."

Walt hesitated. "You sure about the cuffs, sir?" he said doubtfully.

"You heard me, Mr. Downing. I want them off."

Walt shrugged theatrically and removed the cuffs from Charlie's wrists.

"Here, have a smoke and relax," MacNulty said, watching the slight tremor in her hands as she picked up and lit the cigarette.

"That's better. Now we can sit back and talk a bit."

He watched her inhale and blow a lungful of smoke across the shaft of sunlight in front of his desk.

"Mr. Downing, I'm sure there's no need to stand hovering over Miss Mittner like that. Would you please sit down and relax so we can get on with it?"

Walt shrugged and sat stiffly down in a straight chair, his eyes locked on her every move.

"Okay now, everybody relaxed?" MacNulty asked, leaning back in his big padded chair.

"We find ourselves in a difficult position with regard to you, Charlene," he said, arms outstretched and palms open toward the stern-faced woman. "On the one hand, I personally don't think you should have been arrested for anything. On the other hand," he shrugged, "some connections have been made linking you to two different crimes. I'd like to sort things out right now before this goes any further. Once we book you," he shrugged again, "things are sort of out of our hands, understood?"

She made just the hint of a nod and he continued. "Good. As I said, we're faced with two possible crimes here. First, there's the death of your, ah, fiancé, Carl Hoffman, which I don't think you had anything to do with. But then there's the second, ah, situation. That's the disappearance of Harry Potter and his boat. We've been treating that problem as an accident, but I do have a couple of investigators checking things out. Just part of my job to tie up all the loose ends, as I'm sure you can understand.

"Well, you can imagine my dismay in finding out that you also seem to have an interest in Mr. Potter's disappearance. At first, well, I just couldn't believe it, wouldn't believe it. But the investigators have positively identified you. So I wanted to give you the chance, Charlene, to tell us informally just how you're connected to all this."

She was silent a moment, then looked at MacNulty. "I don't have anything to say. Your people must be wrong. I just don't know what you're talking about."

Walt jumped from his chair. "Didn't I tell you the bitch wouldn't talk? This is a waste of time. Let me book her and be done with it."

"Please, Mr. Downing," the sheriff said sternly, "sit down and control yourself. Another outburst like that and I'll have to ask you to leave the room."

"Please excuse his behavior, Charlene. Mr. Downing is a fine police officer, but his overzealous behavior is certainly uncalled for."

"I told you that she and Potter killed her boyfriend, then Potter double-crossed her," Walt said. "She's in this up to her ass."

"That's a goddamn lie," Charlie shouted. "What the fuck do you know about it?"

"Please, please," MacNulty said, holding up his hands. "Both of you are going to have to calm down if we hope to get anywhere. Charlene, don't you see that I'm trying to give you a chance to explain things, to clear the air? Otherwise, I'll be forced to turn you over to Mr. Downing here, whose methods, I can assure you, will be less generous."

"I didn't kill anybody and I didn't break no laws, either," Charlie insisted.

"Just tell us how it was, Charlene," MacNulty urged gently.

She stared at him silently, then glanced away.

"You realize, of course, that when we find the missing boat and talk to Mr. Potter or whoever is operating it, we'll find out for ourselves what is going on. That, together with your silence today, may weigh heavily against you. I'm trying to give you a unique opportunity right now to tell us what happened, without pressure."

She shook her head derisively. "You haven't got a thing on me. I can call a lawyer and be out of here in no time."

"Sheriff, this whore's wasting your time," Walt snapped.

"That's enough, Mr. Downing. Just because there are rumors, you have no right to label Miss Mittner. I don't want to hear that again."

MacNulty noted his prisoner, though silent, had flushed with anger.

"Charlene, if it's what you say, that you haven't done anything wrong, then I find it hard to believe you wouldn't want to cooperate with us, help us find the guilty parties. Do you really understand what kind of person you're protecting by your silence?"

He slid open his top center drawer, removed an eight-by-ten glossy photograph, and leaned forward to place it on the desk near Charlie.

She looked at it, then saw what it was and jerked away. She stared out the window, eyes filling with tears.

"I told you the bitch was guilty," Walt shouted. "Look at 'er, will you? She and Potter beat poor Carl to a bloody pulp. That's why she won't talk."

"You stupid asshole," she yelled through a haze of tears. "I loved him. How could I do that?"

"That's bullshit," Walt said, jumping to his feet. He grabbed the grisly photograph and held it in front of her face. "If you loved him, you wouldn't let anybody get away with this. You'd be trying to get even."

"What the fuck do you think I'm trying to do?" she yelled, standing up and jutting her face toward Walt. Then, green eyes flashing through the tears, she added in a voice shaking with anger, "I'll get even if it's the last thing I do."

"And that's why you're looking for Harry Potter," Mac-Nulty said, not as a question but as a statement of fact. "We're on the same side, Charlene. Sit down and tell us what you know so we can help you find him."

He handed her a Kleenex and she blew her nose. He handed her another for her tears.

"So Harry disappeared deliberately after killing Carl? Is that how you've got it figured?"

She sniffed, blew her nose again and nodded. Walt sat down and relaxed visibly.

"Charlene, why not just explain things, tell us what you think happened," MacNulty urged.

"The son of a bitch is scum. He cheated us, robbed us. When I catch him. . . ." She stopped, tears welling again.

"Charlene," MacNulty said gently, "why don't you just start at the beginning so we can follow along."

She looked at him, green eyes liquid in reddened rims. Then she closed her eyes, squeezing out more tears and shook her head slowly.

"Aw shit," she muttered, "what the hell."

She opened wet, sticky lids and looked straight at Mac-Nulty. "You promise to go after that slime ball Potter?"

"If what you tell us makes sense, Charlene," MacNulty said solemnly. "We'll go after him and get him, my word on it."

She nodded. "Okay, I'll tell you all I know, right from the start," she said in a quiet, weary voice.

"Good. I'm going to tape this, Charlene, so we won't be getting the details mixed up later."

He switched on a small recorder, placed it on the front of his desk, and leaned back.

She blew another Kleenex full and wiped her eyes, then lit a cigarette and started to talk.

"Up off the Quill Mountain Road, where we been cutting, Carl got a pretty good size contract. We only cut a part of it so far. Up that old abandoned road is another piece.

"Anyhow, Carl figured to fix up the old road to take out logs. One day, I think it was a Friday, he decided to go over and put in a new culvert on the old road so we could drive farther in to see where it went and how much work it would take to fix up a landing.

"I didn't think much about it. Hell, he's always off somewhere doing things and I'm out there runnin' a skidder. But that night, he came back to the trailer we got up there and he was real excited. Says 'Charlene,' he always called me that instead of Charlie, 'Charlene, I got a present for ya like ya never had before.'

"I hold out my hand and he plunks this heavy little chunk of what feels like lead in it. Except when I look at it, I can see right away it's a gold-colored chunk. I says, 'Is this thing what it looks like it is?' He says, 'I think so, but I'm damned if I know for sure. We got to show it to somebody who would know, but if it is, it's yours.' "

She stopped and reached into the neck of her shirt for a long chain. "This is what he brought me that day," she said, lifting an object out from under her shirt.

She held out the heavy object in her palm, hefting it. The chain passed through a small hole drilled in one end. "A ten-ounce gold nugget, first thing he ever found over there."

MacNulty shook his head and hefted it, surprised at the weight. He studied the gold patina on the smooth side.

"Solid gold," she said. "Worth forty-two hundred right now."

"So where was it? Just lying around on the ground?" Mac-Nulty asked.

"He was moving dirt; it stuck out of the pile. Said it looked just like you see it now."

"We thought it was gold, but not for sure, so next day he went to town and took it along. He knew Potter was a geologist, so he took it out to the lodge and showed it to him. He said it was."

"So that's how Harry got involved?" MacNulty asked.

"Not right away. Carl and me waited 'til Sunday, when the crew was off, mostly gone to town, and we went back to look.

"We spent the whole day over there lookin', but all we found was some little piddly stuff. The whole works put together wasn't the size of my little fingernail."

She stopped, looked again at the rough lump of gold in her hand, then slipped it inside her shirt and down between her breasts.

"So that convinced Carl that we needed somebody who knew about gold. He was sure there was more around, but we didn't find any more hunks laying around, and we didn't really know what to do next.

"So a couple days later, it was after supper but still sunny out, Harry came to have a look. He spent a couple hours chippin' at rocks, making notes, drawin' pictures, stuff like that.

"Then, I guess it was getting dark, he comes over and says, 'I know there's more gold here because I can see the color, but it's gonna take some work and equipment to get it out and process.' He said he'd help us get it out if we'd go fifty-fifty with him.

"Carl figured it was fair. 'Hell,' he says, '50 percent of somethin' beats a 100 percent of nothin' every time.' So they shook hands on it. Harry said we'd go after it Saturday and Sunday and Carl said okay.

"We kept goin' over there evenings after work, to see if we could find some more pieces laying around, but it was a waste of time.

"So Harry called Carl and told him what to bring and we hauled a lot a shit over there. Friday evening it was two-by-fours, blasting caps, and a case of dynamite, a compressor and drills, some gravel screens. Had to make two trips to get everything.

"We worked our asses off for two solid days. Harry made what he called a sluice, with screens and a box below. We pushed dirt into it with the cat and let the crick run over it; did that all day Sunday. After two days we had a box with maybe five pounds of stuff in it. Harry said it would go about 40 percent gold when it was melted down, so that made a couple pounds. Harry also said it would come to about seven thousand dollars apiece for the weekend.

"We were all pretty excited. Had a couple of drinks and laughed and kidded around 'til after dark that night.

"Harry was pretty mellow by then. I figured he was an okay guy. He said we might just be foolin' around with nickels and dimes when the big stuff was right under our noses. He said the rock cliff just north of where we were diggin' might be the source, said there was color and might be a vein or somethin' in the rock there.

"Carl said he didn't want to be blasting when the crew came back Monday morning, so Harry talked him into drillin' a couple test holes, he called 'em. Knew right where he wanted 'em, I'll say that much.

"Anyhow, we put a couple sticks in each hole and blew a pretty good bit of rock away from the face. So here we are, in the dark and all three of us shined up pretty good, lookin' at pieces of rock with spotlights and flashlights. At first, Harry didn't find nuthin'.

"Hell, we didn't even know what he was lookin' for. He said, 'Don't bother lookin' for gold nuggets in the rock, cause you won't find none.' Finally we hear him talkin' to himself down on his hands and knees in front of some new exposed rock. Says it looked real good, but we gotta blast a lot more rock to get at the best part.

"So we drill three holes and load 'em with three sticks apiece. Then we take cover behind the cat and blow the charges. Shit, the rocks were fallin' for two minutes. Tore half of that cliff all to hell.

"Harry walks over to where the smoke was still rolling out of the rocks, takes one look, and starts gigglin' and laughin'. He was jumpin' around like a drunken Indian, hollerin', 'We're rich, we hit 'er.'

"We go over to look and there's not much to see except

this line running through the rock. Couldn't even tell what color it was. I ran and got the sledge and a cold chisel and we started bustin' rock like a couple a jailbirds.

"He found where this gray-green vein ran down inside the rock and begged us to drill again and blast it open.

"He kept sayin', This could be it. This could be the big one.' So we put in twelve sticks. Blew the whole cliff down.

"This time, when we went back, he shined a light and you could see little gold sparkles in the vein—not solid gold like the nugget but gold enough to know what it was—and it ran about an inch thick through some of the pieces.

"So Carl asked how do we get the gold part out and Harry, he grins like a crazy lunatic and runs to get a propane burner and a big, thick kettle.

" 'Break all the rock away from the veins,' he says. So we break rocks and he starts cookin' the stuff. Once, we stopped and he was hovering over the pot like a crazy witch, talkin' to it. He had what he called molds. Three of 'em I think, and he was pouring the liquid in the pot into 'em.

"We all stopped and had a couple more drinks while the molds cooled, then Harry turned 'em upside down and broke 'em loose. I could'a shit when I saw him take off them molds and leave three bars of gold sittin' there on a plank. It took 'em a while to cool so you could pick 'em up. They were little, but the three bars weighed about thirty pounds apiece.

"By then, we were all jumpin' around like wild Indians. Harry said the bars were worth about $250,000 each, so let's get busy and make some more.

"When it got light, we had nine bars layin' there and there was a lot more of the vein stuff to melt down. At least it seemed like there was.

"By rights, we shoulda been beat, cause we worked all night. But God, it felt so good knowing you're rich that we were all wide awake.

"About then, the problems began. Not problems, as much

as knowing if you could trust the other guy. We decided the fairest way was for me to show up as usual for work and explain that Carl would be gone for two or three days. Then the two of them would finish up the melting process and split the take. That way, neither would have to leave their share with the other.

"Carl and me, we planned to take ours in thirty-pound bars. There looked to be enough for about six of 'em. Harry, though, said he wanted his cast to fit someplace in his sailboat and Carl agreed to help him cast the shape and haul it onto Harry's boat.

"Honest to God, that's the last I seen of either one, that morning with the bars laying around. About a week later, I heard that Harry had disappeared; almost laughed out loud. I figured he had just bugged out with his share.

"Once, I went over to the site but I didn't see anything. Looked like they made some repairs, cleaned up some stuff. There was no gold laying around, of course. I think it was that Thursday or Friday I went over after work.

"Anyhow, that's about it. The first I heard of Carl was when Virgil and I came down the old road to that place where the pickup truck was parked."

There was a long silence as she concluded the story. Mac-Nulty shook his head. "That's the damnedest story I ever heard."

"Honest, Sheriff, everything I said was true. That's the whole story."

"Was it you then who went to Harry's workshop last week?" MacNulty asked. "Looking for some clue of Harry or the gold?"

She nodded slowly. "I never took anything from there. I just looked around and left."

MacNulty nodded. "And then you started following the two fellows who are looking into Harry's disappearance."

Again she nodded. "I figured if there was any way to catch

up with ol' Harry, that'd be the fastest way. I'm sorry about hitting their car like that; they just sort of caught me by surprise. Honest, I never cared much about the money. Hell, I never had any my whole life anyhow. But I wanted to catch up with that snake and make him suffer good. Maybe castrate him, for openers."

MacNulty shuddered. "There are more orthodox ways to deal with him, Charlene."

She chuckled dangerously. "Not near as much fun, though."

"You realize, of course," Walt said, changing the subject, "that the gold would not be your property anyhow. The U.S. government retains all mineral rights to forestry lands."

She gave him a sour look. "No skin off my ass, since I ain't got any of it anyhow."

"I was referring to the little bauble you're wearing around your neck," he said.

MacNulty waved his arms as Charlie reddened with anger. "Whoa there, time out. We sure as hell aren't going to confiscate Charlene's nugget, for God's sake, Downing."

"No, I suppose not, if she cooperates," Walt said. "But forty-two hundred dollars in gold does constitute a felony offense."

"Would you just back off and give her some slack?" MacNulty ordered loudly. "Hell, she's told us the whole story."

"Just want her to know she's still on the hook," Walt said solemnly.

A cold southeast wind carried fog and drizzle to Northport the next morning. Unlike the merchants downtown, MacNulty enjoyed the nasty weather.

"Anything is better than that damn heat wave we've been having," he said to whomever would listen. For emphasis, he continued to wear his short sleeve uniform when all the others had thrown on sweaters and windbreaker jackets.

Walt and MacNulty had spent a rewarding three hours with Charlie Mittner before turning her loose at suppertime. Now it was up to MacNulty to decide the moves that would lead them quickly to Harry Potter.

He sat with a second cup of coffee, watching light rain spatter against the south windows and run down them in erratic rivulets.

Would Harry have done what Charlie suggested? Could he have done it? It was certainly out of character for the man, but who knows what someone would do for a fortune in gold? Would he go so far as to name his boat *Golden Fleece?*

Was she telling the truth? Could she have fabricated the whole bizarre story? Not likely she'd create such a fantasy unless it was true, he decided. He didn't guess she was an imaginative woman, not likely to have conjured up all the details she had described.

So what do you do now, he asked himself, listening to the light rain pepper the windows in wind-blown clusters.

He heard Walt's voice in the outer office and hollered. It would have been more professional to use the intercom, but somehow he never thought of it.

"Get her home safe last night?" MacNulty asked Walt, who entered carrying a steaming coffee mug.

Walt sipped at his coffee and nodded. "She doesn't like me much, though," he said, grinning.

"You surprised?" MacNulty asked. "Hell, if you were really like you acted yesterday, nobody would like you much." He shook his head. "You really took the prize."

"Just following orders," Walt said, "even though it severely tests my sweet and gentle nature."

"Uh-huh," MacNulty retorted. "So what does Mr. Sweet and Gentle think we should do next?"

"I been thinking about it half the night. The boat name is

119

a dead giveaway. Find *Golden Fleece* and we find our man. We've got two routes to follow and I propose we go both ways.

"First, the usual approach. Bulletin all the counties where we think he might have headed. Explain that we're looking for Harry Potter, aka the retired naval commander Trawick, and his boat, the *Fishin' Fool* aka *Golden Fleece*. Wanted for questioning on charges of murder one and grand theft.

"The second route is the one we've been following with Nels. I'd keep him and Graham on the track and explain to them all the latest input we've gotten from Charlie.

"No tellin' which route will pay off, but we've got better odds going two ways at once."

The sheriff gave him a wry smile. "Always said you were a smart young fella, no matter what everybody else said."

"Gee thanks, Ray," Walt replied. "I always did like backhanded compliments the best."

"Somehow I knew that," MacNulty said. "Now you can hear some of *my* brilliant ideas. Incidentally, I agree with your two-pronged attack and I want you to put together the bulletin today.

"I want you to be sure to get the bulletin out to the various highway patrols, too. Not many thirty-three foot sailboats being hauled around on the highways these days, and those boys could get lucky the next couple of days if they keep their eyes open.

"But I think the direct approach, using Nels to track him down, is most likely to bear fruit. I'd send 'em right back to Michigan to find out who loaded the boat and who hauled it. I'd also send our prize witness, Charlie, along with 'em to talk logger talk with the locals."

"Jeez, I don't know, Ray," Walt cautioned.

"The boat was loaded by a logging truck," MacNulty said. "That means they've got to find out which one and talk to the right people. From what I've heard, Charlie never met a logger she didn't like."

"That may not include sailors," Walt said.

"Hell, they're big boys. They can take care of themselves."

"You'll recall that Nels and Charlie have already had one little confrontation," Walt replied. "Neither one of 'em is exactly Cool Hand Luke."

"Figure there might be bloodshed?" MacNulty chided.

"The only blood I'm worried about is yours after Prentice finds out you've sent Charlie along with Nels."

"Who, me? I'm not sending her. Just making a suggestion."

"Well, since it's your 'suggestion,' you get to make the calls and do the explaining."

They met formally in the parking lot outside the sheriff's office. MacNulty was not available, so Walt reluctantly made the introductions.

"Nels, Graham, I want you to meet Charlie Mittner. Charlie, this is Nels Dahlstrom and Graham Jackson. I think you met briefly over in Michigan," he said lightly.

Nels looked at the green-eyed woman coolly and nodded. "You're the one who tried to use my head for a doorstop, right?"

She responded with a swagger and a disdainful look. "That's about the only thing a shithead's good for," she replied.

Nels reddened and took a half step forward. "Okay, sweetheart, read my lips. . . ."

He never finished. Graham saw the roundhouse right starting and jumped between them, catching the blow flush on the ear. He blinked, but caught and held her forearm with a big, powerful hand before she could retract it.

"Le'go, you son of a bitch," she yelled, trying in vain to pull away from his viselike grip.

He waited for her to stop struggling, then spoke very slowly and carefully. "Young lady, if you *ever* try that again, I

121

will turn your brains to a jelly." For emphasis, he increased the force of his grip.

"Owww, it hurts," she whined. "I wasn't even tryin' to hit you."

"Okay Graham," Walt said. "I think she's got the message."

Released, Charlie clutched her forearm which was already red and swelling.

"Charlie, you're very foolish and very lucky that Graham didn't break half your bones just by accident. Lucky, too, that he stopped Nels from killing you right on the spot."

Walt turned to Nels and Graham. "Guys, I know this isn't the easiest thing in the world, but I'd still like you to take her along. If you can handle it, I'll guarantee her behavior."

"I think she can be managed," Graham said. "I'll stand between them at all times."

"How do you propose we keep her in line, Walt," Nels asked tersely.

"Very simple," Walt replied. "Charlie, give me your nugget for safekeeping. You behave yourself at all times and you get it back when you return."

"No way, you bastard," she hissed.

"Let me explain the options to you, Charlie. Either you give it to me yourself, or I take it away from you. If you make me take it, there won't be any trip to Michigan. Instead, you'll go in a jail cell and stay there until they're ready to put you on trial in federal court for grand theft.

"You got thirty seconds to make up your mind," he added. "What could be simpler?"

Tears of rage welled up in her green eyes as she stared hatefully at the chief deputy.

"Fifteen seconds," Walt said calmly.

Hands shaking, she pulled the chain from beneath her checked shirt, looped it over her head, and held it at arm's length. As Walt reached for it, she let it drop on the blacktop at her feet.

Walt smiled, bent down and scooped it up. "Childish games won't work, kid," he smiled.

"I expect it back when I get home," she snapped.

"Only if you earn it, starting now," Walt said.

The long drive was quiet and uneventful, an uneasy truce in the hostilities. Graham, regaining his usual mien, even tried to initiate pleasantries with Charlie, but she was having none of it.

"Buzz off, will ya?" she answered.

"As I understand it," Graham continued, "You're not just along for the ride; you're expected to help us get information."

"So let me know when you need me; 'til then, go jerk off and leave me alone."

They left her alone, dozing quietly in the back seat, as they entered the rugged forest lands of the upper peninsula of Michigan. "I think we should give it another shot with the old fisherman," Nels said. "If we ask the right questions, we might get some answers.

"He knows the boat was loaded on a lowboy trailer pulled by a pickup. Had to be a fifth-wheel rig to handle that kind of weight."

"Isn't that a bit unusual?" Graham asked. "Wouldn't such a boat usually be handled by a larger truck?"

Nels nodded. "Some of these gypsy haulers get into the business cheap that way. Doesn't cost as much to run or maintain, so they can quote lower rates. More than likely, he's from around this area or the vicinity of the destination, one or the other. The C&C 33 would probably be right at the top end of his capacity."

They passed through Marquette and continued east toward Shelter Bay. The day had warmed with sunshine and a southwest wind was blowing the heat up from the prairie heartland of Nebraska and Kansas.

"Strange how we almost freeze in heavy sweaters one day and swelter in shorts and T-shirts the next," Nels said, fiddling with the air conditioning controls. "The water of the lake has a hell of an effect on the weather around here."

Shelter Bay came into view. It was, on this day, a placid cove. Two power boats were tied to the west side of the concrete pier and kids in bathing suits played on the narrow strip of dirt-brown sand. Smoke from a picnic fire drifted over several cars parked near the beach.

"Let's give it a shot," Nels said, turning down the dirt road to the pier. "You never know."

A trail of dust followed them to the parking area, a grassy place where cars simply pulled off the double-rutted lane.

"You want me to do somethin'?" Charlie asked sullenly.

"Suit yourself," Nels answered, removing the car keys and stepping out.

The men went down the small slope to the pier, where they separated. Nels took the beach and Graham the pier, each stopping to ask people if they had been around a few days earlier when a big white sailboat was lifted from the water and loaded on a trailer. After fifteen or twenty minutes of drawing blank stares, quizzical looks, and shrugs, they met again at the foot of the pier.

"Nothing," Nels shrugged, "but at least it was worth a try. Never know when you might get lucky."

"It was a good idea," Graham echoed.

They walked side by side back up the sloping ruts and reached the car, which was empty. "Oh shit," Nels grumbled. "That's all we need now. You see her anyplace?"

"No," Graham answered, looking around. "Ah, there she is."

Charlie had shed her checked shirt and was leaning against the hood of a dusty-looking sedan in hip hugger blue jeans and a flimsy, sleeveless white knit top that bared her belly and clearly outlined her breasts and protruding nipples. She was laughing and gesturing to a short, balding man wearing shorts,

Hawaiian shirt, and brown shoes and socks. He was either sunburned or extremely excited and embarrassed by his first encounter with a green-eyed amazon. Nels and Graham sauntered toward her casually so as not to distrub any progress she might be making.

She glanced at their approach and gave them a dazzling smile. "Hi guys," she said, "I caught up with Ernie here comin' out of the crapper. He's been tellin' me about the fat little jerk who hauled the boat away a few days back."

She turned back to Ernie and put her hands on his shoulders. "You been sweet to me, honey," she said in a husky voice, then pulled him against her in an embrace that nearly smothered him against her breasts.

"I gotta go now, honey," she cooed down at him. Then she stepped back. "You come up to Northport some time and I'll show you a *real* good time, know what I mean? See you, Ernie."

She turned with a wave, gathered Nels and Graham with an arm around each, and led them, arm in arm, toward the jeep.

"Well, wasn't that fun," she exclaimed. "Now we just got to decide how much all that information is worth to you guys. Ol' Ernie, there, is a regular around here. Nosy little bastard."

"Come on now, Charlie," Nels sputtered, caught off balance by her gay and mischievous attitude.

They arrived at the jeep and she stepped back, striking a provocative pose with hands on hips and breasts outthrust.

"I got what you boys want. Now let's just see how bad you want it."

"Okay, Charlie, let's quit screwin' around and get in the car," Nels said, exasperated.

"You wanna quit screwin' around?" Charlie mocked. "Why, we ain't even started yet. How about you, big guy? You want me to whisper little secrets in your ear?"

Graham shook his head, bemused by her sudden change of moods. "I think you should stop the teasing and explain yourself."

She slid her tongue along her lips and her green eyes

glowed beneath hooded lids. There was something dangerous about this taunting woman and Graham could feel it. He watched her fingertips etch light patterns across her hard belly. He had been several weeks without a woman and he could feel himself quicken in spite of his mind's resistance.

"Come to me, big boy," she growled, willing him to respond.

"Goddamn it, you two," Nels said angrily. "Get in the car and let's get going."

He started the jeep and gunned the engine, breaking the spell.

"Just remember," Charlie said tartly. "I got what you need."

She turned to the car door and climbed in, leaving Graham, feeling foolish now, standing alone in the grass.

He finally sauntered to the jeep and climbed in, where Nels shot him a nasty look.

"All right, Charlie," Nels snapped, looking at her in the rear view mirror. "Let's have the story."

"Let's have the story," she mimicked in a whiny falsetto. "Tell you what, ace, you stop and get me a beer or better yet, two beers, to wet my whistle and I'll give you your story."

"No way. Let's hear it now unless you want me to give Downing a bad report when we get back."

"Suit yourself, asshole," she smiled, leaning back on the bench seat with her arms hooked over the seat back.

"Nels, ease up and relax," Graham said. "I could stand a pint myself."

Nels took a deep breath and blew it out noisily. "Don't push me, Graham, okay?"

"Sure. Let's get a beer and hear the lady's story," Graham repeated easily.

Nels held himself in check by a thread. Stiff with anger, he snapped the console-mounted transmission into drive and pulled ahead, making a circle through the grass back to the dusty road. Reaching the asphalt-covered state road, he turned west, back the way they had come. He would acquiesce but he would not forget the humiliation he felt.

Four miles down the tree-lined road, they stopped at a convenience store. Without speaking, Nels stepped out and stalked inside.

"Your friend's got a big problem," Charlie said. "Someday it's gonna get him in trouble."

Graham turned to her. "Nobody likes to be backed into a corner. Just don't press it any further, okay?"

She cocked her head and smiled sensuously. "Sure, honey, I can chill it if you want. Just find a nice place to relax and have our beer, okay?"

"Sure," Graham nodded, watching Nels return with a six pack of Old Style in his hand.

Nels climbed in, handed the beer to Graham, and pulled away from the store.

"Can we find a pullover, like a rest stop, along this road?" Graham asked.

Nels shrugged. "I'll go a few miles and see."

He drove nearly forty miles, halfway to the Wisconsin border, before pulling off onto a gravel parking lot designated as a rest stop.

Graham got out and carried the beer to the picnic table farthest from the road, near the boundary between grass and forest floor. Charlie went toward the rest rooms.

"Still angry?" Graham asked.

"Shouldn't I be?" Nels snapped. "Between the two of you, playing your cute little games, I got a right to be pissed."

"Hey, I'm on your side," Graham replied. "There's a saying you have about catching more flies with sugar than salt, right?"

"No, it's with honey instead of vinegar."

"Okay, well, at least you understand what I'm trying to do, what I think is the best way."

"I just want to find out what the hell she knows," Nels said, relaxing slightly.

"Right, mate," Graham agreed, popping three cans. "I'll drink to that." He handed Nels a can and raised his to his mouth.

Charlie returned, sat down at the picnic table, and took a long pull from her can of Old Style. "Aahh," she said, smacking her lips. "That's more like it."

"So tell us your story," Graham nudged. "I've been waiting an hour."

"For the story or somethin' else?" she grinned.

"The story first," he said, returning her knowing grin.

"Okay. Well, little Ernie back there said the boat hauler arrived about an hour before the logger and got pretty pissed hangin' around waiting.

"He said the hauler was a short guy, fat too, and with a loud mouth. Said he was yellin' at the guy on the boat about gettin' paid and about charging waiting time if the logging truck didn't show.

"The hauler was called Kenny, as best he could remember, or at least something with a K. He said he didn't come all this way to be stiffed, so the guy was paying, with or without a boat ride. Sounds like a real nice guy, don't he? Sorta like you, Nels.

"Anyhow, the boat was going to New Orleans. Little Ernie is sure of that, 'cause they talked about where exactly it was supposed to go. Ernie said he was stationed down near there in the army so he knew what they were talkin' about.

"So that's about it, except that the fat guy was from Florida. Nosy little Ernie asked him that himself, he said. He asked him if he was from New Orleans and the fat little guy, Kenny or whatever, said 'Shit no. I wouldn't live in that pisshole. I'm from Florida.'

"So, it looks like we can just drive on down to New Orleans and find that son of a bitch Potter, right? Not much question that's who it is. Nobody else would think to name a boat the *Golden Fleece* if he wasn't a gold thief, right?"

Graham nodded in agreement. It was a pretty obvious assumption. "Okay, everybody up," Nels said suddenly. "We're heading back to Northport, quick as we can get there. We need to tell the sheriff what we got, then nail down some fast connections to New Orleans.

"He's only four days ahead of us, at least two days of it driving south. If we're lucky, we might just catch up with him at New Orleans."

Charlie continued sitting at the picnic table, sipping her beer. "Shit, I thought we were gonna stay at some nice motel and go swimming and have steaks tonight. It'll be nine, ten o'clock before we get back. What's the hurry?"

Nels eyed her coldly. "You don't seem to give a damn about anything except having yourself a good time. But I've got a boat to catch up with. He's got a big head start, but maybe if we hurry, we can eat up some of it. I don't think he'll hang around New Orleans any longer than he has to, but it may be long enough if we hurry.

"So you got a simple choice, Charlie old girl. Either sit on your ass right there and drink beer, or move your ass into the car. We're leaving, and it doesn't matter to me one bit if you go or stay. Is that clear?"

"Here I got all the information for you and you don't even appreciate it," she sulked. "You're a real pinhead, you know that?"

Nels nodded. "I do appreciate the information. It was very important. Now I'm leaving . . . with you or without you. Understand?"

He walked to the car, climbed in, and started it. Graham leaned in the passenger side. "Give me a minute. I'll go get her."

"Graham, I am leaving," Nels said between tight lips. "She

got her way before, because we needed the information. But no more screwin' around; get in the car. I'll honk a couple times, then wait fifteen seconds for her to start this way."

Nels honked the horn. Graham, standing at the open door, yelled to her. "Come on, Charlie, we're leaving."

"Get in, Graham," Nels said, shifting into reverse.

Graham sat down and closed the door, ready to stop Nels if she made any move at all. But she just sat at the picnic table, holding her can of beer as they pulled onto the thin strip of asphalt that led west through the pine forests of Michigan.

Graham glanced once at Nels, who was wearing a tight smile. He never looked back.

Big Charlie never looked back, either. In ten minutes, she was flirting with a young construction worker as they sped east toward Marquette in his Dodge Ram pickup.

"So my car's got a busted axle and I got to get down to Madison real fast to see my mom, who's real sick," she said. "So I hooked a ride with this pervert and finally made him let me out back there where you picked me up.

"Oh, he was a real sicko, he was," she continued. "Wanted me to do things to him I can't even talk about."

"Really?" asked the young man, his brow furrowed with concern but his eyes feasting on her breasts pressing against the flimsy knit cotton tank top.

"Oh yeah," she went on. "He was pantin' and moanin' and playing with himself right there in the car. I mean, ya know, practically gettin' off and everything."

She stopped and glanced at the effect her talk was having on the young man, smiling to herself at the noticeable bulge in his blue jeans. She enjoyed having this power over men and used it whenever it served her purpose.

"So that's when you got out?" he asked.

"Well, almost. He started grabbin' at me, told me he was gonna pull off in the woods somewheres and do things to me. That's when I told him I'd grab the wheel and put us in the ditch. I mean, I love to fool around with nice guys, but he was a weird pervert, ya know?"

"Yah, I guess so."

"Tell ya what. When we get to the airport, you give me your phone number so I can call you when I get back and show you how much I appreciate this ride. Would ya like that?"

"Well, sure, I guess I would," he said.

"Oooh, I can hardly wait," she said. "Wish I didn't have to go see mom. I could use some good lovin' right now."

"You sure you couldn't put off your trip awhile?" he asked eagerly. "Maybe there's a later flight?"

"No, I can't," she answered sadly. "I got the tickets already and it's the last flight out. But I'll be back in a few days and call you."

They were nearing the Marquette airport. It looked small and tacky, with a single small commuter flight at the terminal. She hoped they would have at least a few flights going out tonight.

"Well, here we are," he said, pulling to a stop. "Reach in the glove box and see if there's a pencil. I'll write my number on this card," he said, pulling out a business card he'd been given.

She found the pencil stub, took the card, and opened the door. "Thanks, hon," she smiled, green eyes sparkling. "You won't regret it." She then slammed the door and turned away toward the little terminal building, rebuttoning her shirt as she went in through the swinging doors.

Charlie scanned the flight schedule, then stepped to the counter and awaited the ticket agent, who was snapping destination tags on a half dozen pieces of luggage.

He turned back to the counter and met her smiling green eyes. "May I help you?"

"Yes please," she said, pushing a VISA card across the counter. "I'd like a ticket on your five-thirty flight to Chicago, with connections to Mobile. I need to get there tonight, if I can."

He tapped the computer, talking as he went. "No problem to Chicago. Hmmm, got an eight o'clock to Mobile with one stop in Memphis. Gets into Mobile at 9:45."

"That would be fine, thank you," she said pleasantly.

The agent completed the tickets and the charge card form, pushing it back for her signature. She signed the forms and retrieved the card.

"Thank you for flying North-Air Commuter Service and Northwest, Mrs. Hoffman. We'll be boarding your Chicago flight in fifteen minutes right over there at gate one. Any luggage?"

"No, just carryon," she replied with a smile.

D riving hard, they reached Northport just as darkness snuffed the blue-gray light of dusk.

Nels pulled into the small boat harbor lot. "I'm gonna get on the horn with Rich Hamilton in Pensacola. See if I can get a line on the boat hauler. I'll be back to get you at eight tomorrow morning. Pack a bag and be ready to travel."

"Anything I could do meantime?" Graham asked.

"No, get some rest. We'll probably be scouring the marinas around Lake Pontchartrain this time tomorrow."

"Toodle-oo, then," Graham said with a half wave. "See you tomorrow."

Nels spun away through the gravel, back onto the highway. In seconds, he'd pulled up in front of his room at Lakeview Lodge. The room was dark. He supposed Tizz was over in the dining room having supper. A quick phone call and I'll join her, he thought.

One call became two. He reached Phyllis Hamilton at home, but she said Rich was at a meeting, or more likely the bar, at the yacht club. He dialed, asked the answering voice for Rich Hamilton, and waited.

"Hamilton here," his friend said. He was an old, regular charter customer and a marine hardware wholesaler who knew people in the boat business.

"You always were partial to yacht club bars," Nels jibed, chuckling.

"Who is this? Surely not crazy Nels from St. Thomas."

"You got the first part right, but I'm up in Minnesota."

"Good God. Is it summer there yet?"

"Last time I looked. Listen Rich, I need some information."

"Shoot."

"Okay, I'm looking for a boat . . . C&C 33, new model. I think it was hauled down your way by a wildcat hauler name of Kenny. Name ring a bell?"

"Sure. Kenny Serkovian. Runs a little marina over in Panama City. I hear he's been hauling a lot of boats. Friend of mine had him carry his thirty footer down to south Florida a while back."

"Short guy? Fat?"

"That's your man."

"Great. And you say he's from Panama City? Is that in Florida?"

"That's the place, about ninety miles east of here. Call information. If you don't get him that way, try Serkovian Marine. I think that's what it's called."

"Listen Rich, I appreciate much. Give you a step-up on your charter next winter."

"Hey buddy, you got a deal. But don't hang up, I can maybe save you a call. Saw Kenny yesterday on his way home."

"Then maybe you already know what I'm trying to find out. Did he say he was coming from New Orleans?"

"No, Mobile. I'm sure of it, because he was bitchin' and moanin' about the people down at Dog River. Said they like to have wrecked his trailer gettin' a boat off a couple days ago."

"Dog River? That's on Mobile Bay?"

"Yup, west side of the bay. Straight down Dauphin Island Parkway. Quite a bit of marine business along the river. Couple marinas, Turner's Marine store, Mobile Yacht Club."

"Rich, I think you just saved me a whole lot of wasted motion."

"Anytime, Nels, just glad I could help. I know a lot of people over there. You just call if you need a hand, hear?"

"Sure, Rich, and you just earned yourself both a step-up *and* a discount."

"Can't beat that with a stick," Hamilton said, laughing, and hung up.

"Damn," Nels said out loud as he placed the phone on the receiver.

The door knob turned and Prentice appeared in the doorway. "Well, this is a surprise. Gone and back already?" she asked, walking toward him. "Ummm, give me a hug. I need to feel you up close and personal."

Nels stood and squeezed her, kissing her cheek. "Strange trip. Very strange," he said.

She kicked off her shoes and sprawled in a stuffed chair. "Oh, I'm stuffed. Shouldn't have had the blueberry pie." She groaned. "So tell me what happened."

"The woman I told you about, the one who went with us, she got the information out of a guy right away. Then she lied to us about part of it. Gave us New Orleans as a destination for the boat when it was really Mobile."

He stared at the flowered, print drapes. "Then, damned if she didn't just sit there. Wouldn't come back. But by then I was steamed. Said to hell with it and came back without her."

Prentice looked at her husband. "So now you're feeling guilty about leaving her. Figure you should have brought her back."

He looked at her and nodded. "At the time, I figured it served her right for being such a bitch."

"Honey, did it occur to you that she may have wanted to be left behind?"

He looked at her, then glanced away. "You mean, she wanted to go after Harry Potter herself, so she gave us bad information and stayed down there where she was close to an airport and could get a head start?" He shook his head. "Jeez, how come I never thought of that?"

"Because you're a man, dear."

"Damn," he said. "Fooled us slick as a fox."

Ray MacNulty sat hunched forward over his desk. His elbows rested on the desk and his thumbs were hooked under his square chin. He was edgy and uncomfortable with the summer heat, though it was only eight-thirty in the morning.

The chair squeaked as he leaned to the side and withdrew his fresh white handkerchief. "Nels, aim that fan next to you a little more toward me; I'm not getting anything off it. Walt, open that other window."

MacNulty mopped his forehead and neck. He looked at Nels, who had just finished telling the story of yesterday's excursion and Charlie's absence. Then he stared out the window at shimmering poplar leaves and scratched his jaw.

"I think this heat affects people; makes 'em crazy," he said. "Otherwise, she'd never pull a damn fool stunt like that, would she, Walt?"

Walt shrugged. "She might, no tellin. Trouble is, we don't know if she's after Harry for revenge or to get the gold and shut him up."

The sheriff looked back at Nels. "You haven't said anything about all this to the folks out at Sawtooth Lodge, have you?"

Nels shook his head. "No way. They don't know he's a

murder suspect and I sure as hell am not gonna be the one to tell 'em."

MacNulty made a thoughtful grunt. "Well, I figure it this way. You boys are hot to jump on a plane and go down to Mobile. I'm sure as hell not gonna stop you. But since we're dealing with a murder and a bunch of missing gold, I'm sending Walt here with you."

"Connie, you out there?" MacNulty yelled through the open door. "Come in here." The short, waistless dispatcher appeared in the doorway.

"Connie, call Seaway Travel and see if they can line up three airplane seats from Duluth to Mobile, Alabama. Noon or later. Fastest way possible."

"Yes sir. They'll want to know who's going."

"Walt, here, Nels Dahlstrom and Graham Jackson."

She disappeared as MacNulty turned to his chief deputy. "Walt, do a fast bulletin on Charlie. You'll need to give it to the sheriff and police chief down there. We sure as hell don't want Charlie catchin' up with Harry Potter before we do."

He stopped. "You know, this is a hell of a mess. We don't even know if the guy we're all lookin' for is really Harry.

"Walt, you can identify Harry, but he can also identify you. Hang back, let Nels go in; see what happens. And remember, you got no authority down there; you're John Q. Public. So for God's sake, don't go blundering into anything and whatever happens, don't get shot again. If that happens, I'll lose all respect for you, understand?"

"Yes sir," Walt answered with a grin. "I better go home and throw a few things in a bag."

"Go ahead. I need to talk with our two jolly sailors for a couple minutes."

He waved Walt out of the office and turned to Nels. "This is Uncle Ray giving you a bit of advice, okay?"

Nels nodded.

"You got hold of yourself too tight, Nels. Ease back, think

things out before you jump. And for God's sake, get hold of that temper of yours. You're not gonna get where you're going if you fly off the handle every time somebody ruffles your feathers."

Nels reddened and nodded silently.

"I knew your dad pretty well. Had a lot about him to admire. He moved quick, like a damn panther. Sometimes too quick for me to follow. But you know, if somebody asked him later why he did it, he always had a logical answer. Never took him long to think things through, but he always did before he made his move. You might want to work on doing the same thing. No offense meant, just friendly advice."

Nels sipped cold coffee, then shook his head. "No offense taken. I'll see what I can do about it."

"You two fellows packed and ready?" MacNulty asked. They nodded and he continued. "Boy, I'm glad it's you and not me goin' down there. I wilt just thinking about that heat. I remember getting off a plane once, maybe it was in Mississippi, and feeling like I had walked into a sauna. I was soaking wet in about two minutes flat."

Connie Roper stepped into the doorway and waited.

"Yeah, what did you find out?" MacNulty asked.

"Got 'em a flight out at 12:47," Connie said, reading from a yellow legal pad. "Doesn't get into Mobile 'til 6:45, though. Long layover in Minneapolis."

Nels shrugged. "At least we get in in time to look around tonight. Ah, how about a rental car? Four-door sedan? If you could reserve it, we'd be off and running when we get there."

"Good idea, Nels," MacNulty said, smiling. "Glad somebody thought of it."

"Everything charged to the department?" Connie asked.

"Yeah, do it that way," MacNulty answered. "We can sort it all out later. Have 'em hold the tickets at the airline desk. They'll pick 'em up."

"Who's driving?" MacNulty asked.

"I was planning to," Nels said.

"Okay, why don't you pick up Walt at his place and head out?"

"Great," Nels agreed. "You ready, Graham?"

"Ready as I'll ever be," he answered.

"Okay, let's head out. I'll see if Connie can leave a message for Tizz; tell her we're on our way south."

The sheriff was right. To the three men accustomed to cool, dry summer weather, exiting the airliner was like walking into a steam bath. They should have been forewarned by the pilot's announcement that it was ninety-six degrees in Mobile. The damp, hot wind waited at the plane door to cover them like syrup, slowing their steps toward the terminal building. There seemed to be no oxygen here.

"I don't care if the car's got an engine," Walt said. "Just as long as the air conditioning works."

"Welcome to the heart of Dixie," Nels said, wiping his forehead as he worked through the crowd of mostly black passengers and their families.

Fortunately, the Taurus that awaited them had not only excellent air conditioning but also plenty of room to stretch out. Nels drove.

"According to the map," he said, "we go east on the freeway to Dauphin Island Parkway, then south to Dog River. Help me look for signs in the dark."

"Shouldn't we find a motel and get settled before we start looking?" Walt suggested.

"Maybe we'll see one down around Dog River," Nels said.

After several miles, an off ramp sign pointed the way to the parkway, which they followed south. There were no motels, only the dimly lit outlines of trees and houses, punctuated by an occasional oasis of light surrounding a convenience store.

They drove along a marshy area, with its pungent smell of

138

warm salt air. A few boats could be seen under flood lights off in the distance.

A poorly lit marina appeared close alongside, with a few sailboat masts outlined against the night. The narrow river was reflected in the lights of a fuel dock on the other side. Then they passed over an old wooden draw bridge, with a nearly illegible sign nailed to the hand rail.

"Damn," Nels exclaimed. "That said Dog River, didn't it? We've got to go back a ways to that marina."

He passed the bridge, found a side road, and turned around. "As long as we're here, let's take a look," he suggested. "Graham and I can wander out there."

Walt remained in the cool comfort of the car as the other two went through an open gate in the fence and picked their way along a dimly lit dock.

Even smells like a swamp," Nels said, batting at a bug that was making a try for his neck.

"Too bad we don't have a torch," Graham said. "Might be hard to recognize the boat."

"Look for double spreaders," Nels suggested.

There were power boats of all sizes and description, from battered shrimpers to sedan cabin yachts. Here and there cabin lights glowed softly in the darkness. Only a few tall masts were scattered among the boats occupying the marina.

As they neared the open river, a flashlight flared ahead. It illuminated rough, graying boards and began moving toward them.

A thick drawl floated across the dank night air. "Can ah hep ya?" It belonged to a slight, weathered man carrying the light.

"We're looking for a boat," Nels responded. "You the dockmaster?"

"Night man," the other said. "Who y'all lookin' for?"

"A 33 foot C&C called *Golden Fleece*," Nels answered. "She came in here a couple days ago."

"She ain't heah na'more," the night man said. "Too much draft. Had the devil's own time gettin' out last night on the tide."

"Where'd she go?" Nels asked hopefully.

"Mmmm. Fella might'a been fixin' to go over ta Fly Creek."

Nels looked puzzled. "Fly Creek?" he repeated.

"Across the way, over in Fairhope. Got good water over there."

"Oh yeah, sure. Fly Creek. We'll run over and find her there, eh Graham? Much obliged."

"Anytime," the night man said, turning away.

Commander Ross Trawick sat at the crowded bar talking with a young couple standing behind him. Laughter and noise resounded through the old building as it always did on a Friday night before a big race. Usually a sedate place, the oak and magnolia-shaded yacht club was alive with boisterous racers and their sleek boats which lay rafted together in clusters at the end of several tee-docks.

Nels and Graham had scoured the bottle-shaped harbor before locating the unoccupied *Golden Fleece* among the race boats. Now they wedged into the crowd at the bar to order a drink and locate the mysterious commander. Walt waited outside in the warm, heavy air, watching for Trawick among the dozens of racers who were coming and going along the docks and darkened lawns.

Inside, now wearing shorts and sailing T-shirts, Nels and Graham blended easily with the bar crowd. Each had been in places like this with people like this dozens of times.

"Too bad we're not here to race," Nels said to his friend. "Gets the old juices flowing, eh?"

"Just so," Graham agreed. "Quickens the blood."

They ordered three vodka and tonics, glancing at the tanned faces around the bar. They did not recognize Trawick, sitting across the bar, partly because his face was turned away in conversation. Equipped with photos of Harry Potter, they had only a description of the much-traveled commander.

"Let's step outside and check with Walt," Nels said.

Graham nodded and followed.

Outside with Walt, they discussed the problem of identifying a midsize, middle-aged man with sandy hair. There were obviously a dozen or more who could fit the description.

"I suppose we could just work our way through anybody that resembles the man," Nels suggested. "Eventually, we'll probably come up with him."

"I'll know Harry by voice, if nothing else," Walt said. "But what if he overhears us questioning people? He might just be off and running again."

They puzzled over the problem until Graham provided the obvious answer. "I say we wait at the boat. He may not be staying aboard, but surely he'll be out to lock up. Three sailors standing on the dock won't raise his suspicions. Not with this lot crawling about the boats. Nels, you and I can engage him in polite conversation and Walt can stay back out of the light to hear his voice."

"You hit the nail on the head," Walt said. "Let's do it."

Golden Fleece was tied alongside the dock end, her cockpit awash with light but her bow in virtual darkness. Three other boats, all apparently racers, were tied side by side outboard of her in the oily, black water. A steady stream of sailors were clamoring across the decks like a huge ant colony at work.

They stood near the bow of *Golden Fleece,* lounging against pilings with drinks in hand like three sailors in casual conversation. After what seemed like a long time, but was only a half hour, one of the sailors broke formation and stepped into

141

Golden Fleece's cockpit. Backlit by the light, his face and features were indistinct.

Nels moved forward. "Racing her tomorrow?" he asked.

"No, 'fraid not," the man replied, coiling the loose main sheet.

"Too bad," Nels said. "I crewed on one just like her this spring. Did real well for her rating."

"Oh really?" asked the man, now sparked with interest. "I haven't raced her much; just passing through."

"Too bad. She'd hold her own in this fleet," Nels added. "Which way you headed?"

"I thought I'd go east, over into Florida," the man replied.

Another figure walked forward into half light.

"Long way from home, eh Harry?"

"Beg pardon?" the man answered, frowning.

"I said it's a long way from Northport, Harry," Walt said.

" 'Fraid you're mixed up, friend. The name's Ross Trawick."

"Sure, Harry, and mine's Santa Claus," Walt grinned, coming closer. "Your disguise is great. I really wouldn't have known you. But your voice," he shook his head. "Dead giveaway."

The man stood frozen in the cockpit, staring at the familiar face of Walt Downing.

"This fellow you've been talking with is Nels Dahlstrom," Walt continued. "You knew his dad, Bob Dahlstrom. This other man is Graham Jackson."

"Why don't we just sit down in your boat and have a little talk," Walt said, stepping over the life lines. "Come on guys," he said, motioning to Nels and Graham.

The man retreated defensively to a corner of the cockpit and was joined by his discoverers.

"Harry," Walt said, staring at the man whose face was now lit by the dock lights. "You should'a fixed yourself up like that a long time ago. Makes you look ten, twelve years younger."

142

"This is not what you think," the man said cryptically.

"No, I'm sure it isn't," Walt agreed, "and you'll have plenty of time to tell your side of it, Harry. These fellows with me have been tracking you and now that they've found you, their job is over. But I'm here because you're a murder suspect and we want you back in Northport for questioning."

The man's eyes opened wide. His mouth fell open. "Murder? I don't know what you're talking about. I'm no murderer."

"Well, now," Walt replied, "your buddy and partner, Carl Hoffman, is dead and his girlfriend Charlie says you're the one, Harry."

"I'm no murderer," Harry rasped. He licked his lips. "They're the ones," he hesitated, "after me. I didn't kill Carl Hoffman, you got it all wrong. I didn't even know he was dead."

The words came faster now as Walt, Nels, and Graham listened in silence.

"They threatened me. I ran, hid. Had to get away to save myself. They're killers, both him and her. Kill me without thinking about it; never should have got mixed up with 'em." He shuddered suddenly. "You don't know how it's been, knowing they're after me, trying to stay alive. Hell, I didn't know what to do.

"Me? Kill Carl Hoffman? That's crazy. I could never do that."

"Well, Harry," Walt said, shaking his head. "You got a lot of explaining to do; we got the whole story from Charlie. About the gold, the three of you workin' all night, the whole nine yards. So now you get to go back and tell your side."

Potter rolled his eyes beseechingly, then closed them and shook his head. "I've been running for my life, Walt, trying to stay alive. Those people will stop at nothing. Now you say *I'm* guilty of a murder I know nothing about? Craziest thing I ever heard of, absolutely nuts."

"All you got to do is come back and convince us," Walt said quietly.

"You're darn right I'll come back," Potter said. "All you got to do is protect me from that crazy woman, Charlie."

" 'Fraid we don't have a handle on her right now, Harry, but we think she's down here lookin' for you," Walt said.

"Right now?" Potter wailed. "I told you she'd try to kill me, shut me up. You probably led her right *to* me."

"According to her story, she's out for revenge," Walt said. "Seems as though she's pretty serious about getting your hide."

Potter hunched down and made himself smaller. "If Hoffman's dead, then she did it. She wants me dead, all right, so I can't talk. How could you believe her? If she killed her boyfriend, you can bet she's not hung up on telling the truth. God, I'd hate to think what lies she's got you believing. You fellows have got to protect me until I can get back and set the record straight."

"You'll come back of your own free will?" Walt asked.

"Oh yes," Potter answered emphatically. "Just as soon as we can go."

"I'm curious," Nels interjected, "about what happened to the gold. Charlie claims you must have got it all."

"Ha, ha," Potter said without mirth. "Oh that's wonderful, very funny. Once we started finding it, and it wasn't easy, they got greedy. We agreed to split the take, but suddenly it was a raw deal, or so they claimed. I was very lucky to get anything, let alone my share."

"Let me guess," Nels added. "You've got it hidden in the bilge."

"That's a good guess. How did you come to that conclusion?"

"We saw the lead you'd removed from the bilge when we went through your workshop."

Potter stared at Nels. "How would it have gotten there? I took it out to the mine, left it there. It wasn't anywhere near the workshop."

"It was there the night we were out there looking around. Two pieces of it."

"That just doesn't make sense," Potter replied. "Unless they planted it back there to point the finger of guilt at me." He shook his head. "As I say, it's a miracle I'm still alive."

"Before we go," Walt said, "I'd like to see it."

"Sure, but it's not much to see. Best piece was a nugget that sort of vanished. At least I never saw it again."

"How big was this nugget?" Nels asked.

"If I remember correctly, about ten ounces."

"Hmmm. Same size as Charlie's," Walt mused. "That's interesting."

"Actually, that's the only nugget, or solid piece, that we found. Most was mixed in with sand. Sort of like a high grade ore that needs further refining. Come on down below, I'll show you."

They descended the narrow companionway steps and crowded into the small main cabin, where Harry pulled up a dark-stained, teak floorboard. In the hollow recess was a small white cloth bag.

"Heavier than it looks," Potter said as he hefted it.

"How much you got there, Harry?" Walt asked.

"Oh, maybe twenty pounds. Here, you lift it yourself."

"And that's twenty pounds of gold?" Nels asked.

"No, that's a combination of dust, grains, and little pieces. Still got to be melted to get out the impurities. Probably ten to eleven pounds of real pure gold."

"And that's the lot?" Graham asked.

"Well, yes, that's it. Nothing to sneeze at, though. Ten pounds. Let's see, we're talking 160 ounces or about seventy thousand dollars at today's prices. Pretty amazing, really, to find that much in one place. Do you realize there's never been more than a trace find on the North Shore before this?"

"You know, of course, that the gold belongs to Uncle Sam?" Walt asked.

Harry blushed, then nodded. "I know the mineral laws, and I broke them. That's what started this whole mess. Thank God it's over."

"It's not exactly over, Harry," Walt said.

"No, of course not. But just being able to present you with this bag of dust is a big weight off my shoulders, believe me. I realize I'll still have to answer to the Forest Service for removing it in the first place, not to mention trying to explain all this to Agnes. Don't know if she'll have me back. God, what a mess I've made of everything." Potter paused, hanging his head from hunched shoulders. "At least I'm alive. I never would have survived those people if I'd stayed put."

Walt watched Harry Potter as he talked. So far, he thought, Harry's details were pretty much at odds with those described by Charlie. But they were plausible. Maybe more so than hers. He itched to dig for the truth, ask more questions, but checked himself. Let Potter talk himself into thinking he was home free. For now. Just get the man back to Northport willingly and in one piece.

"Graham," he said, "I want you to go ahead of us and give the place a good look before we leave.

"Harry, you get what you need to take along home so we can get going. Can you leave the boat here?"

"No problem for now," Potter replied. "It's not in anybody's way. I can call from Northport in a day or two and work out the details."

Nels watched the man rummage around for clothes to fill his sea bag and knew he was telling at least part of the truth: here was someone who had shed a heavy weight. The wariness was gone, replaced by cheerfulness and easy talk. That much was true, he thought, but what about the rest?

It was after midnight now, and Walt knew the airport would be deserted. He'd find them a motel and they could fly out in the morning. He went up into the cockpit, noticing that things had quieted down around Fairhope Yacht Club and the Fly Creek harbor.

Nels handed up the heavy little white bag and came up the stairs, followed by Harry Potter, who switched off the batteries and locked the boat.

They waited for Graham, then went down the dock to the parking lot.

There was no sign of Charlie Mittner.

R ay MacNulty sat at his desk, halfheartedly shuffling a stack of documents and forms requiring his attention. Finally, at 10:00 A.M., he set the stack aside, got a fresh cup of coffee, and devoted his thoughts to the phone call that had awakened him eight and one-half hours earlier.

So Harry Potter was really alive and was coming back voluntarily to tell his side of the story. According to Walt, it was different from Charlie's in most respects. Any time this afternoon Harry would be sitting in front of him, telling the whole thing.

MacNulty slurped from his cup and swiveled to stare out at the shimmering poplar leaves that obscured his view. The breeze had come up off the lake this morning, cooling Northport by twenty degrees and dispersing his fatigue. The half hour long phone call had been followed by a hot, sleepless night listening to the clatter and hum of the bedroom fan.

But today, revived by cool weather and buoyed by the anticipation of Harry Potter's return, MacNulty felt wonderful. He had already called the Hoffman and Sims Logging office to verify Charlie's current absence from work. Then he had made the difficult call to Sawtooth Lodge and talked to Fred Marquardt, who had babbled almost incoherently about the miracle that was somehow responsible for Harry's impending return.

MacNulty had not provided any details, explaining only that Harry was alive, apparently in good health and spirits, and was coming back with Nels and Graham no later than tomorrow noon. He promised to call Marquardt with more details as soon as they were available. How Marquardt would want to handle things with Agnes Potter was not MacNulty's problem, a fact he thanked God for.

If their plane arrived in Duluth on schedule at noon, Harry Potter would be sitting in front of his desk no later than midafternoon. All of this still seemed so improbable that MacNulty had not yet framed his approach.

Harry was nobody's fool. MacNulty had watched as Sawtooth Lodge was transformed in ten years from a ma and pa log cabin operation into a resort destination of regional importance. Harry had paid his dues in the community, was a popular leader, and had never been touched by scandal or questionable dealings. And now this strange turn of events had cast an entirely new light on the man. That he had staged a disappearance was fact. His involvement in an illegal gold mining scheme was also fact. What MacNulty could not know, but must somehow determine, was whether or not Harry Potter was responsible for the murder of Carl Hoffman.

Harry's a talker, thought MacNulty, visually lining up his window sill with the horizon. I think we'll let him talk, maybe he'll talk himself into a convenient corner.

But it's not likely, he thought, not likely at all. He's not stupid. He'll take us down the road he chooses.

Restless, MacNulty pulled himself out of his chair and stood momentarily at the desk, trying to think of anything that absolutely had to be done today. Then he strode into the outer office.

"Connie, I'm gone 'til two, two-thirty. Anybody calls, tell 'em I'm out catching bad guys, okay?"

She smiled and waved. MacNulty returned the wave and went out. A drive along the lonely forestry roads always helped him relax and clear his head. He wanted to be ready for Harry Potter.

Walt was right, MacNulty thought as he first saw Harry Potter in the outer office. Looks different, but a lot younger. Hell, he could probably walk in here and I'd never know him unless he said something.

Walt came into MacNulty's office. "Fastest damn trip I ever made," he said in greeting. "Do you realize we were gone from this office only twenty-nine hours?"

"Hello to you, too," MacNulty answered, smiling. "Think how happy your wife'll be."

Walt nodded. "I imagine you want to get started. Any angles?"

"Nope. We'll just play it straight, ask a lot of questions, be skeptical. Better send Nels and Graham along home."

"They'll be disappointed," Walt replied.

"That's their problem. If we need technical advice about sailboats, we can get it later. I don't like talking in a crowd."

"You're the boss. I'll bring him in."

Walt went out to the large office and spoke to Potter, motioning him to go into MacNulty's office.

Harry walked into the doorway and stopped, stroking a nonexistent beard. MacNulty was standing behind his desk, knuckles touching the glass top, staring at him.

"It's me, Ray, honest to God, come back from the dead."

"Walt said you looked a lot younger and you do. Hell of a disguise, Harry."

"No disguise. Just shaved off the gray whiskers and put a little color in the hair. Otherwise, it's the same old me."

"Well, sit down then. Want some coffee?"

"No thanks. Been drinking the stuff all morning. Feel like I'm about to float away."

"C'mon in, Walt, and close the door," MacNulty said. "Harry, I'm gonna record our conversation so I can listen to it

149

after if I forget some details." He pressed the switch and placed the small tape machine toward the front of the desk.

"Just one thing, Ray," Potter said, raising his hand for emphasis. "I'm here as a completely voluntary witness. I agree to tell you everything I know, as openly and honestly as I can. If you agree to play by those ground rules, fine. Otherwise, I'll have to call Freddie Eckols to come up here and represent me."

MacNulty scratched his chin and stared at the recorder. "Harry, the reason you're here is for questioning. I want you to tell your story any way you want, but then I expect we'll have some questions. Probably quite a few of 'em. And if you're here as a volunteer, like you say, well then I expect you to try to answer 'em so as to help us get to the bottom of all this."

"No pressure tactics?" Potter asked.

"I don't operate that way, Harry. You know me better than that. You try to help us and we'll get along fine."

"Okay, I guess that's fair enough," Potter said. "You want me to just start in?"

"However you want to do it," MacNulty agreed, "and don't forget the details. We like to know about the little stuff, too."

"Well, okay, I guess it goes back to when Carl Hoffman found that big gold nugget up on that land he was getting ready to cut. He brought it to me to see if it was really a gold nugget. I told him it was the genuine article, almost completely pure. I also told him how rare it was to find such a nugget, even in traditional gold mining country.

"He was pretty excited about the find, but didn't really believe what I told him about the rarity of the nugget. I think he expected to find others, just by pushing dirt around."

Potter stopped, thought of something and chuckled to himself. "People get pretty rabid about gold, especially when they find some. Carl was like that. I think he spent several days searching the site for more. He came back to see me at the lodge one evening looking positively haggard. Wanted me to look at a few other little pieces he'd found.

"He had several very small pieces in a little box, probably not a half ounce all told. He was very discouraged. Actually, that was when I first took an interest. Finding one nugget; that's a fluke. Finding ten or fifteen flakes and pieces, no matter how small, in less than an acre, is a different story.

"At that point, I didn't know where he was finding it and I didn't want to know. As you realize, Ray, summer is our busy season at the lodge; 80 to 85 percent occupancy right through the week. I was not exactly loafing around at that time.

"He asked me to help. Said he knew there was more gold up there. Offered me half to come up there and show him how to find it. I told him I'd be glad to show him how to set up a sluice and screen operation on paper that could work well with a bulldozer.

"Then I made my first mistake. Carl didn't seem to grasp the diagrams I was giving him. Said he'd try to put it all together, but begged me to come up in a couple days, say on that Saturday, and take a look. I guess by then I felt sorry for the guy, so I said sure, I'd come up and have a quick look Saturday afternoon to see if he'd assembled the system properly.

"So he showed me on a big map exactly where it was, up near Quill Mountain, off the road where they were logging. And I drove up and walked over to where they were trying to mine the gold."

Potter stopped, shook his head, and stared out the window. "That's when I met the green-eyed monster. Carl was on the cat and she was in the water with a shovel, pushing dirt around.

"I could see immediately that they had the whole setup backwards and I started explaining it to Carl. Next thing I know, she's calling me names, suggesting that I somehow caused it to be wrong so I could come back later and get all the gold.

"Carl tried to calm her down, but she was really out of control, like a rabid dog. I'm sure she'd been drinking. Meanwhile, Carl's yelling at her and begging me to help, wanting to give me half. The scene was a chaos and that's when I made mistake number two."

Potter looked straight at MacNulty and spoke: "You know how it is when you walk into a situation that's all screwed up and people are bickering and blaming each other? Your first reaction is to stop the confusion and take charge. It happens at the lodge, and I bet it happens to you, too, Ray.

"So I took charge. I told her to shut up and pay attention if she wanted any gold. And I told Carl I'd fix his mess and ramrod the effort until dark for half of what we found.

"She started in on me again and I told her, 'Lady, just shut up and do what I tell you.' Then I turned to Carl and said, 'Carl, this is a take it or leave it offer; no more fooling around.'

"Carl finally got her calmed down enough to start working, and we rebuilt the sluice and screen in an hour or so. Then we started moving dirt and water through it.

"After a couple hours, about six o'clock, I stopped and took a look in the sluice box. It was amazing how much we had found.

"We kept on until almost dark. Our best yield was from the dirt near the creek. It fell off as we moved further away. At the end, we were getting virtually nothing.

"At that point, we had about forty pounds of the dust and dirt that's in the white bag I gave you. Doesn't really look all that much like gold, but about half of it is, weightwise.

"I told them right then and there that my involvement in the project was over, that I'd take my half and go home. I told them I thought we'd done well, really well, but that the best was over. Of course, they were completely free to keep looking as long as they wanted.

"By then, they'd both been sucking on a bottle of Canadian for awhile and she started getting mean again. Told me I'd cheated them and she wouldn't stand for it. Carl didn't say much, just stood there with a glassy-eyed look, holding his twenty-pound bag next to him like a baby.

"So I went home with my ill-gotten bag and said goodbye

to the little gold mine. I was really euphoric just thinking of all the nice things I could get for us with seventy thousand dollars. I figured the woman would calm down and be happy with what she had.

"At that point, however, I took the precaution of hiding the bag. Before going home, I went to the boat and pulled two chunks of lead out and replaced them with the bag. Figured nobody would look there.

"After that, things just went downhill. Monday night, somebody broke into my workshop cabin and trashed it. The next night, both of them followed me over to the courthouse where I was going to a planning meeting and stopped me in the parking lot. She was just her usual mouthy, nasty old self but she had somehow gotten to Carl. He was hard-eyed and cold. Told me I'd taken advantage. Said they'd wait for me at the lodge.

"I was scared, but I was also stubborn about keeping my share of the gold. A deal's a deal. Without my help, they would have gotten nothing. So instead of going home after the meeting, I went down to the boat to sleep."

He stopped, wrapped his arms around his body, then continued. "That was the worst night of my life. They found me on the boat. Carl pulled out a knife and told me he was afraid he'd have to kill me. Said it wouldn't be the first time; I believed him. Here I was with their gold within an arm's length and I couldn't tell him. Somehow, I figured he'd kill me quicker if I gave him the gold than if I didn't. Then she started hitting me in the stomach and ribs. I couldn't get a breath, threw up. She kept at it 'til I thought I'd die. She was enjoying it, laughing her head off.

"Next day, I could hardly move. Told people it was the flu. Truthfully, it was worse than the flu. That night, they hung around the bar at the lodge, waiting. Then they left a note. 'We'll let you sweat 'til Saturday, then it's over for you. Tell the cops and it's over for your wife and kid, too.'

"Thursday morning, I suggested to Aggie that we go over

to Isle Royale for a little minivacation. I planned to take her over there where I could tell her what was happening and buy a little breathing room. Figured on leaving Northport early Saturday, before the two crazies showed up.

"But I kept thinking about it, and getting more nervous, so I said I'd go a day early and meet her there. I really did plan to meet her, but the fear kept gnawing at me, it really did. I expected them to kill me, I knew they'd do it, and the fear just made me run.

"I guess that's about it. You know the rest, or most of it at least."

MacNulty sat forward, elbows on the desk, and lit another cigarette. "Damn, that's quite a story, Harry; pretty convincing stuff. You got anybody who saw Carl and Charlie hanging around the lodge or talking to you in the parking lot of the courthouse?"

"Well, there's the bartenders at the lodge. They see a lot of people, but they might remember them, especially her. Then there's Ab Junker, the county commissioner. I remember going into the meeting with him. When he came along, I just sort of pulled away from them and walked with him."

"We'll check it out with those people, right Walt?" Mac-Nulty replied.

Walt nodded. "I've been wondering about a couple things, Harry, like how you just happened to have the hair coloring stuff and the boat paint with you when you left here. Sounds like you had your vanishing act pretty well planned."

"The day before I left, in the afternoon, I was nervous. Hurting, too. I had to stop by the five and dime for a couple of things and I don't know, spur of the moment I guess, I picked up the hair stuff. As for lacquer and solvent, I had plenty around the resort, so I just took a couple cans along."

MacNulty tapped a ballpoint pen on his desk. "How is it you never came to see me about all this, Harry?"

Potter shook his head and stared at his hands. "I don't

know, stupid, I guess. Didn't want to admit I'd broken the law, afraid for my family." He shrugged. "I just don't know."

"What about the dynamite?" MacNulty asked quickly. "You didn't mention blasting the rock."

"Dynamite?" Potter asked. "I don't know what you're driving at. I don't know anything about dynamite."

"But you know how to use it," MacNulty said.

"Well, I used to know. We used it in seismic testing years ago. But I don't understand what dynamite has to do with anything."

MacNulty changed the subject. "Lining up somebody to pull the boat out of the lake and somebody else to haul it must have taken some preplanning. You do that before you left?"

"Well, not exactly. I made some credit card calls from the boat, talked to people who made suggestions, that sort of thing."

"Sounds a little vague, Harry," MacNulty said skeptically. "We'll need some records on that, names, dates, numbers. Okay?"

Potter nodded in agreement.

Walt cleared his throat. "When we first talked to you last night, you said the two pieces of lead from your boat were up at the mine site. You mind telling us how they got up there? You said you were only there one time."

"The lead? Mine site? No, I didn't mean I took them there," Potter hesitated.

Walt watched him. "Think fast, Harry, you're getting things muddled up."

"What happened was that I removed them from the boat," Potter explained, "and put them on the dock. Next day, they were gone. I figured Carl and the woman probably took them, for whatever reason."

"Harry, you sound tired," MacNulty said, pushing himself up from his chair. "Let's get coffee and take a break for a few minutes."

155

For MacNulty and Walt, the break bought time to think of questions that needed asking, contradictions that needed clarifying. The two lawmen talked in low voices as they poured coffee and returned.

"So, let's get on with it so you can go home and face your next problem," MacNulty suggested, pulling his chair toward him and sitting. He waited until the others were seated, then launched into the questioning.

"They tell me your boat is now called the *Golden Fleece.* Why the name?"

"Sort of a joke on myself, I guess," Potter shrugged. "Running away over a little bag of gold."

"Dumb joke," Walt observed. "We picked your boat to follow because of its name."

"Guess I secretly wanted you to find me."

"Sure your boat name wasn't a sort of statement?" MacNulty asked. "As in 'I fleeced all you guys and got away with it?' "

"No, absolutely not."

Walt changed tacks. "You're a pretty good sailor, right Harry?" Potter shrugged.

"I get along."

"Don't be modest, Harry. You've got a lot of experience, the way I hear it. So with all your expertise, you handled that boat like a rookie, ever since you got it in the spring."

"To make the disappearance more believable, I guess." Harry joked nervously.

"You just said the idea of vanishing came to you only after you got the gold, yet you ran your boat that way since spring. When did you say you started planning to disappear?"

"After I got the gold."

"What were you trying to achieve when you were running it like a beginner before that?"

"I hadn't handled a boat that size for a long time. It takes awhile. Then, too, I never had anybody helping me who knew anything about sailing. We fouled up sometimes, simple as that."

MacNulty couldn't tell whether Harry was becoming more nervous or a bit angry at the questions, but there was a change in his composure, for whatever reason.

"Young Lindner down at the fuel dock said you were a menace, Harry. Did you know that?"

Potter shrugged, said nothing.

"You've got the equipment in your workshop to remove the impurities and turn it into a solid bar of gold, right?" Walt asked. Potter nodded.

"So why didn't you do it?"

"The gold was never there. I put it in the boat. It's easy to think of things I could've done differently now, sitting here talking, but it wasn't at the time, okay?"

"Keep your cool, Harry," MacNulty said with a small grin. "We're just pickin' up some of the little details we might have missed first time through. Got to have those details."

Potter nodded uncertainly and MacNulty continued.

"So where were you planning to go when the fellows caught up with you, Harry?"

"No place. I was thinking about calling Aggie and coming home."

"But you hadn't done that yet."

"No."

"Gosh, Harry," Walt interjected, "didn't I hear you say you were headed for Florida?"

"I was just making conversation. I didn't mean anything by it."

MacNulty reacted. "Uh-huh, and are you just making conversation with us, too?"

"I'm trying to tell you the truth."

MacNulty nodded. "Well, I sure hope so Harry, because

this is a very serious situation. I've got a man dead and you're one of the two people who had probable cause to kill him. So don't think we're just making conversation here.

"Tell you what, Harry. Let's stop here and pick up again tomorrow afternoon. That'll give us time to check with Junker and your bartenders. That'll also give you time to pull together your phone records for the past three, four months and bring 'em along. I also want to know how and to whom any calls were made from the boat.

"I'll give you a lift home so you can have a reunion tonight with your family.

"Walt, you copy this tape and take it over to Nels. Tell him to study it and be here at 9 A.M. tomorrow with the Englishman. I want to talk some things over with them.

"You ready to go, Harry? Don't want to delay your big homecoming."

"**G**ot a call for you, Ray," the dispatcher said, holding a slip of paper in the air. "You just missed it."

MacNulty looked at the wall clock in the bullpen—7:38 A.M. Who in hell would be calling at this hour, he wondered. "Sound like an emergency?" he asked, taking the note.

"To tell the truth, I could hardly understand the man," she answered. "Sounded like he had a mouthful of oatmeal."

MacNulty studied the note as he walked slowly toward his office. He recognized the area code—it was an Alabama number. He stood at the desk and direct dialed long distance.

"Baldwin County Sheriff's office," came the reply.

"Let me talk to Mr. Mattson."

"Undersheriff Madison? Just a moment, please."

MacNulty sat down heavily and fumbled a cigarette from his partially-crushed pack.

"Madison here," answered a voice with deep South oozing out of it.

"This is Sheriff MacNulty of Caribou County, Minnesota, returning your call."

"Ah yes, Sheriff, we have us a woman in custody that you're lookin' for. Name's Charlene Mittner. She was brought in early this morning."

"What was she picked up for?" MacNulty asked, exhaling smoke.

"Let's see here. We responded to a breaking and entering on a boat at Fairhope Yacht Club. Security officer made the call, then apparently made the mistake of going down to the boat to apprehend her.

"According to the report, the security man lost his gun and went into the water. Doesn't say exactly how, but when our two deputies arrived on the scene, she was tearin' that boat to pieces and the security man was still swimmin'."

MacNulty, cracking an amused smile, leaned back in his chair and put one big boot on the desk. "Uh-huh," he said.

"Apparently, there was some kind of ruckus. My deputies called in a backup to subdue her and I've got one man with a broken hand and another with some, ah, groin injuries."

"I gather you're holding her on several charges then," MacNulty said.

"Yup, breaking and entering, destruction of private property, assault, resisting arrest, just for starters. When I got in this morning and read the report, I had to go back and have a look."

"Uh-huh," MacNulty replied.

"My boys put some marks on her but they didn't slow her down much. She's got a nasty mouth on her.

"Anyhow," Madison continued, "I see here she's wanted for questioning up there in a murder. Any warrants?"

"No, not yet," MacNulty replied. "We're still putting it together."

"Well, by rights I should take her before the judge on these charges I got, but if you want her, send somebody down and I'll be glad to hand her over."

"Okay, we'll do that. Someone will be there with paperwork by tomorrow morning," MacNulty said. "One question. Was the boat she trashed called the *Golden Fleece?*"

"Let's see here, Sheriff. Yup, that's the boat. I'll tell the sheriff you'll send someone. Just one question."

"Let's hear it," MacNulty said.

"Are all your women like that one?"

"Pretty much so, yup."

"Whoo-ee. I'm sure glad I got me a little Southern gal."

At 9:00 A.M. with Nels, Graham, and Walt seated in front of him sipping coffee, MacNulty called the meeting to order.

"Let me start by telling you boys about a little phone conversation I had with a southern fella this morning." Grinning broadly, he regaled his audience with the tale of Charlie Mittner's latest exploits and her current whereabouts.

". . . so she trashed his boat, which I'm sure will bring more joy to our friend, Harry Potter. Obviously, she was not after his hide, as he claims, but his gold instead.

"Now that could mean she killed old Carl for the gold and is now after Harry's, or maybe she didn't kill Carl and is now looking for both Harry *and* the gold, as she says.

"So which way do you lean, guys? I've got an opinion, but I'd like to hear yours first. Who wants to start?"

"I'll go first," Nels offered. "I think Charlie killed her boyfriend. She went after Harry because she's crazy with greed and because she wanted him silenced before he could talk to us. Her story sounds like a fantasy; his is more logical. You don't just find veins of solid gold lying around, here or anywhere else.

She slickered us once down in Michigan. I wouldn't give her a chance to do it again. As they say, she's wired a little too tight.

"Anyhow, my guess is that she's the one."

MacNulty nodded without comment. "Okay, who's next? Walt?"

"Sure, I'll be next," Walt agreed. "On the one hand, Harry's story has got some holes in it. But I think the reason is clear; he never expected to have to use it to alibi a murder charge. I think his statement that he was too proud to admit to theft and too afraid to hang around and face the two of them rings true. So does the story of his involvement in the gold mine and his description of how much gold they got.

"Charlie, on the other side, has a hair-trigger temper. She could easily have bashed her boyfriend, and I think she did. Seventy thousand dollars is a lot of money to somebody who never had any. And if she killed once for it, no matter what the reason, she'd kill again without fear to get Harry's share, too."

"Interesting logic, Walt," MacNulty said. "Graham, how are you voting?"

Graham smiled and looked at the floor. "Odd man out," he said. "I agree Charlie could easily be a killer; she would think nothing of doing in Harry. But no, I don't believe she killed Carl Hoffman.

"Sure, her story is somewhat fanciful, but I'm not thinking she would make up something like that. I think they discovered more gold than Harry says. For him to hide it there in the bilge is foolish. First place I would look. It's almost like he put it there to be found.

"Then, too, there's his status. Successful man, worth quite a lot, I should say. Would he run off with seventy thousand dollars? I think not. He could go to the bank for that kind of money.

"She claims he took the money. Sounds right. If she had seventy thousand dollars, no questions asked, would she risk everything to double it? No, it would be stupid, and she's not that. She's angry and wants to get even. She also wants the big payoff. Why else would she tear apart a boat?"

Nels shook his head and grinned. "I knew you two had something going. Don't tell me she actually got to you?"

Graham shrugged, embarrassed. MacNulty held up his hand.

"Come on now, Nels. Graham's got a right to his own opinions. Even if he is outnumbered at the moment."

He looked first at Nels, then Walt.

"I'm siding with Graham. Harry's story is too slick, too simple. My old buddy, Mr. Hunch, isn't buying it. Uh-uh.

"Charlie talks about watchin' Harry make gold bars. Not just one or two, but a bunch. What the hell does she know about gold bars unless she's seen 'em being produced, right?

"No way does Charlie have any gold right now. If she did, she'd be layin' back. Nope, she's mad as a hornet 'cause her boyfriend got killed and she's holdin' an empty bag. She knows who did it and she's after him, plain and simple, the only way she knows.

"So," MacNulty paused, glancing at Nels and Walt, "have I convinced any skeptics?"

Nels shook his head. "Me, I'm stubborn. I just don't see Harry killing anybody. Certainly not killing somebody and running away. If for some reason he did kill the logger, hypothetically speaking, he's too smart to call attention to it by running."

MacNulty smiled. "You'd be surprised what people can do when they're in a bind. Some are all bark, no bite. Others never bark at all, they just up and bite. I think Harry's one of those biters."

Walt joined in. "One thing you said earlier made sense; the idea that Charlie wouldn't be talking gold bars unless she'd actually seen 'em."

"We'll know a lot more," MacNulty said, "when we get her in here to tell us the whole story, one more time. Because this time, we'll know all the discrepancies between the two stories and we can poke around a little bit better."

"I had one more thought," Graham said. "There's always been this question in my mind about the boat."

"Let's hear it," MacNulty urged. "Now's the time to kick things around."

"Well," Graham continued, "why would Harry try to take the boat with him when he disappeared? It's so cumbersome, easy to trace.

"Think of the options. Sink the boat, leave debris scattered about as evidence, then get aboard a bus and just vanish.

"Unless. . .unless you're carrying something very heavy. What did Charlie estimate? Three hundred fifty pounds?

"In that case, the boat could serve as a hiding place and carrying device. We never looked. Charlie wouldn't know where to look, but there are many places, and I can think of several, where you could mold or cast that much gold to hide in a boat. It would be very difficult to find."

"Why not rent a car?" Nels asked. "You could use a car to carry the gold, assuming there was that much, which I doubt."

"Ah, just so," Graham retorted, "useful to carry, but not to hide.

"Remember that drug bust in the islands last winter where the Coast Guard eventually found a ton of marijuana in the sailboat, and the crew wasn't aware of it? It was so well stashed behind fake bulkheads that they never even suspected."

Graham turned to MacNulty. "I think the *Golden Fleece* is a floating treasure vault."

"If you're right," MacNulty said, a small smile creeping onto his face, "Harry is not going to be happy when he hears about Charlie and her wrecking tools."

"Wonder if she found anything?" Walt asked, almost to himself.

"Wait a minute," Nels interrupted. "I just thought of something, something very important."

Three sets of eyes focused on the tall, lean sailor. "I suggested that he could have rented a car. Then I thought about how he'd have to show a credit card to make the rental, which would leave a track. And then I realized that somewhere along the way, someone said that Harry identified himself to the Canadians as this phony Commander Ross Trawick. Right?"

"That's the story," MacNulty agreed.

"Okay, here's the important part. He not only told them, he showed them an ID card and documents on the boat which they seemed to recognize as legitimate.

"So, this may shoot down my earlier theory about Charlie being guilty, but will someone tell me how the hell he came to have an authentic ID card with a different identity? You don't just get threatened on a Wednesday, panic on a Thursday, take off running on a Friday, and somehow manage to have identification papers for yourself and your boat."

MacNulty stared at him. "A fake ID. Set up in advance. Must have been."

He stopped, tapping his Bic against the desk in a drum roll. "Both stories we've heard would lead us to believe that whatever occurred was pretty much spontaneous, actions and reactions. But his fake personality couldn't have been set up overnight. There's nobody around Northport who could handle it, right, Walt?"

"As far as I know," Walt concurred.

"He'd have to have a contact to set it up, and a couple days to get the job done. If he didn't leave town the week of his disappearance, it meant he handled it by phone or already had it."

The sheriff paused. "Make a note, Walt, to check out credit cards issued in the name of Commander Trawick, as well as bank accounts."

He grinned. "Maybe I'll just ask him for the phony ID and papers. See what he says. This is all getting better and better."

He looked around. "Anybody got any other ideas? No?

Well, this has certainly gotten real interesting. Yessir, real interesting.

"We're gonna sit on this thing a day or two. Meantime, Walt, you get all the long distance phone records for Sawtooth Lodge for the past three, four months. Give 'em to Nels and Graham. I want to know if Harry ever talked to the logger with the crane or to the boat hauler from Florida.

"I'll call Harry and get the logger's name. I'll also have a talk with his other so-called witnesses. There's something real strange about all this, but I'm damned if I can put my finger on it.

"Walt, you're headin' back down to Baldwin County to pick up Charlie. Make it a one-day trip. Tomorrow. We can have the paperwork done today. And look at the boat. See if she unearthed any secrets.

"I'd like to hear her story again, start to finish. I also want to use each of our two suspects to help us snare the other. Damned if I know how to do it right now, but I know there must be a way."

MacNulty chuckled. "Maybe we just turn 'em loose together and whoever survives gets charged with murder."

He shook his head and doodled on his legal pad. "You know, those TV cops and book cops always find some way to pin down the real killer. Madlock or Madigan or whatever his name is could probably wrap up this whole goddarn mess in a half hour and still have time for a dozen commercials. How come we never get any clues like that? Maybe we got 'em and we're too damn stupid to know it.

"Hmmm," he mused, shading in a triangle on his pad. "Let's just keep at it and see what happens. Not much choice in the matter. Maybe I'll have one more go with Virgil Sims and his loggers, too. Ya never know."

He looked up suddenly. "Sorry to bore you guys, but it sometimes gets me going in circles. Let's get up and at 'em. We got a lot of questions to answer. And so does our friend Harry."

165

Pushing his creaky chair back, MacNulty stood. The others did likewise. "Walt, see that the phone bills get to Nels."

He looked at Nels and Graham. "Fellows, you've been very helpful. I want you to know it. If you could check out the phone business, I'd appreciate it. And say 'hi' to Prentice for me. I want to stop by and see how your mansion is coming along."

They turned to leave. "Walt, stick around a minute."

Walt turned back and sat down, watching MacNulty rub his face in his big hands.

"You okay, Ray?"

"Sure. Just tired, I guess. I get wore down tryin' to think of a way to go on this. You realize we ain't got shit on either one of 'em? Just a bunch of hunches and two stories with holes in 'em."

Walt nodded. "It'll crack, Ray. All we got to do is keep piling up the facts 'til the answers come clear."

MacNulty looked at his desk calendar.

"Shit. Do you realize it's Sunday? We'll never get the paperwork done 'til tomorrow noon on Charlie, and you'll have to wait 'til tomorrow for the phone records. Better fly later tomorrow and come home Tuesday. That'll give you more time to look at that boat while you're down there anyway.

"Tell you what. I'm gonna get home and surprise hell out of Muriel by taking her to church. 'Bout time I show my face up there. Then what say about three, four o'clock, you and me take the canoe up to this secret little lake I know and see if we can catch some of those big brookies that hide in there. Hell, I'll even bring the worms, minnows, and beer."

"I'd like that," Walt grinned. "Why don't we take the Scout in there? Save some walking."

"You mean use the department vehicle for personal pleasure?" asked MacNulty in mock shock.

"Sure, this is official business, right?"

"Right," MacNulty smiled. "Official monkey business."

Northport basked in high summer. A beautiful Sunday folded into a perfect Monday, calm and clear. Half a hundred boats prowled the reefs for trout and salmon. Cars and pickups bearing shiny canoes were loaded with provisions for back country treks. Shops selling northwoods clothing, souvenirs, fishing tackle, and camping gear were getting down to bare shelves as they collected the money needed to survive another long winter. The city campground, recently enlarged to three hundred sites, was turning away sleek Airstreams and ponderous Winnebagos at an alarming rate.

A few miles from town, Ray MacNulty circled the Sawtooth Lodge parking lot for a second time before pulling into a vacant slot marked Handicapped Only. He wondered how anyone with a business like this could get screwed up enough to run away. Made no sense at all, he decided.

Inside, he walked through the noisy lobby to the administrative section and asked to see Harry Potter. He was told Fred Marquardt would see him.

He entered the now-familiar office. Marquardt was standing at the desk, scowling.

"Mornin', Fred. Looks like you got a full house."

"No thanks to you, Sheriff. Cops hanging around in uniform make our guests want to go somewhere else. So what can I do for you?"

"I'd like to talk with Harry if he's around, Fred," MacNulty replied, ignoring the insult.

"He's in no shape to talk to anybody, least of all you. You ought to be ashamed of yourself, treating him like some kind of common criminal."

MacNulty's eyebrows shot up. "You heard his story, then?"

"Oh yes, you can save your breath, 'cause I heard all about

it. Doc Johnson came out yesterday to look at him and said it's a wonder he hasn't had a nervous breakdown. Told him to get bed rest.

"I called Freddie Eckols myself after I heard what happened. He said you had no right to detain Harry like that. Said if you want anything else, you got to see him about it. Said that just because Harry's natural goodness made him go out of his way to help you, you got no right to grill him like that. Just between you and me, Sheriff, I wouldn't be surprised to see Freddie file a lawsuit against you for the way you handled things."

"He said that?" MacNulty asked, his mood sliding from amazement toward anger.

"He did. And I'm pretty busy this morning, so if there's nothing more. . . ."

"Nope, that's about it," MacNulty said, rubbing his jaw. "Amazing how Harry can walk back in and wrap you right around his finger like always. This time, I think you'll end up kicking yourself for bein' so stupid.

"And just for your information, Fred, your lily-white son-in-law's gonna stand trial in federal court for illegally removing gold from forest service land, not to mention that he's the number one suspect in a first degree murder case. So I'll talk to him anytime I fuckin' well please, even if I've got to charge him with murder to do it, understand?"

Marquardt reddened and pointed a shaking finger. "The door is right there, Sheriff. Use it."

MacNulty stalked angrily through the lobby and out to his car. Bullseye. Another nice day shot in the ass, he thought. My reward for one day of fishing.

Frustrated, he turned in at the Dahlstrom construction site to have a look at the progress. He could hear what sounded like a lot of hammering as he eased himself out of the car.

Walking down the well-traveled path through the spruce, he soon understood; Axel and his crew were nailing on the siding. Prentice appeared in the doorway as he approached. She waved.

"Pick up a hammer and get some exercise," she joked.

"No thanks. The way my day's going, I'd only hurt myself."

"Starting to look like a house, don't you think?"

"Yup. You gonna leave that cedar sort of natural looking?"

"Axel has a finish that brings out the honey gold a little bit. A secret formula, I think."

"So where's Nels? Still banned from the site?"

She laughed. "When I left, he was embroiled in a long discussion about the mast section. Something about the dimensions."

MacNulty shielded his eyes from the sun as he looked up at Axel giving commands to a helper. "Lookin' good, Axel."

"Oh, you bet. This cedar we got, she's good stuff. Nice an' clear."

MacNulty watched as another wide board was overlapped and nailed in place. "Gonna be a real showplace when you get her done," he told Prentice.

"You mean 'if we get her done,' don't you?"

"Looks like it's goin' fast to me."

"You wouldn't say that if you were here every day," she said. "We're still not finished with the plumbing or the electrical inside."

"You'll be in by October," MacNulty said.

"I may not last that long," she laughed. "Want a cup of coffee? I've got a thermos."

"No, but thanks. I gotta go catch some bad guys." He turned to leave.

"Nels told me about the latest exploits of your friend Charlie," she said. "She sounds like a handful."

"Baddest of the bad," he said, waving goodbye. He walked back along the sun-dappled path to the cruiser with a spring in his step.

169

Charlie Mittner wore the purple bruise beneath her left eye and the split lower lip like badges. She strode into Mac-Nulty's office, right up to his desk, and glared down at the seated sheriff. "Here I am. So what do ya want?"

MacNulty leaned back and looked up at her, trying to act casual. "Looks like you had a little trouble. Sit down and tell me all about it."

"Big deal," she replied with contempt. "You sure as hell didn't send your pet moron after me just to hear about how I got into a fight."

She was arrogant; MacNulty hadn't expected that. He hesitated, then pulled himself up out of his chair until he could look down at her. "Sit down, Charlene, and take a load off," he commanded evenly.

MacNulty had expected her to be subdued, maybe sullen, but certainly not aggressive, not haughty. He was relieved when she finally complied, sprawling carelessly in an easy chair. "You could start by thanking me for getting you out of the southern jail system," he suggested.

"You're all heart," she shot back.

"I have my days," he said, glancing to the doorway as Walt appeared and shrugged, as if to say 'what could I do?'

MacNulty looked back at Charlie. "I had a little talk with your boss while you were gone." He stopped, got no reaction and continued.

"Says he's had it with your games. Says he's gonna fire you on sight. Told me he cleaned your stuff out of the trailer and wants both you and your stuff out of there."

"Virgil's a stupid asshole," she said. "Wouldn't know shit if it hit him in the face."

MacNulty shook his head, smiling like a contented cat. "I don't know about that. Surprising what he suddenly remembered about you and Carl."

170

Her green eyes flared, and he could see a nasty-looking bloodshot section in her left cornea.

"What's that supposed to mean?"

"Only that you're getting close to having more trouble than you can handle."

"Bullshit," she snapped at the smiling sheriff. She was edgy now; he could see it and hear it.

"Virgil tells me that you and Carl weren't exactly on the best of terms toward the end. Some yelling and some pushing and shoving. Even some threats." He held up his hand to cut off her response.

"Don't bother denying it, Charlene. You're not one of the boys up there anymore, and most any of the fellows will be glad to testify that Virgil's telling the truth. Sorta puts you out on a limb, sorry to say."

She locked eyes with him, her face reddening.

"I already told you what happened. You got it all on your little tape machine, dammit." Her voice was shaking, angry.

"You want the one who killed Carl and stole our money, go see your buddy, Potter. I hear he's still walkin' around free as a bird, the son of a bitch."

MacNulty studied the woman as she spoke, watched the tears well up in her eyes. Either you're one hell of an actress, he thought, or you're dead serious.

She wiped a bruised fist across her eyes. It came away wet. She blinked, looking down at the floor.

"I'm probably a sucker," MacNulty said, "but I'm gonna release you for awhile. But I give you fair warning; you're a suspect in a first degree murder investigation. Do not leave Caribou County. Go out to the camp, pick up your stuff and your check, and find another place to bunk. Then call us and tell us where you're staying. Finally, keep the hell away from Harry Potter and Sawtooth Lodge. You break any one of these orders and you'll be spending a lot of time as a guest in my hotel, you got that?

"And wipe that goddamned smug look off your face, because no matter what happens in this case, you're going back to Alabama to face about a half dozen charges, and I guarantee you that you'll be doing time down there."

She was still sprawled carelessly in the chair, but now her chin was on her chest and her face was red and puffy.

"One screwup, Charlene, and you're history," MacNulty added, sighting along the finger he had pointed toward her. "Now get the hell out of here."

She lifted herself out of the chair, pulled her long hair back with her fingers, and moved toward the door.

Walt, leaning against the door jamb, stepped back to let her pass, then stepped forward into the office and sat down, arms folded.

MacNulty relaxed, stretching in his chair with fingers laced behind his head. He yawned, then bent forward, elbows resting on the arms of the chair with hands still locked. "Did I screw up letting her go?"

Walt shrugged. "Time will tell."

"Any problem coming back?"

"Nothing unusual. She's just a smart-mouthed broad."

"I figure, let her have enough rope to hang herself, same as Harry."

"Still nothing solid?" Walt asked.

"Nope. Prosecutor'd throw up his hands."

"I gave the boat a real good look," Walt said, changing the subject. "She'd made a mess, thrown stuff out of drawers, pried loose a couple seat backs, but no real damage. I don't think she found anything."

"Is that what she said?"

"Yeah. Said she was too busy kicking deputies in the balls. Didn't have time to do much looking; but I did. Looked every place I could see with a flashlight. Pried some panels loose, checked every damn nook and cranny."

"And?"

"Nothing. Zilch."

"Anything else on your southern adventure?"

Walt laughed. "Charlie was really doing a number on those southern boys. She had two or three wishin' they could marry her, and the rest wantin' to kill her."

MacNulty snorted and grinned. "She's got the brags, all right. Won't stand for anybody bein' neutral."

"Anything else happen while I was gone?"

"Ol' Harry figures he's done us enough favors. He's poor Harry now around the lodge. Out to win the sympathy vote. We talk to him only through his mouthpiece, Freddie Eckols."

Walt shrugged. "Kinda figured that might happen, even though we treated him with kid gloves."

"Freddie's not wasting any time. This morning, he called to say he had statements from two bartenders and the Lindner kid down at the dock to the effect that his client had been hassled by the big green-eyed woman and her rough-looking friend. Said all that, plus the stress of running the lodge, forced Harry into a state of nervous exhaustion and caused him to make some minor errors of judgment which he naturally regrets at this time."

"Sounds like Harry's working hard to avoid being charged with anything," Walt agreed.

"Does indeed," MacNulty said, his eyes twinkling. "I still think he's the one."

T he Whitetail Saloon was a tourist attraction owned by Mel and Jean Johnson, who had operated it for two years since buying it from Butch Berger. They had completely renovated it in a northwoods motif. Under Berger, it had been known simply as Butch's, a place whose reputation was as dark and soiled as its interior.

With Butch behind the bar, a logger or construction worker could get a cheap, stiff drink and let off some steam.

Since it was not a large place, most of the steam spilled out on the sidewalk.

Under threat of a revoked license, Butch had sold out to the Johnsons, who paneled the place in knotty pine, hung snowshoes and bearskin rugs on the walls, and put rustic signs on the restroom doors labeling one Bucks and the other Does. With lively music and clean-cut waiters, it was a popular and safe place for tourists and their wives.

Into this benign scene walked Charlie Mittner, who leaned against the bar and ordered a double whiskey and draft beer chaser. She surveyed the half full saloon, realized she was a stranger among strangers, and turned back to accept the tumbler of bourbon.

Without hesitation, she lifted the glass and drained the raw liquid. She shuddered, exhaled loudly, and set the glass down with force. "Hit me again," she demanded of the bartender who had looked up at the clank of her glass against the bar. He stared at her ravaged face, cocked his head in indecision, then picked up the glass and refilled it.

"You a farmer?" she asked the fat-faced man in bib overalls sitting closest to her at the bar.

"Sure enough," he grinned, "from Iowa. How'd you guess?"

She tilted the second tumbler and emptied it, then belched. " 'Cause you smell like cow shit, asshole."

The farmer's face pinkened perceptibly. A number of people, hearing the remark, turned to look at the foulmouthed woman before turning away in whispered conversation. Finally, the bartender walked to Charlie, wiping his white hands in a dish towel. "I'm afraid we can't tolerate that kind of language here," he said quietly. "Please finish your beer and leave."

"I tell it like I see it, Jack, so fuck off. Go pour some more horse piss and quit hasslin' me."

Heard by everyone in the room, her remarks caused shocked silence.

The bartender picked up a phone receiver and dialed 911.

174

He knew the police station was only two blocks by way of the alley.

He talked quietly and succinctly into the phone, then turned to Charlie. "The police will be here in one minute. You can explain yourself to them."

She picked up her beer glass and threw it at him. It missed, but hit a decorative mirror that exploded with flying glass.

"How'd you like it if I got some dynamite and blew this shit hole to pieces. You better start worryin', cause I'm gonna do just that."

She turned, knocking down a bar stool and pushing aside an elderly couple on their way in. Then she was gone, leaving the Whitetail Saloon patrons buzzing with speculation.

When the Northport police arrived, the bartender met them on the sidewalk. He explained her behavior, described her, and pointed out the direction her pickup had taken.

The two officers looked at each other and nodded. "Big Charlie," one said, then looked at the bartender.

"Welcome to the club."

It was a warm summer evening at the Sawtooth Lodge. A relaxed ambience, softened by the lavender of dusk, belied the fact that the place was full.

Outside, the lake heaved gently beneath its slick skin, sending a muted surge against the sand and shingle rock beach. At the river, two men in waders cast expertly to an unseen trout as a small audience watched their efforts.

Inside, the dining room was busy, but beginning to empty as patrons were drawn to the lively piano music in the Tepee Lounge.

Charlie Mittner sat at the bar, listening to the melody of "Oklahoma" and nursing a beer. The young bartender had seen she was tipsy and unsteady as she came in, but mistook her for a guest and served her.

He came back to wipe off the bar and she asked him, "Where's a boss?"

He looked at his watch. "Be here in about an hour."

"Potter?" she asked, staring at her glass.

"Oh, you mean the big boss," he nodded. "Don't see much of him in here. Try the front desk."

She nodded loosely and raised her beer, ending the conversation.

The bar was filling and the bartender paid little attention to her for the next few minutes. She seemed to be talking to a young man who had come in and sat next to her. In the barkeep's eyes they were a draft and a Heineken. A short time later, when he drifted along the bar, he found the young man sitting alone. "She gone?" asked the bartender, noting beer in the glass.

"Guess so," the young man replied. "Said she had to see the boss."

The bartender shook his head. "Hope she's not interviewing for a job."

"Yeah, for sure," the customer agreed. "She was pretty sloshed."

F red Marquardt came out of the dining room into the lobby and stopped. He recognized the woman at the front desk as Charlie Mittner. Retreating to the dining room maitre 'd station, he picked up the phone and called the police.

He identified himself and spoke to the dispatcher. "Charlie Mittner is hanging around here again. You tell MacNulty he better shape up and send somebody out to pick her up right now. He promised to keep her away from here. Looks like his promises are as worthless as he is."

Marquardt hung up and looked out at the front desk. The woman was gone. He went to the front door of the lobby and looked outside in the darkening twilight, but she had vanished.

Ray and Muriel MacNulty were sitting on the back deck, drinking coffee, and watching the light fade, when the phone rang. "Ahhh," MacNulty growled, pushing himself out of the wrought iron chair, "I'll get it."

He went inside through the screen door and caught the phone on the third ring. A minute later, he came back out and sat down.

"I gotta go. Big Charlie's hanging around Sawtooth Lodge again. Fred Marquardt's upset, so I better handle it myself. Looks like I'll have to lock her up this time. She must have a screw loose, pulling a stunt like this after I warned her not to."

"Want me to ride along?" Muriel asked.

He thought a minute. "Hon, it's not likely to be a pleasant trip. I'll be back within an hour, though, if you're still interested."

"I'm always interested," she said meaningfully, and they both chuckled.

George and Verna Walton lingered over dinner in the Sawtooth Lodge dining room, sipping coffee and spooning their desserts as the room emptied. They had reserved the same table for the last three nights, a window table for two where they could watch the light fading through the pines.

This was their first visit to Sawtooth Lodge since they had honeymooned there for three days in the fall of 1954.

George lifted a spoonful of dessert, then paused. "This is sure good, you know? Wonder what's in it?"

Verna tasted, looked thoughtfully at a point above George's head, and said, "Well, I think there's. . . ."

Her description hung in midsentence as a loud but somehow muffled report echoed from the darkness outside.

"What on earth was that?" she frowned.

"I dunno. Sounded like a shot. . . ."

George's response, along with dessert, was blown away by a blast that sent the picture window, now missiles of sharp glass, flying fifty feet into the dining room.

He found himself on the floor, confused by the pain on the right side of his face and body, listening to shrieks and screams. Opening his left eye, he saw glass, red, smudged glass, on the floor. With his left arm, George pushed himself up to a sitting position, an effort that brought dizziness. He closed his eye and remembered. "Verna," he called, "Verna where are you?"

There was no response.

MacNulty was within a mile of Sawtooth Lodge when he felt the explosion. It was more like a sudden gust of crosswind, combined with a dip in the road. He guessed that it was an explosion, but having never felt one in a moving car, he wasn't sure.

One thing he was sure of, the dirty orange glow looming up from the horizon ahead was fire, a big fire that was growing fast.

He reached down by his left foot, found the flasher, and stuck it on the car roof above his head. Then he flipped on the VHF radio, keyed the mike and spoke, "This is MacNulty."

"Go ahead."

"I've got a signal nine at Sawtooth Lodge. Have you got verification?"

"Affirmative. Northport volunteers are rolling. Ambulance requested and notified."

MacNulty was on the lodge road now, driving fast toward flames that were flickering through the pines. The southern sky was bright with smoky orange and yellow.

At the entrance to the parking lot, he slowed to avoid hitting backlit figures running across the road. Though his adrenalin was pumping and his senses racing, he willed himself to slow down, observe accurately, make the correct decisions.

He felt glass beneath the tires. Windshields blown out by an explosion. He saw the entire fire now, flames fifty feet high as they fed hungrily on the dry logs of a cabin.

The side wall of the lodge was no more than twenty-five feet away. A second cabin about the same. A pine tree exploded into flames, lighting the faces of onlookers unable to get close enough to help. Two garden hoses sprayed water, one against the smoking lodge wall, the other into the flames. Worthless, he thought. Keying the microphone, he spoke, "MacNulty with instructions in the clear."

"Go," came the crisp response.

"I want the Northport volunteers to bring their portable pump; they'll need it. Alert the forest service. They'll need a tanker out here right away. Has Walt been called?"

"Affirmative."

"I want every deputy we've got out here. Off duty included."

"Yes sir."

"You said they called for an ambulance? Make it two. They'll need 'em."

"Affirmative."

"And Connie, stay alert. You'll have your hands full tonight."

"Yes sir."

"MacNulty out."

He replaced the microphone and climbed out of the car. A small explosion showered onlookers ahead of him with burning and smoking debris.

He pushed through the onlookers and turned his back on the fire to face them.

"How many of you are employees?" he asked. A young man in busboy jacket, another in shirt and tie, and a waitress all raised their hands.

"All right, I want you three to move this first row of cars

out of here. Get whatever help you need. Get somebody with a four-wheel drive and a chain. Push 'em out. Do whatever you have to do but move 'em fast. We've got to make room for fire equipment." Then he addressed the others watching from the parking lot.

"Folks, I want all of you off the parking lot. You'll be in the way here. Everybody move over there off the pavement. That's right."

As he herded people ahead of him, the big diesel and wailing siren of the Northport volunteers sounded its approach, helping to scatter the crowd.

MacNulty moved around the fringe of heat, seeking someone in authority. Mostly, he saw only the confused and frightened faces of tourists lit by the roaring flames.

Reaching the lakeside of the inferno, he spotted Fred Marquardt gesturing to a garden hose firefighter with one hand and holding a fire extinguisher with the other. Looking up, his eyes were wild in the firelight, his face streaked with soot and dirt.

"You son of a bitch," yelled Marquardt. "How dare you show up here after what you've done. You're a disgrace to the badge."

MacNulty grabbed his arm at the bicep, yanked him around angrily, and force marched the hysterical man through the crowd, away from the fire.

"Get ahold of yourself, Fred," MacNulty commanded, releasing Marquardt from his grip.

Tears were furrowing the grime on Marquardt's face. He blinked to clear his eyes, then turned away and began to sob. After a half minute, he turned back toward MacNulty.

"You're supposed to protect people, protect their property, goddamn you. Now he's dead, the place is ruined, and it's your fault."

"What do you mean, he's dead? Harry's dead?"

Marquardt nodded and pointed. "He was in there, in his workshop. She was here. Goddamn you, anyway."

"I can't protect somebody who won't protect himself, Fred. Out there in that cabin, he made an easy target."

MacNulty softened. "If I've neglected my duty, then I'll take the full blame when all this is over. But right now you've got what, a hundred, two hundred guests who need you.

"That wall's gonna catch fire," MacNulty added, pointing to the west wall of the lodge. "You need to evacuate the rooms on this end. Then get the coffee pots going and get people inside, in the lobby, out of the way."

"How many were hurt?"

Marquardt shook his head. "Several. I don't know. I been out here." His body was still heaving with sobs.

"Okay, both the ambulances are coming. I'll see to the injured, you get this end of the lodge evacuated, and start looking after your people. Now go."

Marquardt wiped his dirty face, blew his nose, and nodded. "Okay, you're right, but this isn't over. Your day will come."

MacNulty watched him go, then turned back to see that the flames had jumped the gap in two places and were now climbing a portion of the lodge wall and licking at a section of the eave. To the west of the burning cabin, two more pines were afire and the flames had crept hungrily through the dry brush for one hundred feet. The Northport volunteers had not yet put any water on the fire, though they were running out the hoses.

Inside, he found the lobby intact. Two or three small groups, including several employees, were talking in low tones. They stopped as he approached.

"Injuries?"

Several arms pointed him to the dining room, which showed the effects of the blast. The glass crunched under his boots as he crossed the long room, stepping around a fallen chandelier and several overturned tables.

The victims were mostly at the west end of the room, attended by people who were friends or employees.

"Anyone in charge here?" MacNulty asked of nobody in particular.

A young woman, whose cream-colored waitress uniform was smudged with red, looked up and pointed. "That man in the blue shirt is a doctor. I think another one of them might be, too."

Thank God the lodge was upscale enough to attract a few doctors, thought MacNulty as he threaded his way toward the man in blue.

"You're a doctor, sir?" MacNulty asked the man kneeling over a woman who seemed to be bleeding more than was possible.

The man looked up, then leaned forward to instruct a busboy. "Keep this on the pressure point. Don't ease up."

"Can I talk to you, Doctor?" MacNulty asked more firmly.

The doctor put his hands in a linen napkin to wipe away blood as he stood. He was a thin, dark-haired man with a mustache. "Who are you?" he asked MacNulty bluntly.

"I'm the sheriff in this county. What's the situation here?"

The doctor took MacNulty's arm and led him away from the clusters of wounded. He spoke in a confidential tone. "Where in hell are the ambulances? I've lost one and could easily lose another two. You *do* have ambulances coming?"

"We've got two. First one should be pulling up right about now," MacNulty replied.

The doctor nodded. "Paramedics?"

"Every one of them," MacNulty answered.

"Okay. See if they can pull around the lodge to the front door of the lobby. That would be a help. And tell 'em our biggest problem is loss of blood and shock, so they'll know what to bring. Every minute is important. Some of these people are gonna need a lot of sewing. They look like sieves."

"Okay, I'll go handle the ambulances. How many are going to need transport?"

"Let's start with ten or eleven. That's a rough guesstimate, Sheriff."

Both men turned away.

"What's the quickest way to the parking lot?" MacNulty asked the same waitress who had pointed out the doctor.

"Through that door to the kitchen and out through the pantry," she said, pointing.

He followed the instructions and exited at the back of the lodge into chaos. The parking lot was a din of engines and shouts. Bathed in the eerie firelight, crisscrossed by rotating red and blue flashers, were hundreds of faces.

An ambulance was crawling toward the scene along the approach road narrowed by rows of parked cars and clogged with onlookers arriving on foot. Its shrill siren seemed to have little effect on the pedestrians mesmerized by the blaze.

Then MacNulty saw Walt Downing across the lot, trying to clear a path for the frustrated ambulance crew. He hurried to Walt through the sea of lights and faces.

"Walt. Thank God you're here. Take this ambulance to the left here, away from the crowd. Make an end run around the lot and the lodge building to the front door. We've got ten casualties to transport, two criticals. Tell the guys they'll be dealing with severe lacerations and shock. Got all that?"

Walt nodded. "The highway's a mess. Accident between here and town. Had to stop and work it a few minutes 'til the Highway Patrol arrived. The other ambulance is transporting from the wreck."

MacNulty shook his head. "Shit. Anybody else here?"

"I saw Jess down there helping the volunteers with crowd control. He's the only one so far."

"Okay, hustle the ambulance along and help with the injured. I'll catch you later."

He turned back toward the fire, which was throwing heat across most of the parking lot as it fed hungrily on the log structure.

The volunteers were pouring water against the main lodge and had knocked down the fire on it. MacNulty knew the truck's one thousand-gallon capacity would be expended quickly. He hurried toward the firefighters silhouetted against the flames, spotting Fire Chief Johnson near the truck.

"How's it going, Ed?" MacNulty shouted over the roar of the equipment and the fire.

"I dunno yet, Ray. Depends if we get the portable pump pretty soon. I've got ten minutes of water left to keep the lodge wet down. I figure that's priority."

"Can't you knock down the main fire some?"

Chief Ed Johnson, a plumber by trade, smiled ruefully. "Shit, Ray, that's like tryin' to kill a moose with a fly swatter."

"Can't you get some help from the forestry boys?"

Johnson looked through the woods where the flames were marching steadily away from the resort, then spat tobacco juice. "I'd say those boys got their own problems, you know?"

"Anything I can do for you?" MacNulty asked. The heat of the fire forced him to shield his face with his hand.

Johnson shook his head. "I've got trucks coming up from Silver Bay and Two Harbors, but we're talking another hour. I need that pump. Then I can throw the whole goddamn lake on 'er."

"I'll see what I can do," MacNulty yelled, turning away toward his car.

The parking lot was now impassable, blocked by hastily-parked cars and hundreds of onlookers. People he knew were yelling questions at him as he threaded his way to his car.

"How's it going, Ray?"

"Anybody hurt?"

"Hell of an explosion, eh Sheriff?"

He waved in acknowledgment but said nothing. Must be half the town here, he thought. What a god-awful mess.

Climbing into the car, MacNulty slammed the door behind him and took a deep breath. The first thing he noticed was the quiet. He lit a cigarette and took a deep drag. The radio began to chatter. He listened. Ambulance talk.

He keyed his mike and got the dispatcher. The pump was

184

on its way. Somebody with a pickup was hauling it. They were still clearing away the wreck. Traffic was backed up.

MacNulty felt suddenly detatched, tired. Things seemed out of control, beyond his reach. He had tried to help the others. Now the parking lot was hopelessly blocked; it was his own fault. Crowd control was his first responsibility. Somehow, he had forgotten. Now it was too late; what a mess.

He drew on his cigarette, felt his body sag. Just sit in the car a few minutes, catch your breath, he rationalized.

Someone was pounding on the window. He turned slowly and looked out with smoke-reddened eyes.

It was the two boys, Nels and Graham. He wondered why they were there. What the hell, he thought. Everybody else was here to watch the fire, why not them? He pushed the door open.

"You okay Ray?" Nels asked. "You look sort of dazed."

"No, I'm fine. Had to check some things with the office," MacNulty answered.

"We'll help," Nels said. "Tell us what to do."

MacNulty caught sight of Prentice standing behind Graham. "See you brought the brains of the family along, too," he said.

"Right," Nels said, ignoring the comment. "So what should we do? Where's Walt?"

"In the dining room, helping with the injured."

"Go find him, Graham, and bring him here," Nels snapped, "and hurry."

MacNulty grabbed the door and pulled himself slowly up out of the car. "Hell of a mess," he said, staring out at the scene.

Nels stared hard at MacNulty, trying to read him. "You're beat, Ray, but we can help. Just tell us what you need to get done."

MacNulty gave him a lopsided grin. "I need to clear this whole damn parking lot," he said with a laugh that sounded more like a snort. "Got to get ambulances and fire trucks through. So you tell me how we're gonna do it."

185

Nels looked at the tangled scene. It really was a mess. "I'm no expert, but I know we can't do it if we don't try."

MacNulty looked at the younger man soberly. "You're right. We gotta try. Over by the fire truck, you'll find Jess Anderson. Tell him I want him and any other of the deputies he can see to get over here right away."

Nels pushed through the crowd and was gone.

MacNulty turned to Prentice, who was watching him. "Sometimes, the road ahead gets to looking like a mountainside. Makes you feel your age. Sort of takes the wind out of you."

"Ray MacNulty, I've never seen a mountainside even slow you down, let alone stop you. As far as I'm concerned, there isn't anything you can't do if you set your mind to it."

She was looking at him with soft, serious eyes and he could feel his jaw set with new determination.

"Prentice, I do believe you're right, as usual," he said with a grin.

Walt and Graham arrived on the scene, followed shortly by Nels, deputy Jess Anderson, and another deputy in blue jeans and sweatshirt.

"Okay men, here's what we're gonna do," MacNulty said, matter-of-factly explaining the seemingly impossible task of clearing hundreds of people and dozens of cars to open routes to and through the parking lot.

By the time he finished telling deputy Anderson to block off all nonessential traffic entering from the highway, he had talked himself and his listeners into believing it really could be done.

Within ten minutes, the group had cleared a narrow path, though not without incident, through which the fire department's pump was delivered to the beach and the ambulance was able to escape with two critically injured guests.

The owner of a sports coupe threatened to sue after seeing that its bumper had been ripped loose while being towed. And two large young men reacted to Nels's zealous efforts to move

186

them off the parking lot by pushing him away. This escalated into a scuffle which ended only after Graham stepped between them, apologized for Nels, and quietly explained to his adversaries that they would be taking their beer through a straw if they continued the hostilities.

"Goddamned Canuck," one was heard to say as they swaggered away.

After a lane was cleared, and people realized the sheriff meant business, drivers were more than eager to remove their vehicles voluntarily. "We were gonna leave anyhow," said one.

"I had to park here. There was no place else," said a second.

MacNulty had regained control. He intended to keep it.

"Run this line from that tree back to the corner of the lot. Walt, you run another line from the pantry door to where the Bronco is parked."

"Folks, these are police lines," he yelled, walking through the crowd with arms raised. "You'll have to get back behind them and stay there.

"Ron," he said, motioning to the deputy in blue jeans. "Patrol these lines and see they're observed."

The portable pump was pulling water from Lake Superior now and a three-man hose team was aiming it at the main fire. If anything, the heat was more intense than before, though the flames had diminished from the lack of fuel.

"Walt, come over here," MacNulty called. "We got some work to do."

Walt stood, hands on hips, listening to the sheriff's instructions.

"It's a dark-colored pickup. Call Connie and get the tag number. It's worth a look, just in case."

"Nels, Graham," he waved the two over. "You guys ought to be deputies. Hell, I got you working like a couple of 'em. C'mon over here,"

They followed him to his car and waited while he rummaged around in the glove compartment. Finally, he emerged, a wide grin creasing his soot-lined face. "Found 'em. I knew I had 'em someplace."

In his hand were two silver shields, each designating the bearer as a deputy sheriff of Caribou County, Minnesota. He handed one to Nels, the other to Graham.

"You boys earned 'em." Then he laughed with a bark. "Course, it don't mean I'm gonna pay you, and it don't mean you can go around arresting people, but you never know when they might come in handy, especially if you keep turning up when I need something done."

"Any time, Ray," Nels said, genuinely touched.

"Thank you," Graham said, smiling broadly.

"Now if you really want to help, I got a couple more things you could do. . . ."

They agreed without knowing what he had in mind.

"Well, since you're on good terms with old Fred Marquardt and I'm not, here's what I need."

He explained and sent them toward the lodge. As he turned back toward the fire, he saw Prentice, looking for Nels.

"Prentice, hey Prentice," MacNulty waved. "They went to the lodge to see Fred Marquardt. You can catch them if you hurry."

MacNulty walked toward the fire and the short, square figure of Fire Chief Johnson, whose bull neck made him appear permanently hunched down in his heavy black neoprene coat. Johnson looked up, his dirty face glistening with sweat and water.

"This is arson, Ed, maybe a murder to boot. We're gonna have to sift through what's left for evidence."

"Figured as much," Johnson replied, spitting tobacco juice. "Silver Bay should be here any minute. Then we'll knock this fucker down fast." He looked at the indistinct pile of flaming timbers that had once been a cabin. "Hot fire. Won't be much left."

MacNulty shrugged. "Do what you can."

188

He left chief Johnson staring at the fire and began to circle the site, walking through blackened, still-smoking weeds. The crowd had begun to disperse, having seen enough of the cabin fire and having decided they would not be treated to the sight of a burning lodge or a forest fire.

Off to the west, MacNulty could hear the forestry team at work on what seemed to be an effective fire line. The forest service had moved fast with chain saws, a bulldozer, and water to stop the racing woods fire and was now knocking down hot spots. A small group that he judged to be a family stood close together near the side of the adjacent cabin.

"You folks staying in this cabin?"

"We were, 'til the windows blew out," the man replied.

"Anybody hurt?" MacNulty asked.

"No, we were pretty damn lucky," the man replied.

"We could have all been killed," his wife added.

MacNulty nodded. "Can you tell me what happened?"

The couple looked at each other, then the man spoke: "Me and Helen were in the kitchen doing up the dishes. The kids were back in the bedroom. That's why nobody got hurt."

"Tell him about the gunshot," his wife prompted.

"I was coming to that."

"We heard a gunshot," she said.

"Oh? When was that?" MacNulty asked.

"Let me tell it, okay? About five to ten seconds before the explosion, there was a gunshot. If it was a gunshot, it was heavy caliber, like a .357 or a .45 or maybe a 12-gauge. Something big. Didn't sound like a car backfiring."

"You said it could have been a backfire," the woman corrected.

"I know that's what I said, but I don't think it was. Anyhow, when the blast hit, the windows blew out. We sort of ducked down behind the counter for a minute, then I heard what sounded like a fire and I took a look. That's when I saw the fire and got everybody out."

MacNulty saw the woman was shaking her head.

189

"There were at least two more explosions," she said. "That's when the fire really started."

"Oh?" MacNulty asked, making notes on his small spiral-bound pad.

The man explained. "It was the kind of explosion you get from a can of gasoline or solvent, you know. Pretty fair blast but nothing like the big one."

"Did you folks hear anybody yelling or screaming, anything unusual, before the gunshot or the big explosion?"

"No, I didn't," he said. She shook her head in agreement.

"You've been a big help. Let me get your names and address for my records," MacNulty said, writing on his pad.

Completing his notes, he thanked the family, suggested they talk to the front desk about their accommodations, and went on toward the dining room. There he found George Walton, whose right side, from the top of his head to his waist, was swathed in bandages. More specifically, Walton found him, grabbing his shirt sleeve as he walked past.

"You. Mr. Deputy. Gotta help me."

"Let me get the doctor for you."

"No. My wife, they took my wife. Gotta find her."

MacNulty could see the man was distraught, possibly on the edge of shock.

"Take it easy now, mister. They took your wife in the ambulance?"

Walton nodded. "Verna. Got to get to her. She could be dying. Hurt bad. Window cut her face, neck." Tears ran down his left cheek and he began to sob.

"Please. Help me," he implored.

"Okay. Let me see what I can do," MacNulty agreed, releasing the man's arm and walking to the doctor in blue.

He got approval to put Walton in the next ambulance and sat with him, soothing and talking. He learned the man was George Walton, an insurance adjuster from southern Minnesota. He also learned that Walton had an almost uncanny recall of the events up until he found himself on the floor,

190

covered with blood. His recollections matched identically the observations of the family he had just interviewed.

MacNulty got Walton into an arriving ambulance, interviewed another victim with less gratifying results, talked briefly to a doctor in blue, and walked back toward the lobby.

A gunshot, followed closely by an explosion, he mused. A picture formed in his mind, then a scene he played out. He tried other pictures, other scenes, but he kept coming back to the one in which Harry Potter was holding the gun and Charlie Mittner the dynamite.

"Ray", a familiar voice called. MacNulty turned to see Walt Downing hurrying toward him.

"I've got it," Walt breathed excitedly. "Her truck's still in the parking lot."

"You sure?"

Walt nodded. "I think you should come see for yourself."

MacNulty nodded and followed the chief deputy back through the kitchen and out into the roaring engines and moving lights of the parking lot.

The pickup had been backed into a space on the far side of the lot, away from the fire scene. Walt played his light across the grill and license plate, then led the way to the door on the passenger side.

"Her stuff is still in boxes in the back end. Looks like she hadn't landed anywhere after she left the logging camp."

MacNulty noticed that Walt had referred to Charlie in the past tense. He wondered if his sidekick had formed a similar mental picture to the one that was becoming indelibly etched in his mind.

Walt opened the door and handed him the light. "Here, have a look for yourself."

The cab was a dirty mess. A nearly empty pint bottle of vodka lay on the seat, along with some clothing and a pair of sneakers. On the floor was an open lunch bucket, more clothing, wrapping paper, empty cartons, and gum wrappers.

"Look in the lunch bucket," Walt suggested.

"Hmmm," MacNulty agreed, spotting the dynamite caps and snippets of fuse material. The innocuous brown paper was dynamite wrapper. "Okay," he added, "make some notes and inventory this stuff."

Then, almost to himself, he mused, "What do you suppose got into her? You think the booze did it?"

Walt shrugged. "Almost like she lost everything and just didn't give a shit."

MacNulty shook his head. "Gutsy broad. Maybe crazy, too."

"Maybe dead, too," Walt added.

MacNulty nodded soberly and turned away.

"Go over everything. Don't want to miss anything that could be important later," he said over his shoulder.

Silver Bay had arrived and was pouring water on the flames. The smoke was heavy now, rolling gray and white across the lodge and into the trees. Won't be much to look at, Mac-Nulty thought as he walked heavily across the pavement. Bits and pieces for the boys at the state crime lab to analyze.

"Aha, there you are," Nels called from the darkness. "Been looking all over for you."

The two honorary deputies, as MacNulty thought of them, came up to where he had stopped.

"Got some info you wanted," Nels explained. "Fred's a wreck, but at least he tried to be helpful. Said Harry drives one of two cars, a Mercury station wagon from a few years back or a red Toyota Supra, usually the wagon.

"Well, we found 'em both in the lot; the wagon's open. We looked inside but there's nothing much in it. The Toyota's locked."

MacNulty listened without comment, staring at the pavement a few feet away.

"We went back for the Supra keys but Fred didn't have 'em and didn't want us to bother Harry's wife or daughter.

"Anyhow, Fred started rambling on about how Charlie had showed up, said she started in at the bar, so Graham and I went in there and talked to the bartender who served her.

"He said she was pretty drunk. Said he could tell. But he served her because she wasn't loud or boisterous, and only ordered a glass of beer."

MacNulty nodded and looked at the fire.

"Anyhow, Ray, we thought it might be information you could use," Nels added.

"Oh, it is," MacNulty agreed. "Didn't I tell you fellows that you deserved those badges I gave you?'

Nels nodded. "Hope you don't mind that we already used 'em to get the information from the bartender."

MacNulty grinned. "Why do you s'pose I gave 'em to you?"

D awn climbed over the horizon and cast its gray light on the Sawtooth Lodge fire scene. The ambulances and fire trucks had come and gone. The crowd had returned to town. Guests had been allowed to return to their rooms; the overflow occupied couches in the lobby and the Tepee Lounge. The excitement was over.

In his office, Fred Marquardt's red-rimmed eyes stared vacantly at the opposite wall, worrying over the problems ahead: lawsuits from the injured, refunds to displaced guests, bad publicity in the media. He had been back to the fire scene, glimpsed MacNulty, and left. His granddaughter was curled up on the office couch.

A heavily sedated Agnes Potter slept, while Ivy Marquardt dozed in a chair nearby.

Nobody had seen Harry Potter since he had ambled out to his workshop about 8 P.M.

Ed Johnson, implacable as ever, squirted a stream of tobacco juice at an imaginary target. His portable pump, some distance away, steadily droned as it fed cold water to the hose that still dampened the smoking hulk of what had once been a cabin.

Johnson, holding a half full cup of cold coffee, was flanked by Sheriff Ray MacNulty and Chief Deputy Walt Downing. They watched the open nozzle lay a fine spray of water over the embers. There was nothing more to say about the fire, so they talked fishing.

Johnson sipped his bitter brew and spoke.

"Me and the boy were up at Musquash Lake last week. Got a half dozen nice Splake. Amazing there's anything left, what with all the tourists in there."

MacNulty nodded. "I took Muriel over to Bath Lake and we got two fourteen-inch Brookies. Nice place. We had lunch on the island. Bob Rydaff's boy was in there. Said he heard somebody took a four pounder out of there last week. Jeez, that musta been one helluva nice fish."

"I can believe it," Johnson nodded. "Ralph Larson got a six pounder outta there last winter."

MacNulty shook his head in the disbelief Johnson expected. They were silent a minute, watching the water.

"You ever get up into Mouse Lake, Ed? I talked to a couple, older guy and his wife, that had a cooler full of fourteen-inch Brookies outta there. Got 'em on leeches."

"Really?" the chief responded. "I fished Mouse two, three years ago. Didn't catch shit." His tobacco juice sizzled against a still-glowing log.

The light of dawn intensified, bringing early birds outside. One couple in sweat suits watched the rising smoke as they stretched and bent before running off to the east, across the bridge and into the woods.

"So," Johnson said, "you got a line on what happened here? Fire Marshall should be along this morning and I gotta show him around."

"We got some theories, Ed, but I don't know if we'll ever be able to make 'em hold water," MacNulty answered. He explained his thoughts to the chief, who responded with a low whistle.

"I never run into something like this before," Johnson exclaimed.

"Me neither," added MacNulty. "We're gonna have to sift through that shit pretty careful when it cools down, ya know. Send it down to the crime lab. So I don't know who gets first shot at it, me or the fire marshall. He's looking at arson, but hell, I'm lookin' at murder. Guess we just wait and see."

"Why don't I go and give 'em a call; see what he says?" Johnson suggested.

"Suits me," MacNulty agreed.

A car pulled up and Nels Dahlstrom got out, hair tousled. Walt watched him walk toward them. "Thought you went home."

"I did," Nels answered. "Couldn't sleep. Kept thinking I'd forgotten something."

"Did you?"

Nels nodded. "The desk clerk. I talked to the one who saw Charlie last night. Didn't seem all that important at the time. Now that I've thought about it. . . ." he shrugged. "Sorry I forgot."

MacNulty, interested now, turned. "You got our attention, so let's hear about it."

"This girl at the desk, college girl type, she said Charlie came up to the desk. Said she could see she was drunk, or pretty close to it. Anyhow, Charlie asked where the big brass was. Said she was looking for Potter.

"The desk girl figured Potter didn't need the hassle—they seem to be pretty protective of the guy—so she told Charlie that he was gone, away from the lodge.

"Charlie asked when he'd be back and the girl said he'd be gone all evening. So far, nothing much of interest, right?

"But then, she said, Charlie flashed this big smile and said, 'Gee, that's too bad. He'll miss all the fun.' Then she turned and walked out the lobby door.

"Anyhow, that's the gist of it, but I thought you guys

should know that Charlie probably came out here expecting the cabin to be empty."

MacNulty nodded. "Interesting. Me and Walt'll chew on it and see what we make of it."

Nels could see the sheriff was tired and not interested in discussing it at the moment, so he said goodbye and returned to the car. Walt waved goodbye and turned back to the fire. "So, that puts a new twist on the motive, right, Ray?"

Looking into the ashes, he nodded slightly. "Like she only meant to scare him bad and not blow him up. That what you mean, isn't it Walt?"

Cocking his head, Walt agreed. "Things fit together better in my head if that's what happened."

"Yeah, they do for me, too," MacNulty concurred, nodding. "They do indeed."

Ed Johnson rounded the corner of the lodge.

"Fire marshall can't get here 'til afternoon," he advised. "Said if you don't mind, he'll take charge of the digging. Said the explosion and the hot fire and the way it burned all night are gonna make it hard to know what you're lookin' at without some experience."

"Fine by me," MacNulty shrugged. "I'm gonna go catch forty winks 'til he shows up. Have him call my office when he gets here. They can reach me at home."

"I'm right behind you," Walt said.

As they pulled out of the lot, the first of several TV camera vehicles passed them on its way to the scene.

"**M**acNulty here," he grumbled, sitting on the side of the bed with eyes still closed. It was only 10 A.M.

Connie, the dispatcher, explained the problem, a bullpen half full of media types waiting for the sheriff to return and verify the vivid story Ed Johnson had told them.

196

"I can't give 'em that story, goddamnit. I don't even know if it's true."

The dispatcher continued in a barely audible voice, explaining that somehow, these people also knew about Harry's earlier disappearance, the missing gold, and Charlie's apparent vendetta.

"Now how in the name of hell did they get hold of all that? Who the hell is shooting off their mouth?"

She told him it was on the street, making the rounds of Northport.

"Ah shit, Connie, that's all I need. Tell 'em I'm on my way, will ya? I'll be there in twenty, thirty minutes."

MacNulty rarely cut himself shaving, but this morning, he arrived at the office still wearing the pieces of toilet paper needed to blot the flow of blood.

"Give me a minute to get some coffee," he told the reporters. "Then we'll sit down and get everything squared around." He glared at the dispatcher, then strode into his private office. She was right on his heels with a mug of hot coffee.

"I'm gonna kick Ed Johnson's ass from here to the fuckin' border," he muttered.

"Shall I send them in?" Connie asked.

"You do and I'll kick yours, too," he growled. "Let 'em cool their heels a couple minutes."

"You still got paper on your face," she said.

"Oh shit, I forgot. That's all I need, to look like a fuckin' clown," he grumbled, picking gently at his face.

Despite his foul temper and language to match, Connie giggled. She liked her boss, especially at times like this, when she was reminded that whatever he was, he certainly wasn't a phony.

MacNulty sipped the coffee, trying to focus on the problems at hand, but his mind kept flashing images of newspaper headlines that read "Two missing, one dead in revenge bombing and fire," or "Revenge thought motive for lodge explosion," or "Vendetta bombing kills three, injures ten."

197

Shaky ground, he thought, checking his facial cuts for signs of blood.

"Ah, what the hell. May as well let 'em in, Connie. It isn't gonna get any easier."

The dispatcher went out and MacNulty hoisted himself off his creaky chair to greet the media.

As they crowded into his office, he noted that two people were carrying video cameras, while others had their trademark motorized thirty-fives.

"Tell ya what," he said, leaning forward over the desk on his knuckles. "Let's talk first, get the story straight, then you can get whatever shots you need. My time is yours, so there's no need to trample each other."

"Deadlines, sheriff," a young woman replied. "We all got 'em."

"Well, I'm sure we can move this right along so none of you miss any deadlines," he said congenially.

"Already have, sheriff," rebutted a middle-aged man in sweatshirt and blue jeans. "Listen, we got the story. We just need you to confirm it, sorta put your seal of approval on it, okay?"

"Let's hear your story and we'll see," MacNulty replied.

The man started with the murder of Carl Hoffman, the disappearance of Harry Potter, and the strange behavior of Charlie Mittner. He continued with the discovery of Potter, the recovery of Charlie, and the fact that they were both suspects, which led somehow to the explosion and fire, during which both suspects were probably killed and a number of innocent people seriously wounded.

"That about it?" he asked MacNulty.

The sheriff chuckled. "That, my friend, is one hell of a story. Might make a pretty good book."

"Do you deny it?" the reporter shot back.

" 'Fraid I'll have to," MacNulty replied easily. "You people are all from the city, so you might not understand how us small town folks like to tell stories. We take a couple facts, embroider 'em up a little and pass 'em along. Next fella, he fixes it up some more and so on. Pretty soon, you got a hell of a good story, but it's not true."

"So what *is* the true story, sheriff?" barked a young woman.

"I wish I could tell you what I know, I really do, but it's part of a case that's under investigation."

"What case is that?" the sweatshirt-clad man asked.

"The murder of Carl Hoffman," MacNulty answered.

"Are you denying that Hoffman's girlfriend was at the lodge last night looking for Harry Potter?"

"Sorry, no comment."

"Was anybody killed in the fire?"

"I understand there was one fatality caused by the explosion before the fire."

"What about Harry Potter?"

"What about him?"

"Was he killed?"

"Not that I know of. You people will have to realize that the fire marshall and I have not yet combed the site for evidence. Anything we find will go to the pathologists and the state crime lab, so we're talking several days before we have any answers."

"What about the gold?" asked a woman. "We understand there was a lot of gold found but not accounted for. Hundreds of pounds of it."

MacNulty chuckled. "If you can find several hundred pounds of gold, ma'am, I'll give you half."

"Where was the gold found?" she snapped. "We heard it was near a place called Quill Mountain."

"Ma'am, I hope you can understand that I don't want a gold rush in Caribou County when there's no gold to rush for.

We were told of a site during the investigation that I can't identify for obvious reasons. I can assure you we found no gold there."

"When Charlie Mittner was brought back from Alabama, why was she released?"

"I'm sorry, I can't comment. That's part of the ongoing investigation."

"Fred Marquardt, Mr. Potter's father-in-law, says you deliberately turned her loose to go after him, with inevitable results."

"No comment, but that's a damn lie." MacNulty could feel his pulse rising and fought to maintain his composure.

"We've talked to a county commissioner who claimed you were, excuse the pun, 'playing with fire' in this case."

"No comment, I can't be responsible for somebody else's opinions."

"We understand you were reelected just this year without opposition. In light of this tragedy, do you still intend to serve out your term?"

"Yes, of course I do. Now I think we've about chewed over everything worth chewing, so if you want any pictures, fine, but the interview is over."

MacNulty posed obligingly for several minutes of film and stills, then thanked the reporters as he herded them from his office. They went out, still whispering among themselves.

He wondered what they would do with his information, imagining photos with captions that read "Beleaguered sheriff: MacNulty refuses to take blame," and "Lawman fostered revenge killing." Somehow, he had felt their hostility, real or imagined, and feared the worst.

He knew he could expect the story to be featured tonight on at least two regional newscasts. After that, his phone would start ringing. He needed all this like a hole in the head.

It didn't take long for a rumor to make the rounds in Northport, especially a juicy one. Between the stories already spreading and the news coverage on television and newspapers, MacNulty knew his reputation and image were about to take a dive.

"Fuck 'em," he muttered to himself. "Let 'em think what they want."

He took a large plastic bottle of Rolaids from his bottom left drawer and shook two of the tablets into his hand.

T he fire site was about thirty feet long and thirty feet wide. Chief Ed Johnson stood next to a tall, thin, balding man with a gray fringe of hair, occasionally pointing a hairy arm to emphasize his description of the fire.

MacNulty and Walt Downing pulled up in the department Bronco and got out.

The older man was introduced as Earl Perkovich, state fire marshall. Together, the four men stood looking at what was now a mostly flat area covered by gray-black ash. A few charred timbers ringed the blanket of ash and two or three wisps of smoke still circled lazily from within.

"So, what can we expect to find?" MacNulty asked.

Perkovich shook his head. "Not much, I'm afraid. As I was telling the chief here, you couldn't have done a better job of burning this cabin if you'd tried.

"Chief tells me he used his water to save the lodge, then had to wait for his portable pump. I told him he better get some more decent equipment. Can't fight a fire like this with just one or two hoses. Imagine if a downtown building catches fire. You could lose the whole downtown."

MacNulty shot a glance at Johnson, who was staring at the ruins.

"Chief Johnson explain to you how it started with the explosion?"

Perkovich nodded. "You've got eye witnesses?"

201

"Written and oral testimony. I can send you copies when we get everything typed up."

"Good. It's arson, of course, but I'll need the testimony. Sure not gonna find evidence in there that would prove anything."

MacNulty's eyebrows raised, furrowing his forehead.

"What about human remains? We think there's a couple of bodies in there."

"Sheriff, what's in there is not bodies; let me explain. You start with an explosion that was certainly strong enough to blow a human body into pieces. Then you spray those pieces with exploding gasoline, solvents, propane, whatever. Then you let what's left burn in direct flames for what, six or seven hours? Sheriff, I'm no pathologist, but what's in there isn't bodies. Might as well have put them through an incinerator."

"But there'll be something left, won't there?" MacNulty's face was etched with concern. "I need some evidence that those people were in there."

Perkovich shrugged again. "We should get some bones, or fragments at least, but not enough to prove that such and such a bone belonged to Mr. X or Miss X. With a fire like this, you're way past that point. When we get in there and start raking it apart, you'll see for yourself what I'm talking about."

MacNulty nodded and looked at Walt, who shook his head.

"Walt," the sheriff said, "I'm gonna put you in charge of finding whatever evidence is in there. Call the office and get yourself some help."

"Gee thanks, Ray. You can't imagine how long I've been wanting to wade around in hot, muddy ashes looking for bones."

"Well, somebody's got to go back to the office and put this all into a report," growled MacNulty. "I don't look forward to that, either."

MacNulty turned away, then stopped. "Ed, can I have a word with you before I go?"

Chief Johnson sauntered over and looked up. "What's up?"

"I just wanted you to know how much I appreciate you shooting off your fucking mouth to the reporters this morning. It really puts my ass in a sling."

Johnson spat the ever present tobacco juice near MacNulty's feet. "I just told 'em what you said."

"Goddamnit, Ed. This is part of an ongoing investigation. Half what I told you is pure speculation and the rest is confidential. From now on, just practice fighting your fires and let me handle the police work. It's hard enough without your help."

He turned away with Johnson glowering at his back.

S omehow, the day passed. MacNulty spent it at home. When Muriel arrived home from the library at five, she found him sitting out in back at the picnic table. He was drinking a glass of milk and eating chocolate chip cookies. She took a long look at his choice of snack. "Home early from camp?" she asked.

MacNulty grinned and shook his head. "Does my food give away my mood?"

"Usually," she answered. "Right now, I'd say you're feeling a little punk and need some comforting. I gather this was not your best day?"

"You gather right. I'd say we'll get a better assessment of the damage in about an hour."

"What happens in an hour?"

"That's when we find out how the TV stations will handle all the information they got about the fire."

"What did you tell them?"

"Nothing. Didn't have to. They got all they needed from Ed Johnson, Fred Marquardt and every other blabbermouth in town. All they wanted from me was confirmation."

She looked at him silently.

"I didn't give 'em any. Told 'em it was part of an ongoing case and couldn't talk about it."

"What's wrong with that? It's true."

MacNulty was touched by his wife's loyalty, but remained unconvinced. "Doesn't keep 'em from frying my ass.

"If they use any of the rumors, I'll end up looking like a goat. A lot of people figure I screwed up letting Charlie loose. That's one I'll have to live with."

"Just curious, but why did you release her?"

He sighed. "First reason is I didn't have anything to hold her on. Plus I figured she'd stir something up to help solve the case. Never figured she'd go bananas with an armload of dynamite."

"You're sure she caused the explosion?"

"No getting around the evidence. If I defended her this time, I could start lookin' for another line of work."

She got up from the back step and hugged his head against her. "You always got me in your corner, so just do whatever you think is right.

"Meanwhile, I need to fix some supper. How'd you like some walleye filets in dill sauce? Cousin Ed brought them by the library for us and they look good. Said he caught 'em yesterday evening in Devil's Track Lake."

"That might perk me up some. I'll give you a holler when the news comes on."

MacNulty scanned the newspaper headlines before settling into the sports section. His favorite team, the Twins, had won again and were challenging for the lead. He read the entire section, as he usually did, including half the major league box scores and statistics.

Suddenly, it was five 'til six. Amazing, he thought, how you could lose yourself in the sports section.

He went in and flipped on channel three with the remote control. Might as well get the worst over with, he thought, recalling the snappish reporter from this morning's session. He called Muriel and together they endured a dozen commercials preceding the news.

The anchor man came on to preview the lead story.

"Good evening. At the top of the news tonight, one person is dead, two people are missing, and a dozen more are injured following a major explosion and fire last night at the Sawtooth Lodge near Northport. We'll have the details on that story and more following these messages."

The report began in straightforward style, with an on-the-scene reporter describing what had apparently happened as she stood before the still-smoldering ruins.

"So far so good," Muriel said hopefully. Then the reporter returned.

"Caribou County Sheriff Ray MacNulty this morning refused to confirm the fact that the missing woman, Charlene Mittner, known locally as Big Charlie, and the missing lodge owner, Harry Potter, were both suspects in last month's murder of logging company owner Carl Hoffman. According to Caribou County officials, Hoffman and the two people who are missing and believed to have perished in the fire, were partners in a gold mining scheme that went awry.

"According to local sources, the three took several hundred pounds of gold worth millions of dollars from the mine shortly before Hoffman was murdered.

"MacNulty, who was unable to make an arrest after interviewing both suspects, is today the focus of widespread controversy in Northport. Resort manager Fred Marquardt, in a public statement, claims MacNulty is responsible for last night's devastating explosion and fire because he knew Mittner had sworn to kill his son-in-law, yet refused to level charges against Mittner and released her.

"MacNulty shielded himself from reporters this morning by refusing comment and denying any wrongdoing. Meanwhile, Marquardt heads a new group who are seeking the state attorney general's help in having the sheriff dismissed from office for malfeasance. MacNulty, who was unopposed in this year's election, said he intends to serve out his term."

The picture switched from reporter to anchor, who said, "Sandra, sounds like you've uncovered some big news up there in Northport in addition to a disastrous explosion and fire."

"Yes, Ted, we'll be bringing more details on this story to our viewers at ten, and by tomorrow, we hope to have an on-the-scene story from the gold mining site near Quill Mountain, which experts say may be the biggest gold strike ever in Minnesota and perhaps the largest in the lower forty-eight states in our generation."

"Aw shit," MacNulty said, pushing the control button. The screen went as black as his heart.

"Goddamn that bitch," he said, staring at the pictureless screen. "Managed to squeeze it all in and then some. Can you believe how it's all so matter of fact? Half that stuff may not even be true, but she reports it like it's the gospel. I can't believe it. Talk about stirring up trouble. Goddamn that woman, anyhow."

"Now, now, Ray. It's only one report. Maybe the others will be more, you know, discreet; won't speculate so much. Anyhow, people around here know you, know you wouldn't do something without good reason, so quit sputtering. Lord knows it's not worth getting so upset about. You'll make yourself sick."

"I am sick."

"Maybe some walleye will make you feel better. Come in and fix your plate now, so you can watch the sports."

"God almighty, what am I supposed to do when a couple thousand gold miners from Minneapolis show up in their bermuda shorts to look for nuggets?"

"You could sell 'em maps," Muriel teased.

"Dammit, this is no joke. Forest service is gonna have a fit, since they own all the mineral rights anyhow."

"Maybe they could sell little gold mining claims. Probably take in more than they'd get from the loggers."

"God, I wish we could go somewhere on vacation for a

couple weeks," MacNulty said, filling his plate with three wall-eye filets, buttered mashed potatoes, and fresh garden peas. It was one of his favorite meals, and she knew the food would make him feel better.

T he morning paper carried a less inflammatory but still highly speculative story on the explosion and fire. Mac-Nulty skimmed the account with his coffee, then set off early to face the expected deluge of phone calls at the office. But there, the phone was strangely quiet. Phyllis, the dispatcher, handed him two messages, both routine.

MacNulty poured his coffee and looked at the message slips. Then he grinned and shook his head. The usual well-wishers were conspicuously absent. As for the local wolf pack, he figured they'd wait awhile to make sure he was really in a jam before attacking. Still, the silence was unsettling. He knew the residents were talking, but they weren't talking to him.

He started the laborious process of writing reports on the explosion and fire, stopping only to talk with deputies at the shift change. He noted Walt Downing was late for work, which surprised and irritated him. He needed to talk to someone, and Walt was the only one who knew all of what had happened.

The office emptied quickly at the shift change, leaving him alone again except for the dispatcher. He couldn't concentrate, so he filled his coffee cup for the third time since arriving.

"Call Walt at home," he told Phyllis. "See what's keeping him." Then he walked heavily into his office and looked out at the poplar leaves hanging lifelessly in the summer calm. Shit, he said to himself, I don't have any answers and I don't know how to get them. If both suspects are dead, do I just close the Hoffman case and claim victory? I sure as hell can't get any more information out of a pile of ashes. Probably never know what the answers are.

His mind had leaped from gold mining to goose hunting

and he was diagramming a set of decoys on his scratch pad when the chief deputy appeared in the door frame.

"Just because I'm in deep shit doesn't mean you have to hide at home," MacNulty growled.

"Who says I'm hiding," Walt shot back. "I been down to the Bus Stop Cafe having breakfast."

"They gettin' up a lynch mob downtown?" asked the sulking sheriff.

Walt studied his boss momentarily. "I went down there to see what people were talkin' about, because I was concerned about it, too."

MacNulty eyed him warily.

"What I found out is that we don't know diddly about human nature."

"What's that supposed to mean?"

"It means that while you're sitting up here under your private little rain cloud, most everybody in town is talking about gold.

"Nobody cares much that Charlie and Harry Potter might have got themselves blowed up, or that you didn't solve Carl Hoffman's death. Hell, the whole town is catching a serious case of gold fever. I bet there's a hundred guys lookin' around Quill Mountain already for any little crick to put their pans in. Half of 'em are out-of-towners who drove up from around Duluth during the night."

"Oh shit. The forestry people are gonna have a fit," MacNulty said, staring at his coffee mug.

"So far, they're not stopping anybody," Walt replied. "In fact, rumor has it they may work something out with anybody that wants to go prospecting, like a twenty-five dollar permit fee and a percentage of the find."

"They'd really do that?" MacNulty was incredulous.

"Guess they're on the horn right now with Washington. Said there would be a decision by noon."

MacNulty shook his head.

"Ray, I talked to some of the merchants who think this

208

gold thing might set off the biggest boom ever seen around here. They're predicting thousands of big city miners by Saturday and they can hardly wait to sell 'em supplies and gas and groceries."

"Hell, those people aren't gonna find any gold wandering around in the woods," MacNulty scoffed.

"I know it and you know it but those weekend prospectors don't know it. Hell, somebody might actually stumble onto something. Then, think of the gold fever."

MacNulty almost smiled a little, imagining the consequences of an additional gold discovery. "Come to think of it," he said, "that woman TV reporter said she was gonna hang around here and do a report on the location of the gold mine on tonight's news. That ought to really bring the crazies out. Talk about hysteria, we may actually have to assign people to handle the traffic problems this weekend."

Walt agreed with a nod and a grin. "Crazy but true," he added.

"So sit down and tell me what you found in the rubble yesterday," MacNulty said, gesturing to a chair.

"Truthfully, I don't know what the hell we found," Walt answered, "but I can tell you it's a nasty job. Wet ash feels like clay, heavy, ya know. We did find some pieces of what might be bone fragments, along with other stuff. But everything is in little pieces or so deformed that it's hard to identify. I kept expecting to find skulls grinning up at me, but we didn't see anything like that. Fire marshall wasn't very surprised."

"But you did find *some* things, right?" MacNulty asked.

"Yup. We were there 'til dark. Raked through all that shit. You know all that silver and copper and stuff he had around?"

MacNulty nodded.

"Melted right down to liquid. Cooled in flat pieces sorta like bubbly pancakes. We bagged up all the stuff and Perkovich took it with him to Duluth. Said he'd send it along to the crime lab down in the Cities this morning."

MacNulty nodded again.

"So where does that leave us?" Walt asked. "What should I be doing next on the case?"

The sheriff shrugged and raised his hands, palms up, like a minister instructing his congregation to stand.

"That's what I've been chewing on ever since I got up. Truth be known, I'm stumped. Dead ends in all directions. If they're both dead, I might as well be talkin' to that chair over there. We got nobody to question, nobody to charge with the crime. I'm stuck, unless you got some ideas."

Walt shrugged. "Maybe the stuff we sent to the crime lab will give us some answers, but Perkovich said not to hold our breath. If I was in your boots, I'd close the Hoffman case. Hell, it was narrowed down to two suspects, either of whom had a motive. If they're both dead, the suspects, I mean, then there's no reason to pursue it, right? Either way, the killer's dead. Case closed."

MacNulty nodded. "You're probably right. Which still leaves the explosion and fire at Sawtooth. There's charges to be filed in that one, too. Maybe murder, certainly manslaughter. There's gonna be a lot of insurance claims, maybe some law-suits, too, so we'll have to pursue it, maybe even establish a verdict of guilt, just to satisfy the insurance companies and all the lawyers.

"Why don't I talk to the county attorney and handle the paperwork on the Hoffman thing. You start on the Sawtooth Lodge business, Walt."

Downing nodded as the speaker on MacNulty's desk came alive.

"Sheriff," it was the dispatcher's voice. "I got a long distance for you. Can you take it or should I get a message?"

"I'll pick it up. Thanks, Phyllis."

He lifted the receiver. "Sheriff MacNulty here."

"Sheriff, this is Sheriff Coats from Baldwin County. Thought I'd call and see if you or your office talked to anybody down here about that sailboat that fella's got sitting down heah."

210

"No, I never talked to anybody." He covered the mouthpiece: "Walt, see if we logged any long distance calls about Potter's boat."

Uncovering the mouthpiece, MacNulty addressed the southern sheriff. "I'm checking on any calls we got. Why? What's the deal?"

"Dockmaster at the yacht club called us last night. Said the boat had to be moved on account of the storm we got comin'. Said he called for the owner, but was told he wouldn't be available. I told him to call ya'll and work somethin' out."

Walt came back into the office with a phone message. He handed it to MacNulty.

"Sheriff," MacNulty answered, "it appears we got a call but the dispatcher forgot to spindle the message, which was to call a number in the 205 area code. So it looks like nobody talked to anybody down there."

"Huh," Sheriff Coats drawled, "dockmaster just called us to see where we moved the boat. Figured we moved it, but I said we're not in the boat movin' business. Appears the boat was moved last night."

"Where was it taken?"

"Damn if I know. Thought you might know."

"No, we don't. Could you assign a deputy to find it?"

"Might could do somethin' after the hurricane"—he pronounced it hurri-cun—"but my hands are full right now."

"Is this a serious storm you got comin'?" MacNulty asked.

"Reckon so. Fixin' to make landfall with 140-mile winds tonight or tomorrow. Might be lookin' for a lot of boats after ol' Ethyl comes through."

"Who's that you said?"

"Ethyl. Storm's called Ethyl."

"Oh yeah. They give 'em names."

"Yessir, they got names. Best be goin' now. Might be that somebody stole the boat, I guess, since it happened at night. Lotta that before a storm. Things get moved, nobody notices. Boat vanishes, insurance company pays."

"Uh-huh," MacNulty said.

"Bye now," Coats said, and hung up.

"What was that all about?" Walt asked.

"Damned if I really know," MacNulty mused, fingering the phone. "Maybe it's what we been waiting for. Give me a couple minutes to think about it."

M acNulty stood at his window, looking at poplar leaves, but not seeing them. He'd been standing there, almost motionless, for fifteen minutes.

"Walt," he said sharply without turning, then listened to a desk chair being moved and the approach of footsteps.

"Yeah, Ray," Walt said from the doorway.

MacNulty continued to stare into the poplar foliage.

"Calls Nels and Graham, would ya? See if they can stop by. Tell 'em I got some questions. When they get here bring 'em on in."

"Sure, Ray," Walt answered, turning away. He'd seen MacNulty like this before, staring out the window, pondering one of his hunches.

A single call to the small boat harbor caught the pair at work repairing damaged stanchions. They were at the sheriff's office in five minutes, wearing cutoffs and sweatshirts.

"Your undercover squad reporting as ordered," Nels said cheerfully at the door. MacNulty was back at his desk, writing on a yellow legal pad.

"Come on in," he waved, standing up behind the desk as Nels and Graham came in, followed by Walt.

"Sit down and relax, guys. I'm gonna use a little of the famous MacNulty logic on you and see what you think," Mac-Nulty said, hitching up his pants.

Walt had seen that sparkle in the eyes before and shook

his head, grinning. *The old man thinks he's onto something,* he thought.

"Okay kiddies, listen close now 'cause Uncle Ray's gonna tell you a little story.

"Once upon a time, this fella name of Harry Potter decided to run off on his sailboat. A couple of us in this room think he did it after killing Carl Hoffman and hiding a pile of gold, probably on the boat.

"Anyhow, old Harry went to considerable lengths to avoid being found. He changed the boat, illegally I might add since it was a documented craft, and he changed himself, too. At least a couple of us figure old Harry wasn't planning to come back, ever.

"But we caught up with him. Surprised the hell out of him when we did, too. But old Harry was pretty crafty. Right away he volunteered to come on back and straighten things out. Of course, that was the only smart choice available to him, but he pulled it off with a lot of class. Gave us all pause to think maybe he was innocent after all.

"Now old Harry had one minor problem, a big, tough woman name of Charlie. And he could pretty well figure she'd keep after him as long as we let her do it. Course, we played right into his hands by letting her loose to go after him, as I shall shortly explain.

"When we let her loose, Harry could have stayed out of sight and well protected. After all, according to his sympathizers, he was close to having a nervous breakdown. But old Harry was eager to get it over with, so he was out in his workshop, where Charlie could find him real easy.

"Now Charlie played right into his hands. I don't think she wanted him dead, just scared real good, so when she heard he was away from the lodge, she went to the workshop cabin, the one place she was familiar with, to plant a little dynamite.

"But guess who was there to surprise her? Good ol' Harry and his revolver. My guess is she planned to set the charge when she got inside. Probably wouldn't have had it ready in advance, since she was somewhat, if not totally, inebriated.

"So the way I see it, Harry holds her with the gun, maybe even ties her up. As we know, he's familiar with explosives, particularly dynamite. He sets up the explosive package, waits until the coast is clear, then shoots her either out of choice or necessity. He's timed the charge to give him about eight or ten seconds; enough to get into the parking lot and behind a car for protection.

"Now, in the confusion, Harry simply walks away to where he's got a car stashed for just such an opportunity. There's several vacant cabins within easy walking distance where he could have parked it. Then he drives leisurely to Minneapolis and pays cash for a plane ride south the next morning. That would have been yesterday.

"Naturally, it would take him until noon to get there and a few more hours to get to his boat and figure out a plan. So the first time he would dare to take it out was during the night, last night. Especially convenient because of the confusion caused by an oncoming hurricane, which will also serve to obscure his tracks and screw up the search afterwards.

"Right now, I'd say he's pulled in somewhere's provisioning the boat for his getaway."

MacNulty glanced at his watch and nodded.

"And in twenty-four hours, gentlemen, he could be anywhere."

There was momentary silence in the room.

"Jesus," Nels exclaimed. "That's a hell of a story. But is it true?"

"Some parts are true," MacNulty replied. "The fact that Harry put himself at risk, the timing between gunshot and explosion, the disappearance of *Golden Fleece* last night, all are true. The rest is theory, based on my theory that Harry killed Carl Hoffman."

Walt, silent in thought until now, spoke, "Am I right in

guessing that your next suggestion is for us all to jump aboard a plane and go chasing after Harry and his treasure ship? If that's the case, I think we should look real close at your scenario before we buy our tickets. Seems to me, and I'm not doubting the possible truth of parts of it, but it just seems there's some awful big jumps between the few facts we've got. First off, I'm not convinced Harry even killed Hoffman, which makes the rest of it suspect."

"Walt, I'm glad you're a skeptic," MacNulty said. "So tell me how someone just walks onto the boat and steals it without keys or knowledge of the master switches."

Nels answered his question. "It can be done if you know how. Electrical controls don't require a key. Once you're inside, you can bypass the ignition key. It's not common knowledge, but possible."

"A lot easier with the key, though, right?"

"Infinitely so," Nels agreed. "Especially there in Fly Creek where you haven't got much room to maneuver by sail."

"So, Graham, what do you think of my theory?" MacNulty asked.

"I don't really know," Graham admitted. "Bloody good story, though."

"What I'm saying, you guys, is that this is what might have happened. Or it might not have happened." MacNulty shrugged. "But if there's a possibility it happened like I described it, then we're obligated to find the boat and close the book on it, one way or the other.

"My strong feeling is that if we don't find and apprehend whoever's got that boat right away, we'll never see it again. And we'll always be left with the big nagging question, Who took the boat?, and, coincidentally, Who killed Carl Hoffman and what exactly happened in the Sawtooth explosion?

"As for me, I hate nagging questions. Especially when they're questions I'm supposed to be able to answer in my job as sheriff.

"Walt, if you were in charge, could you live with the question hanging over you, knowing you might have had the answer to at least two murders if only you'd followed it up?"

Walt frowned, thought for several moments, then shook his head. "No, I'd have to go for it, try to learn if the jigsaw puzzle really fits, even though I don't think it does."

He stopped and a smile flickered. "Want me to check the flight schedules?"

"No, that won't be necessary," MacNulty answered, matching Walt's smile. "I already made the reservations."

When the laughter subsided, MacNulty outlined his plan.

"Graham, I'd like you to stay here and call all the marinas around the bay. Try to locate the boat. Nels and Walt, I want you both along. Our flight goes out of Duluth at 1:30 P.M. and arrives in Mobile at six-thirty. That's the best I could do. I've got a car reserved when we get there. We'll call back here for Graham when we arrive. And Graham, if you could, make your calls from here. That way, we've got a direct billing on them."

"One thing, Graham," Nels added. "The Mobile Bay chart's down in the nav station. If you don't come up with anything in the bay, try east and west along the intracoastal waterway. Some good hurricane holes along there, if I remember correctly."

"I figure we need to leave in twenty to thirty minutes," MacNulty said. "Any questions?"

"Just one, about the hurricane," Nels said. "When's it supposed to make landfall?"

"Sheriff down there said late tonight or early tomorrow," MacNulty replied.

"Okay, that means rain and wind by the time we arrive," Nels warned. "Just hope they keep the airport open 'til then. I've been through a couple of 'em, and they're serious business; not something you can drive around in. Depending on where it makes landfall, we could see a big tidal surge, too, so we'll have to be careful not to get caught in the wrong place. Just so you know it's not gonna be a picnic down there."

"I understand," Walt said. "I rode out a typhoon in the Pacific. Like you say, it's no fun."

"Okay, fellas, you can compare storms later," MacNulty suggested. "Run home, get what you need, kiss your wives, and be back here in thirty minutes."

T hey could feel the buffeting and turbulence of the approaching storm as the Northwest Airlines DC-9 descended into Mobile. It was fortunate the progress of the storm had slowed, holding winds to a sustained twenty-five to thirty knots with gusts to forty in Mobile.

According to the pilot of Northwest flight 403, parts of the city were already experiencing flooding due to the heavy rains. He alerted continuing passengers to stay on board since the stop would be shortened. Had the flight been an hour later or had the storm advanced a bit faster flight 403 would have bypassed Mobile entirely.

As they touched down on the puddled pavement, Nels pulled his sailing bag from beneath the seat. In it were three waterproof sailing jackets with hoods.

"I figured you guys would enjoy staying dry," he remarked, handing jackets to Walt and MacNulty.

"Extra large?" MacNulty asked.

"With Graham's compliments," Nels replied.

"Let's hope he's got a lead for us to work on," Walt said. "Be a bitch tryin' to find marinas in this shit."

The plane pulled up to the terminal and a ramp was rolled into place by three men in long, yellow slickers. There was no jetway for protection against the rain and wind that pasted their jackets against their bodies as they exited the airplane and groped down the steep stairway.

Crouching against the wind, they splashed forty yards through standing water to the terminal door near which the outgoing passengers clustered. Inside, they found the terminal quiet, almost empty.

MacNulty unzipped his rain jacket. "Damn, it's humid down here. Between that and the heat, I'm already wringing wet."

Walt glanced at Nels with a grin but said nothing. They had already listened to MacNulty complaining about the heat and humidity in Memphis.

It was a quarter mile, maybe a bit more, to the National Car Rental counter where they were met by a worried-looking, dark-haired woman.

"Hi, my name is MacNulty. You got a car for us?"

"Yes sir. Thank goodness you got here before we closed down." Her worried face was instantly transformed by a smile.

"They planning to close the whole airport?" MacNulty asked.

"Oh, yes sir. Fixin' to do it right soon, I expect," she replied. "You must be insurance fellas."

"Why's that?" Walt asked.

She shrugged. "Hurricanes always bring you insurance men. Guess you come to inspect the damage, figure out how much the losses are."

"Guess you got us pegged," MacNulty said. "That's why we're here, all right."

She took the form and returned it with copies of the agreement and car keys.

"Blue Buick Century. Parking place seven in row A. It's right here on the map; X marks the spot. Y'all be careful, hear?"

She turned and began pulling on a plastic rain coat. She looked worried again.

MacNulty turned toward Walt, then spotted Nels talking on a phone fifty feet down the hall.

"Looks like he got through," Walt said. MacNulty nodded as their footsteps echoed in the empty concourse.

Thankfully, traffic was light on the rain-swept parkway. The city lay quiet but alert, awaiting the storm. Preparations had been made, Nels saw, as they splashed past a blocklong strip of darkened store fronts; plywood sheets covered a few windows, many others were heavily taped. People had not forgotten the fury of Hurricane Frederick in 1979. Judging from a steady stream of reports on the car radio, Ethyl was packing an equally brutal punch.

They were headed for Dauphin Island, a barrier island that lay at the southwest corner of Mobile Bay and in normal times separated the bay from the gulf. Dotted with vacation homes and cottages, the island had been swept by hurricane surges three times in fifteen years.

According to the manager of Dauphin Island Marina and Boatyard, *Golden Fleece* was tied off to leeward of the docks and riding easily in the chop. Graham said the boat had apparently come in around noon but appeared to be unattended at the moment. The manager hadn't noticed it arrive and had not seen anybody aboard, but was adamant that the boat would have to be moved before the storm arrived.

After plodding generally northward across the gulf, Hurricane Ethyl now lay wobbling and nearly stalled ninety miles south-southeast of the entrance to Mobile Bay. The National Oceanic and Aeronautical Administration Hurricane Center said the storm, packing winds of 130 mph on its dangerous right shoulder, was expected to resume forward movement in a northwesterly direction during the night, making landfall sometime shortly after daylight. Reports from around Mobile Bay indicated that tides were already running three to four feet above normal.

Walt stared past the steadily-beating wipers at the slick, black asphalt ribbon ahead. He leaned the car into a strong gust that blew a heavy sheet of rain against them. A palm frond skidded across their path.

"How far to where we're headed?" he asked Nels, who was navigating with a road map.

"Looks like fifteen to twenty miles to the bridge, then three or four miles across the bridge to the island."

They pulled up under a red light swinging in the wind. On the corner was a small liquor store, still doing a brisk business. A man was taping the windows.

MacNulty sat in back, drowsy from the close, wet warmth and the metronome-steady swish of wipers. He had been silent since the car had pulled away from the airport parking lot.

He stared out the rain-distorted side window at an alien landscape. People who spoke in a strange dialect were performing curious rituals of taping and boarding up their property. He remembered the newsreels, but had never seen, firsthand, a city braced for a hurricane or the actual storm itself. A foreigner, he thought. I feel like I've been dropped in a place where rules, weather, people, trees, everything is so different.

MacNulty searched for a word to describe it all. Eerie, he thought, like the setting for the kind of ghost stories he'd heard around the campfire as a kid.

Intent on reaching the boat quickly, Walt drove steadily south. The only traffic on the road was coming at him, heading north away from the slowly spinning beast in the gulf.

Funny, he thought. Nobody's mentioned supper or a place to sleep. Finding the boat, that's all that matters now. Everything else can wait.

"Assuming we find the boat," Nels said, apparently sharing MacNulty's thoughts, "then we've got to secure it for the storm. That could be one hell of a problem at night in strange water."

Walt glanced at him. "How do you mean?"

"Well, if the boat's got to be moved and the storm's due in twelve hours, somebody's got to take it out in this rain and wind and find a safe place. Mobile Bay is gonna be a bitch in this weather."

"Can you do it?"

"If it comes to that, and if you'll go with me, and if we know where the hell we're going. . . ."

"That's a lot of 'ifs.'"

"You're right, and even if we succeed, we may have to ride out the storm on board, which is not exactly a fun prospect."

"Maybe there's a safe place close by."

"Yeah, and maybe pigs can fly," Nels said, grinning darkly.

The city fell away and the land flattened as they neared the Dauphin Island bridge. Ditch water stood bank deep along the two-lane asphalt and in places covered the surface in thin sheets. Walt plodded on, slower now, between open fields of wind-battered marsh grass.

They came to a darkened intersection with a four-way stop. The red signs were shimmying in the gusty wind.

"Hang a left here," Nels instructed, looking at the map.

Walt turned the blue car onto another dark path through the grass.

"How far to the bridge?" he asked.

" 'Bout a mile," Nels replied. "See those flashing lights up ahead? That's probably it. The yellow light's likely to be a warning flasher for the bridge. Blue one's a cop car, handling traffic. How we gonna do this?"

"You mean they'll want to keep us off the island?" Walt asked.

"Yeah. You want to handle it?"

"I'll handle it," came MacNulty's sandpaper voice from the back seat. "Nels, let me look at the map a minute."

MacNulty switched on the overhead light and studied the road map.

"Okay," he said, switching off the light and laying the map on the floor.

As Walt neared the yellow flasher, a state trooper in a reflectorized rain slicker stepped out of his patrol car to halt them.

The car stopped and the trooper came to the driver's side. MacNulty rolled down his window and the rain slanted in.

"Sorry fellas, the bridge is closed. Island's bein' evacuated."

"Police business," MacNulty said, holding his badge wallet up for a quick scan by the trooper's flashlight. "I'm Sheriff MacNulty from Cahokie County. We been called down to help get everybody off."

The trooper hesitated momentarily, shining his light at the front seat occupants. He saw Walt and Nels were also holding badges and snapped the light off.

"Okay, but be real careful on the bridge. That wind like to carry you off sometimes."

"We'll do that," MacNulty said with an easy wave as Walt pulled away toward the bridge.

After a few seconds, Nels turned toward the sheriff. "Cahokie County?" he asked, eyebrows raised.

"Yup. Rural county about sixty to seventy miles northwest. Trooper probably never met anybody from there before. Sorta stopped him cold."

"I think it was the Yankee accent that stopped him," Nels replied.

"Heard you fellas talking about going boating tonight," MacNulty said, noting that the water being blown across the bridge was not just from the rain. He looked down at the dark, white-crested shapes crashing against the concrete pilings, sending spray across the roadway. "I don't think I'd be too quick to go out there on a night like this."

"If the boat's there and has to be moved to save it, I've got no choice," Nels replied. "I don't like the idea so well myself, but what can we do? Let 'er sink?"

A gust buffeted the car and stopped the conversation. They were climbing now, as the bridge rose to allow sixty-five feet of vertical clearance in the waterway. Beneath them, jagged waves raced westward, having grown to six or seven feet in their twenty-mile journey from the bay's eastern shore.

"Ugly bastards," Nels muttered, looking down.

Then they were off the bridge, protected from the worst of the wind by pines and magnolias that had somehow survived earlier assaults. To the right, Nels spotted sailboat masts.

"Let's hang a right here," Nels said. "That could be the place."

They drove toward what appeared to be a small collection of shacks and docks along the bank of a cove. Several shrimpers were tied alongside, and a handful of sailboats bobbed at anchor in the chop. Two slicker-clad men were adjusting heavy lines that cleated one of the shrimpers to the dock.

"Let me go talk to those guys," Nels suggested, and climbed out, following the headlight beams toward the boat.

He was gone less than a minute.

"Wrong place. Marina's over east of the bridge. Not a bad place to ride out the storm, according to the shrimpers. Tricky getting in here, though, if the visibility's bad. Might give it a shot, if it comes to that."

"Let's head for the marina, Walt," MacNulty instructed. "You know how to get there, Nels?"

"Yeah. Go straight back to the highway, then south another block, then left. Should be a sign."

They followed the road through a wooded residential area. The houses were dark, their occupants gone. Then, a lighted parking area, dimmed by slanting rain, appeared on the left. An old wooden sign, paint peeling, identified the Dauphin Island Marina.

"God almighty," Walt gasped as the docks came into view. Waves were breaking over the small protective jetty and cascading knee-deep over the planked walkways. Two power boats, Nels guessed they were about twenty-four footers, had managed to climb onto the dock where, still tied to pilings, they were being battered and ground to ruin. There were no other boats in sight.

An older man in a two-piece yellow foul weather suit stood

in the lee of the wind near a white frame office and ship's store building.

They pulled up to the building and got out.

"Howdy," MacNulty shouted over the noise. "We called earlier about the sailboat, the *Golden Fleece.*"

"C'mon inside. Can't hear a damn thing out here," the man shouted back, and motioned toward the office.

They followed him inside, puddling the planked floor.

"Pretty nasty out there," MacNulty said, pulling back the hood of his rain jacket. "We're the people who called about the sailboat, the *Golden Fleece.* You're the manager, the fella we talked to?"

The man stopped mopping his wet face long enough to nod.

"I don't see the boat," MacNulty continued. "Gather it's long gone, right?"

The marina manager nodded again. He pulled out a smoke and lit it, the white cigarette contrasting against his tan, heavily creased face.

"I was out on the dock, saw the man on the boat, so I told him somebody was lookin' for him, had called asking about the boat."

"What did he say when you told him that?"

The man shook his head. "Don't remember him sayin' nothin', just sort of nodded."

"Tell me, what did this man look like?"

The man stared at the counter, his arms folded. "Hmmm. Sorta average, I guess. Midsize. Middle age. Ya know, forty to forty-five years old."

"What color hair?"

"Don't really remember. Not gray or silver, probably like a light brown, sandy-colored."

"So when did he leave?"

"Didn't see him go. Probably pretty soon after I talked to him. Had my hands full."

"When was it? Rough guess at least, how long ago?"

A shrug. "Maybe an hour and a half, two hours."

"Which way did he go?" Nels asked.

"Didn't see that either. Look behind you at the chart. You can see he could'a gone damn near anyplace."

Nels turned, looked momentarily, and pinpointed their current position with a jab of his forefinger.

"Could have run west, under the bridge, north, back up the bay, or out through here, into the gulf. Can we get out here by car?" he asked the marina man.

"Out to the pass? Sure, just stay on the road you turned in here offa. Takes you to the cut. Parking lot overlooks a little beach and the channel."

"Ray, let's take a run over there," Nels suggested. "I want to take a look at that pass."

"Well, thanks," MacNulty told the manager. "We appreciate your help a lot. Just so you know, that's a stolen boat we're chasin' after."

Eyebrows raised, the older man exhaled. "Guess that's why he took off so quick, eh?"

"Guess so," MacNulty nodded.

They went out through the rain and piled into the car.

"Straight ahead, right?" Walt asked.

"Right," Nels replied.

"Sounds like our man, eh Ray?" Walt said to the rear view mirror. "Mister sandy-haired average."

"Harry's a hard man to describe, but that old fella was describing him, all right, or somebody damn similar." MacNulty paused. "That son of a bitch is one slippery bastard."

The car ground through wet sand drifted across the asphalt as they came out of the woods and skirted grass-covered dunes.

"Where you takin' us, Nels?" MacNulty asked.

"Just a crazy hunch. He's got three ways to go. He could beat back across the bay, which is damn near impossible in this weather, he could run straight west down the waterway under the bridge, which is like threading a needle in the dark, or he could try to run out the pass, then bear off west and run from the storm. Once I get a look at the pass, I'll know a lot better."

Walt drove carefully along the narrow road, buffeted by rain and blowing sand. After a mile and a half, the road ended in a parking lot.

"Go to the far side and put your brights on," Nels instructed.

Walt drove across and stopped, then flipped on the high beams. The sight was frightening.

"No fuckin' way," Walt muttered. "That's scary just lookin' at it from here."

The pass was a boiling kettle of huge waves, whitecaps, spindrift and blowing spume. Though less than half a mile across, the far shore was invisible in the rain and darkness.

"You can't seriously think a sailboat could go through that," MacNulty admonished. "Hell, those waves look ten feet high."

Nels nodded. "Probably ten to twelve in the pass, maybe fifteen to twenty in the gulf. Depends. He's alone. That makes it real tough. I don't know what kind of sails he's got for storm work. With a storm jib and trys'l, a good sailor might have a chance. Bad current coming in though."

Nels was talking almost to himself as he watched the savage fury of the pass, putting himself in Potter's place, gauging the odds of survival.

"You guys just want to sit here?" Walt asked.

"Yeah, if we could," Nels suggested. "I don't know of anyplace else to go looking."

"We'll give it awhile," MacNulty agreed.

Nels unzipped his sailing bag and pulled out a pair of Steiner waterproof binoculars. "Light sensitive," he said.

Ten minutes passed. MacNulty smoked a cigarette, lit a second.

"I got something," Nels said. "Big ship, comin' in off the gulf. Running for cover."

In five minutes, the freighter was visible to the naked eye, in five more, it was broadside to them, sliding swiftly on the current through the night. Nels followed it with his glasses.

"Wouldn't want to be on that ship tonight," Walt shuddered.

"Hold it," Nels snapped.

"Hold what?" Walt asked.

"Hold the fuckin' phone. It's a boat, sailboat, coming south. He's gonna try it." Nels was talking excitedly, as if he, himself, were at the helm of the careening, wave-tossed boat.

"You serious?" MacNulty asked.

"Yup, there he is. Oops, out of sight again. There. Yes. Definitely. Making slow progress. Reaching under storm trys'l. Probably got the diesel running full-out, too. Should be able to see him with the naked eye soon. Here, Walt, you take a look. Keep those wipers on."

"That way?" Walt asked, pointing.

"Yeah, midchannel. He's out of sight a lot, then he gets bounced up on a crest.

"Had him. Nope, gone again. There. I see the boat. Shit. You'd think he'd be washed overboard. Ooh, big wave almost covered it."

"He's wearing a safety harness, maybe two," Nels replied.

Walt handed the binoculars back to Nels. "I don't believe it. The sucker's got guts, I'll say that."

"Okay, I got a look at someone at the helm. Red foul weather gear. That fits, doesn't it?"

"Yeah, but is that the boat we're lookin' for?"

"All I know is I'm lookin' at a C&C 33 right now," Nels answered. "Oh, shit, man, sheet in or ease off, ah, that's better."

"Damn, he's doin' it. He's got a long way to go to clear the pass, though, and it won't get any easier." Nels put down the glasses.

"Sounds like you want him to get away," MacNulty growled.

"Well, if you put it that way, Ray, yeah I do. It's all or nothing. Either he makes it or he dies trying. I admire his guts."

"Ah, I see him now without the glasses," Walt said. "Jeez, can you believe it?"

"Yup, I see him now, too," MacNulty observed, leaning forward.

"Slid over a bit to this side of the pass," Nels pointed out.

The white-hulled vessel, though thirty-three feet in length, was dwarfed by the waves. It rose and fell precipitously in the breaking sea, sometimes disappearing for several seconds in the deep troughs. It was hard to believe it could keep afloat in the raging fury.

The wind was up, now, buffeting and rocking the car steadily. Nels put the glasses back to his eyes to watch the sailboat, now almost abeam. He studied it in silence, then exploded.

"Holy shit, there's someone else aboard."

"You sure?" MacNulty snapped. "Let me see."

He took the glasses for the first time and leaned forward over the seat back.

"Second person's in red, too, Ray. Leaning out of the hatch," Nels explained.

"Ah, I got the boat. Son of a bitch. Who do you s'pose?" He put down the glasses. "There's two on board, all right. Ya know, I always wondered if he had some gal stashed down here, waitin'. We got to get 'em before they get out into the sea. How we gonna do it, Nels?"

"We're not, Ray. Nobody, repeat nobody is going to go out there on a night like this, not the Coast Guard, the navy, nobody. If they survive, they're gone and there's not one damn thing we can do about it."

"Let's get outta here. Drive back to the marina, Walt. I want to ask that old man about the second person on board. He never said a word about more than one person."

228

Walt turned on the sand-covered asphalt and drove back toward the protection of the trees. MacNulty raged at himself in speculation as to the second person aboard *Golden Fleece*.

They pulled into the rain-slicked marina as the old man was starting his pickup to leave. He switched on the headlights and pulled up even with the car.

"Find your boat?" he shouted into the wind at their open windows.

"Yup," MacNulty answered. "You forgot to tell us there were two people aboard."

"Oh, did I?" The wet-faced old man replied. "Guess that's 'cause you forgot to ask."

"Then there *were* two on board?"

"Oh yes, oh yes indeed."

"Could you describe the second one at all?"

The man nodded down at MacNulty.

"Yup, reckon I could try. First off, it was a woman. She was a big one, best I could tell from the height of her, but the thing that stood out, and I ain't seen any like that for a long time, was she had what we used to call cat eyes."

"You mean bright green?" Walt asked slowly.

"Yup, green as emeralds," the old man said. "Well, I think we all better be getting off this island while there's an island left to get off of. See ya around, boys."

He pulled away without an answer, leaving the blue car sitting motionless in the rain.

EPILOGUE

In the last week of September, at the end of a crisp, cloudless day, Ray and Muriel MacNulty and Walt and Helen Downing joined Nels and Prentice Dahlstrom for dinner at their newly finished home overlooking Lake Superior.

The sun was gone, drawing a lavender sky in its wake across the cold, still lake and over the yellow-forested shoulders of the Sawtooth Range.

Three silhouettes, bulky in heavy sweaters and jackets, stood over the still bright embers of a driftwood fire set on the blue-black ledgerock. Two large trout, split open and wired flat against a heavy oak plank, sizzled alongside the coals.

Nels basted the fish with a brush, stirred the coals, and stood up. The evening was still, a silence broken only by the gentle heave of water against granite and the sizzle and pop of the fire.

"So," Nels asked in a low voice, hesitant to interrupt the quiet, "you never heard anything?"

Walt looked at MacNulty, who was staring into the fire, then turned back. "Nope, not a word. Papered the whole damn coast with notices and posters, but nothing."

"Well, as I said that night, they were going against long odds."

"You ever get paid by Marquardt for locating Potter?"

Nels nodded. "Yeah. A check in the mail about three weeks later. No note, no nothin'. I don't think he was very happy about it by then."

"What the hell," Walt shrugged. "You did your job. You hear the stunt he and his lawyers tried to pull afterwards?"

Nels looked up at Walt. "Huh-uh."

"They wanted Ray to declare 'em both dead in the fire. Said we had no real evidence to the contrary except heresay."

Nels looked at MacNulty, who was sipping his bourbon. The sheriff lowered his glass.

" 'Fraid I had to disappoint them."

"I'd say they were more scared than disappointed when they came runnin' out of your office, Ray."

"Guess I wasn't very polite," MacNulty explained.

"Gold fever about died down?" Nels asked, changing the topic.

MacNulty chuckled. "Looked like a boom town there for awhile, 'til the forest service clamped down and kept those idiots away from there. Forestry people brought a couple mining experts in; they checked the site, said that from the looks of things, our friends Harry and Charlie had been working up there all summer. They didn't just work it one day and split, like we heard.

"The experts also said it was probably a freak of nature, I guess they did placer tests all over that little creek, didn't come up with any color at all, except in some of the tailin's right there."

"We'll never know how much they really took out of there," Walt added. "Considering what they gave us with no argument, they must of had a lot more."

MacNulty cleared his throat, "Too bad Graham couldn't

be here tonight to see the final result of old Axel's handiwork. Built you a real showplace."

Nels nodded. "Graham's getting the charter business ready for the season so Tizz and I can enjoy our new place a little while. Axel did a hell of a job and he and I buried the hatchet over a few beers one night awhile back."

The three men fell silent again, staring at the embers of the cooking fire. After six weeks, they were still uneasy talking about it.

They had raced into the storm, only to be greeted by a truth that had stunned them. They had sat a long time in the marina parking lot, shocked and disbelieving. Finally, running before the oncoming hurricane to the safety of an airport motel, they had come to terms with the truth over a bottle of good bourbon as the storm raged outside.

"I can't get it off my mind," Nels began, "keep rolling it around, looking at it from different angles. The clues are there; I just never saw them."

"Nobody did," Walt replied. "We've chewed on it 'til there's nothing left to chew on. They played their parts and we sat there clappin'. We believed 'em, so we saw everything the way they wanted us to see it."

MacNulty cleared his throat again. "Fella once said if it walks like a duck, quacks like a duck, swims like a duck, and looks like a duck, then it must be a duck."

He looked up from the fire to the two men who were watching him. "Don't you believe it, fellas. Don't you believe it for a minute."

They shook their heads. Being fooled, and embarrassed in the bargain—a hard lesson.

"Wonder if it's really over," Walt mused.

"I'd say the odds were about seventy-thirty against them making it," Nels replied, adjusting the fish, "but you never know."

MacNulty remained silent. They don't know the half of it, he thought ruefully, but they'd have to be told. He'd waited for the right time, but there just didn't seem to be any right time. This was the final humiliation, the turn of the knife, and there was no way to make it hurt less.

"Aw shit, forget the odds," he muttered, shaking his head. "Sometimes when you get your ass kicked, it's hard to admit it. It's even worse when you've got to let the world know about it." He reached into the inside pocket of his jacket and withdrew a well-fingered post card. Nels and Walt watched silently.

"Got this little gem in the mail a couple days ago. Didn't know what the hell to do about it. Made me mad, I guess. But I can't very well just ignore it, pretend it never arrived, so you two better have a look."

He handed the card to Walt, who glanced first at the colored photograph of a small mountain village with a caption in Spanish, then turned the card over.

Adjusting it toward the light of the fire, he held it between Nels and himself, so they could both read the two stanzas of hand-written verse.

With riches in her holding tank,
  away the Fleece did steal,
Through fire, storm and raging seas
  to a shore I won't reveal.

With Charlie's brawn and my small plan,
· *we made events unfold.*
Now it's easy street for the two of us
  'cause we're worth our weight in gold.

The Commander